HERGÉ
★
THE ADVENTURES OF
TINTIN
★

THE CASTAFIORE EMERALD

LITTLE, BROWN AND COMPANY
New York   Boston

This edition first published in the UK in 2007

by Egmont UK Limited

Translated by Leslie Lonsdale-Cooper and Michael Turner

The Castafiore Emerald

Renewed Art copyright © 1963 by Casterman, Belgium

Text copyright © 1963 by Egmont UK Limited

Flight 714 to Sydney

Renewed Art copyright ©1968 by Casterman, Belgium

Text copyright © 1968 by Egmont UK Limited

Tintin and the Picaros

Renewed Art copyright © 1976 by Casterman, Belgium

Text copyright © 1976 by Egmont UK Limited

casterman.com

tintin.com

Little, Brown Books for Young Readers is a division of Hachette Book Group, Inc.

The Little, Brown name and logo are trademarks of Hachette Book Group, Inc.

First US Edition © 2009 by Little, Brown Books for Young Readers, a division of Hachette Book Group, Inc.

Published pursuant to agreement with Editions Casterman.

Not for sale in the British Commonwealth.

Little, Brown and Company

Hachette Book Group

1290 Avenue of the Americas, New York, NY 10104

Visit us at lb-kids.com

The publisher is not responsible for websites (or their content) that are not owned by the publisher.

L.10EIFN000666.C008

ISBN 978-0-316-35727-2

20   19   18

APS

Printed in China

THE CASTAFIORE EMERALD

Ah, the merry month of May!...
Spring, the sweet spring ♪♩
Cuckoo, jug-jug, pu-we, tu-witta-woo!

The chorus of birds . . . the woodland flowers . . . the fragrant perfumes . . . the sweet-smelling earth! Breathe deeply, Tintin. Fill your lungs with fresh air . . . air so pure and sparkling you could drink it!

As far as perfume goes, I wouldn't call this exactly fragrant.

You're right!

No wonder! Look at that disgusting rubbish dump. The filth from every dustbin in the neighbourhood is chucked over there.

Good heavens! Some people seem to be attracted by the stink! ... Fantastic!

Gipsies!

No sense of hygiene, the guttersnipes. Incredible!

Ssh!... Listen! That sounds like a child crying . . .

BOO-HOO!

A little gipsy girl . . .

BOO-HOO-OO!

She must have wandered away from that camp.

Hello! . . . What's the matter? What are you crying for? Are you lost?

?

It's all right, don't be afraid. What's your name? I'm Tintin. Who are you?

Speak up little'un.

Thundering typhoons, don't be so timid! We're not going to eat you!

No, no, Captain.

HI-I-III!

YEOW!

GNAA!

Billions of blue blistering barnacles!

Little spitfire! Just wait till I catch you!

Look at that! She's drawn blood, the little wildcat!

So she has; but you scared her.

WOOAH! WOOAH!

Now what's happened?

?

WOOAH! WOOAH!

Oh, poor little thing?

Poor little?. . .

WOOAH! WOOAH!

Good gracious! She tripped over the brambles and then bumped her head on the tree root.

You haven't cut yourself, have you? . . . No, there isn't any blood. I expect you'll have a lump, that's all.

Little goose!

Please don't be frightened. We'll take you back to your mother . . . Can you stand up?

KILIKILIKILI!

OK now?

A few minutes later . . .

Mama!

Miarka!

To think that people live in the midst of all this filth!

I know.

Good day to you!

We found her in the woods; she must have wandered off. When she saw us she . . . er . . . she ran away. But then she fell over and bumped her head on a tree root. So we brought her home.

You are a good man. I will tell your fortune. You cross my palm with silver!

No, thanks. Definitely not!

Er . . . It might be as well, for a clear conscience, to let a doctor have a look at her.

A doctor! I suppose you think we have money to pay for a doctor!

Kind gentleman! I'll tell your fortune . . . you cross my palm with silver!

No, no! Please leave me alone!

OOOOOH!

What is it? . . . Tell me!

Trouble!

Well, if that's all you can see, I can tell your fortune, too!

You must be careful . . . otherwise I see an accident . . . But not serious . . . I see you in a carriage . . . AAAH! A beautiful stranger approaches . . . She is coming to visit you . . . AAAH! She has wonderful jewels, and . . . OOOH! . . . A terrible disaster . . .

Go on, go on!

The jewels are gone . . . vanished! . . . stolen! You cross my palm with silver and I tell you many more things.

No, no! That's enough! Let go of my hand!

Just a little silver . . . otherwise you will suffer great misfortune! . . . The jewels will disappear!

Me too! . . . That's enough mumbo-jumbo for one day.

Well, goodbye, and take care of that little cherub. But if you take my advice, you'll camp somewhere else, and not on this rubbish dump . . . In the first place, it's unhealthy . . .

D'you think we're here because we like it? D'you imagine we enjoy living surrounded by filth?

You mean . . .

Quiet, Mike, let me talk to this gajo.

Me, a gajo?

That's what we call anyone who isn't a Romany . . . Listen, we arrived here yesterday with a sick man, and this was the only place where the police would let us camp.

So that's it!

Blistering barnacles! Now, just you listen to me. You're not staying here! . . . There's a large meadow near the Hall, beside a stream. You can move in there whenever you like.

Making people live on a dung-heap like this. It's revolting!

I'm glad you could help them.

?!

THUMP

Poor Professor!... Anything broken?

Yes, a piece several inches long!

That confounded step! Still not repaired! When's that sluggard of a builder coming?

I telephone him constantly, sir, and he assures me he'll come...

Well, I'll show you how to deal with him!

Hello?... Hello? Mr Bolt?... What, that isn't Mr Bolt?

No, sir, this is Cutts the butcher ...Yes, sir... Not at all, sir.

Hello?... Is that Mr Bolt?

Yes... oh, yes sir... Yes, I do know... I... Yes, a sudden rush of work... Yes, very tiresome... What? Oh yes, sir, it's very dangerous too... When?... Well, yes, I... I'll come along... er... tomorrow. Yes, first thing tomorrow... You can rely on me, sir. Goodbye.

That's how to get results, Nestor. Just a touch of firmness, that's all. He'll be here tomorrow, as you heard.

Seeing is believing, sir!

Now for a little drink: the fresh air makes me thirsty!... All well, Tintin?

A letter from Chang in London: he's fine, and sends you his regards.

What a nice lad he is.

Yes, and another letter ...You'll never guess who from: Bianca Castafiore!

Bianca Castafiore! Ha! ha! ha! The dear old Milanese nightingale!

AAAAAH ♩ My beauty... ♪

SPLOTCH

...past compare ♩ Ma-a-aargarita ♩♪

Hello, there's a storm brewing.

And what has that delightful creature to say?

No, it's passed over.

That she's arriving here at Marlinspike tomorrow!

7

Castafiore? . . . Tomorrow?? . . . Here??? You're pulling my leg!!! Read it yourself.

My dear young Tintin, it is so long since . . . blablabla . . . two recitals in your country . . . blablabla . . . escape from the press . . . blablabla . . . May your simple and unaffected friend (not half!) invite herself to Marlinspike Hall? . . . blablabla . . . I shall arrive on the 17th . . . What?

Castafiore?! . . . Here!? . . . Cataclysm! Calamity! Catastrophe!
Er . . . there's a little postscript for you . . .

Kindest regards to Captain Bartok.

Haddock, by thunder, Signora Castoroili! . . . Haddock!

NESTOR!
Coming, sir!

Nestor, pack my bags this instant! I must be out of this house in an hour!
Very good . . . sir . . .

It's no good protesting: I'm weighing anchor!

THUMP

Er . . . it's the step, sir.

But, thundering typhoons, you knew the step was broken! . . . I've made myself hoarse reminding you about it!
DONG
Er . . . yes, sir . . . The doorbell, sir.

I'll go. You get on with my packing.

Pity he's going; the fur would really fly with Castafiore here . . .
MRRAW

A telegram for you Tintin. Who knows: perhaps Bianca Cataclysm is held up.

Well?
It's from her, all right!

Sincere regrets. Stop. Cannot come . . .

Splendid!

HOORAY!

!

Good gracious me, I shouldn't have come without my umbrella.

Happy day! She isn't coming, Cuthbert old friend!

No, but I don't suppose it will last.

But . . .

Nestor! . . . Nestor! . . . You can stop packing! I shan't be going!

That isn't all, Captain . . .

Er . . . very good, sir.

Sincere regrets. Stop. Cannot come 17th. Stop. Arriving 16th. Stop. Regards, Bianca.

WHAT?!

The 16th! . . . The 16th! . . . But it's the 16th today!

Exactly, Captain.

All hands on deck! Abandon ship! Every man for himself! I'm off!

But where?

I don't know! Doesn't matter where. Milan perhaps. I've never dared go there in case I met that thundering typhoon!

But . . .

Nestor! . . . Nestor! . . . My bags! . . . At once!

CRRUMP

?

THUMP

BUMP

Captain! Captain!

Billions of bilious blue blistering barnacles!

Thundering typhoons, that step! . . . That confounded step! Just wait till I see that bone idle builder!

Nothing broken, I hope?

Luckily not. Though I might easily have sprained something . . .

YEOW!

It's a bad sprain . . . and you've pulled the ligaments.

?

Tomorrow I'll put it in plaster . . .

In plaster!! . . . A sprained ankle?! . . . But doctor, I'm leaving today for Italy.

Out of the question. Absolute rest with the foot in plaster for a fortnight. Think yourself fortunate you didn't break a leg.

And my advice to you is, get that step repaired. Someone else might not have your good luck . . . Goodbye.

Goodbye, doctor.

Luck? If that's luck, give me disaster!!

CUCKOO

!

Ah, dear Captain Fatstock! . . . How too divine to see you again!

How . . . how did you get in?

Misericordia! What has happened to you?

A sprain! But . . . how did you get in?

Just as we arrived, dear Tintin was showing someone out. So we didn't need to ring.

"We"? There can't be more than one of you!

But of course! Irma, my maid, always travels with me . . .

And so does my accompanist, Igor Wagner, who obviously has to . . . ha! ha! ha! . . . accompany me!

10

Excuse me, signora, may I introduce our old friend Professor Calculus.

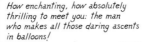

How enchanting, how absolutely thrilling to meet you: the man who makes all those daring ascents in balloons!

POP
!

I am deeply honoured, signora. What a rare pleasure for me to meet so great an artist . . . an artist of such charm, such distinction, such . . .

Professor, you make me blush!

I sincerely hope so, signora. Tintin has often spoken of your pictures . . . the delicacy of the drawing in perfect harmony with the boldness of the colour. And your portraits, I know, always display an amazing likeness.

Nestor, please show the signora to her room.

Yes, sir.

How kind . . . But first . . . er . . . Irma, where is the . . . er . . . the little something for dear Captain Drydock?

In the taxi, madame. I'll fetch it.

!

I thought . . . I thought that an old sailorman like yourself must feel very lonely in his little boat . . . Il povero capitano!

That's very kind of you, but . . .

I knew you'd adore . . .

Here, madame.

?

. . . this pretty polly to be your constant companion.

?!¿?

I . . . What a . . . surprise! . . . What a delightful surprise! . . . Nothing could have given me . . . er . . . greater pleasure.

Aha! I knew it!

Here, Irma, put him on his perch.

Yes, madame.

I can't stand animals who talk!

They've unloaded the luggage. This is where she's staying . . . To work, Gino!

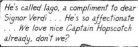

He's called Iago, a compliment to dear Signor Verdi ... He's so affectionate ... We love nice Captain Hopscotch already, don't we?

Stroke him, Captain, don't be afraid; he wouldn't hurt a fly.

KILIKILIKILIKILI!

How sweet! ... He's taken to you already ... Ah, animals have an unfailing instinct: they immediately attach themselves to those they love.

You think so?

CRO!

YEOWWW!

Billions of bilious blue blistering barbecued barnacles! ... Cannibal! ... Bashi-bazouk! ... Vampire!

Hello-o-o! I can hear you!

Please, Captain Stopcock! Such language! ... Poor pollikins might learn it! ... Show me your hand.

CRO!

Now, now ... our finger is just a teeny-weeny bit sore ... Irmaaa! ... The first aid things, please!

Here is the case, madame ... and ... this ...

Of course, I forgot! Dear Tintin, this is just a little gift from me to you.

There we are ... A pretty little butterfly to comfort the poor sailorman.

The Jewel Song!

I'm very grateful, signora. It was very kind of you to think of me.

Not at all, not at all! I thought it would remind you of our first meeting in Syldavia. Do you remember?

Shall I ever forget it! Of course, that was the first time I heard you sing the Jewel Song from "Faust".

Ah, yes, the Jewel Song ...

MERCY! ... MY JEWELS!

Here madame; I've got your jewel-case.

Oh, so you have. I can breathe again!

Now, my man, if you'd be kind enough to show me to my room...

As the signora wishes.

Oh, I almost forgot... The reporters will probably run me to earth here. May I ask my brave sailor to protect me?... Not a single interview, no publicity, no photographs ... nothing! I came here incognito; you must help me to escape.

Of course!

May I point out to the signora that the fourth step is broken.

Yes, yes, I see.

The signora's room.

Ravishing!

What delightful old furniture! ...and a four-poster bed. It's... er... Henry the Tenth, is it not?

Charles the First, signora.

DONG

Precisely what I meant, of course.

If the signora will excuse me: the doorbell.

You may go.

Fiddle! What is it now?

Oh dear!... The step!

Well done, Nestor ...always keep your head!

I'll put the telephone here, Captain, where you can reach it.

Thanks, Tintin, that's very kind.

Oh sir! . . . In the drive . . . a whole horde of gipsies! . . . They say you told them to come, sir . . . you invited them to camp in the grounds.

That's right, Nestor. Show them into the big meadow, down by the stream.

But sir! . . . If I may make so bold, sir . . . Gipsies, sir . . . Nothing but a bunch of thieving rogues . . . They'll only make trouble for you, sir.

Trouble!!

How can I be in worse trouble? . . . Go and see to them, Nestor . . .

But . . . I . . . er . . . Very good, sir.

Would you like me to go, Captain? Nestor has so much to do in the house already.

Thanks.

Inviting gipsies to stay!

He's mad . . . He's absolutely mad! . . . He'll come a cropper one of these days! . . .

THUMP

Blistering barnacles, that step! Why can't people look where they're going!

RRRING

Hello . . . Yes, Haddock here . . . Who's that? . . . The police! . . . What?!!

Ah, Captain: my men report that some gipsies who were camping by the main road have moved . . . It seems you invited them to pitch camp on your land . . . Is that so?

Quite correct, Inspector. I think it's intolerable! Those wretched creatures forbidden to camp except on a rubbish dump! And as I have a meadow . . .

Hello-o-o! I can hear you!

Hello? . . . What? . . . You can hear me? . . . Well, I can hear you. And since we can hear each other, let me say I quite understand your action, Captain. It's most generous . . . I beg your pardon . . . Did you say shut up?

No . . . not you! . . . I'm talking to this pestilential parakeet! Will you shut up, you . . .

Hello-o-o! I can hear you!

Ah, I see. You're still addressing your parrot . . . Now, about those gipsies. Of course, you're free to do as you like. But I should warn you: you'll only have yourself to thank when they make trouble for you.

Trouble! . . . Ha! ha! First I'm bitten by a little wildcat, then by a parrot! . . . I sprain an ankle . . . Castafiore descends on me with Irma and that budding Beethoven . . . And they talk about trouble! . . . Ha! ha! ha! ha!

Meanwhile . . .

Mission completed: all settled in.

I hate them, the gajos. They pretend to help, but in their hearts they despise us . . .

Not these, Mike, not these.

GRRR! WOOAH! WOOAH! GRRR!

Hello, what's up? Snowy's got wind of something.

WOOAH! WOOAH! GRRR! GRRR!

Snowy! . . . Here, Snowy!

?

WOOAH! WOOAH!

Hey, who are you? . . . Stop!

WOOAH! WOOAH!

The gap! . . . They're going through the gap in the wall!

WOOAH!

A car!

VROOMM

WOOAH!

!

What's the meaning of that? . . . And what shall I do? . . . Tell the Captain? . . . No, he's got enough on his plate already.

RRRING

Hello? . . . Hello? . . . Can you hear me?

?

Rrrring
Rrrring
Rrrring

KRRTCHMURTZ!

Mercy, my jewels!

I'll lock my jewels in this drawer, Irma . . .

. . . and I'll hide the key to the drawer in this vase, over here. Try to remember, girl.

Yes, madame.

That's that, Captain. Our gipsy friends are installed. They're delighted with their new camp.

Good. I'm very glad.

Hello-o-o! I can hear you!

That parrot! . . . It'll drive me crazy! . . . Anyway, its nearly bedtime! Then at least I'll be free of it for the night! . . .

Nuts!

That night . . . .

AH! MY BEAUTY

E-E-EEK!

!

O Dio! ... Dio mio! ...

What's happened?

There ... in my room ... at the window ... a monster!

A monster?

There's nothing here, signora. Absolutely nothing.

But I did; I saw a monster, I tell you ... A ghost or something ... It was horrible ... I heard a long, mournful cry, and I saw two eyes shining like diam ...

MERCY! MY JEWELS! IRMAAA! MY JEWELS?!

No, no, madame: they are quite safe.

TUWIT-TUWOO

O Dio! That voice!

The cry of the monster! ... Listen!

That? ... But that's only a bird: just a poor old night-owl!

Are you sure? And the footsteps on the ceiling?

On the ceiling?

Yes, I heard someone walking about upstairs ... It was a man, I'm certain.

Impossible, signora. It's only the attic above, and no one lives up there.

But I assure you ...

Don't be afraid, signora. Go back to sleep ... and close your window; then you won't need to worry.

The next morning...

I might just have a look under Signora Castafiore's window.

That's the one ...

Well, well, well ...

17

Fooptprints! . . . Right under the window! . . . Was she telling the truth, then?

The ivy?

No. It would never support a man's weight . . . A child, maybe? . . . But then there'd be traces of the climb . . . Anyway, the footprints are those of an adult . . .

. . . But whose? That's the problem . . . Someone from the house? . . . One of the two strangers I chased yesterday? . . . A gipsy?

Here, Snowy. We'll take a walk down by the encampment.

If there are any footprints, they'll show up in the mud. So let's go where they water their horses.

No, none like those we saw in the flowerbed.

SPLASH

?!

WOOAH! WOOAH!

? ? ?

Come on, Snowy. We shan't find our humorous friend by staying here . . .

There he goes. Ha! ha! He didn't wait for a second round, the little brat. I don't like the way he's always snooping around.

So, that's who it was . . . that gipsy . . . he threw the stone. But why?

We don't seem to be much further on . . . Come on Snowy . . . home.

That's the doctor leaving: he'll have put the Captain's foot in plaster. But there's another car . . . Who does that belong to?

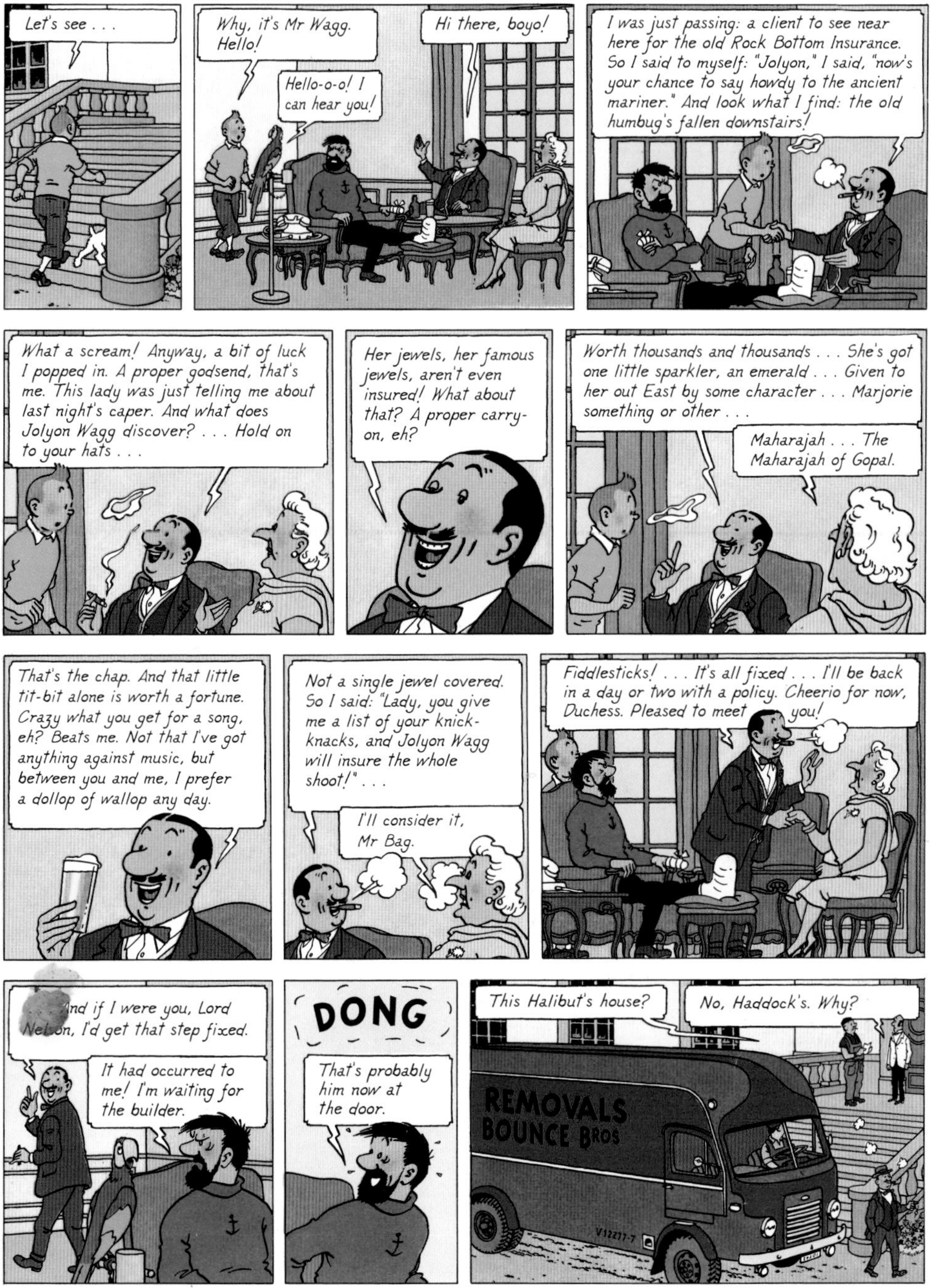

Let's see . . .
Why, it's Mr Wagg. Hello!
Hello-o-o! I can hear you!
Hi there, boyo!
I was just passing: a client to see near here for the old Rock Bottom Insurance. So I said to myself: "Jolyon," I said, "now's your chance to say howdy to the ancient mariner." And look what I find: the old humbug's fallen downstairs!
What a scream! Anyway, a bit of luck I popped in. A proper godsend, that's me. This lady was just telling me about last night's caper. And what does Jolyon Wagg discover? . . . Hold on to your hats . . .
Her jewels, her famous jewels, aren't even insured! What about that? A proper carry-on, eh?
Worth thousands and thousands . . . She's got one little sparkler, an emerald . . . Given to her out East by some character . . . Marjorie something or other . . .
Maharajah . . . The Maharajah of Gopal.
That's the chap. And that little tit-bit alone is worth a fortune. Crazy what you get for a song, eh? Beats me. Not that I've got anything against music, but between you and me, I prefer a dollop of wallop any day.
Not a single jewel covered. So I said: "Lady, you give me a list of your knick-knacks, and Jolyon Wagg will insure the whole shoot!" . . .
I'll consider it, Mr Bag.
Fiddlesticks! . . . It's all fixed . . . I'll be back in a day or two with a policy. Cheerio for now, Duchess. Pleased to meet you!
And if I were you, Lord Nelson, I'd get that step fixed.
It had occurred to me! I'm waiting for the builder.
DONG
That's probably him now at the door.
This Halibut's house?
No, Haddock's. Why?
REMOVALS BOUNCE BROS

We've brought the piano.

The piano?

Piano??

Piano???

Oh, yes, the piano! ... It's mine. I hired a piano, to practise with Mr Wagner. I do hope you don't mind ...

Of course not, I'm overjoyed.

You sweet old thing! ... In that case they can put it in here, so we can cheer you up.

I ... er ... thank you; but the maritime gallery would be better for you.

Admirable! ... Mr Wagner, just see to it, will you?

Certainly, signora.

Thundering typhoons, she'll have a juke-box next!

Is that piano for you?

Yes, it is.

Excuse me, your shoelace is undone.

Why, so it is.

!

RRRRING

Drat that parrot!

RRRING

Hello, yes ... Speaking ... 'Paris-Flash International'? I beg your pardon? ... What? An interview? ... I ... er ... I'm very flattered ... Gladly ...

I can hear you!

Oh! An interview with Signora Castafiore! ... I ... er ... I'm very sorry, but Signora Castafiore has asked me to say ...

Allow me ... 'Paris-Flash'? ... Hello-o-o! ... I can hear you!

?

Yes, this is me ... Of course I'm me ... An interview? ... Naturally ... with pleasure. Whenever you like ... Very well. I shall look forward to tomorrow ... Ciao!

Those footprints ... they were made by the little pianist ... Very odd

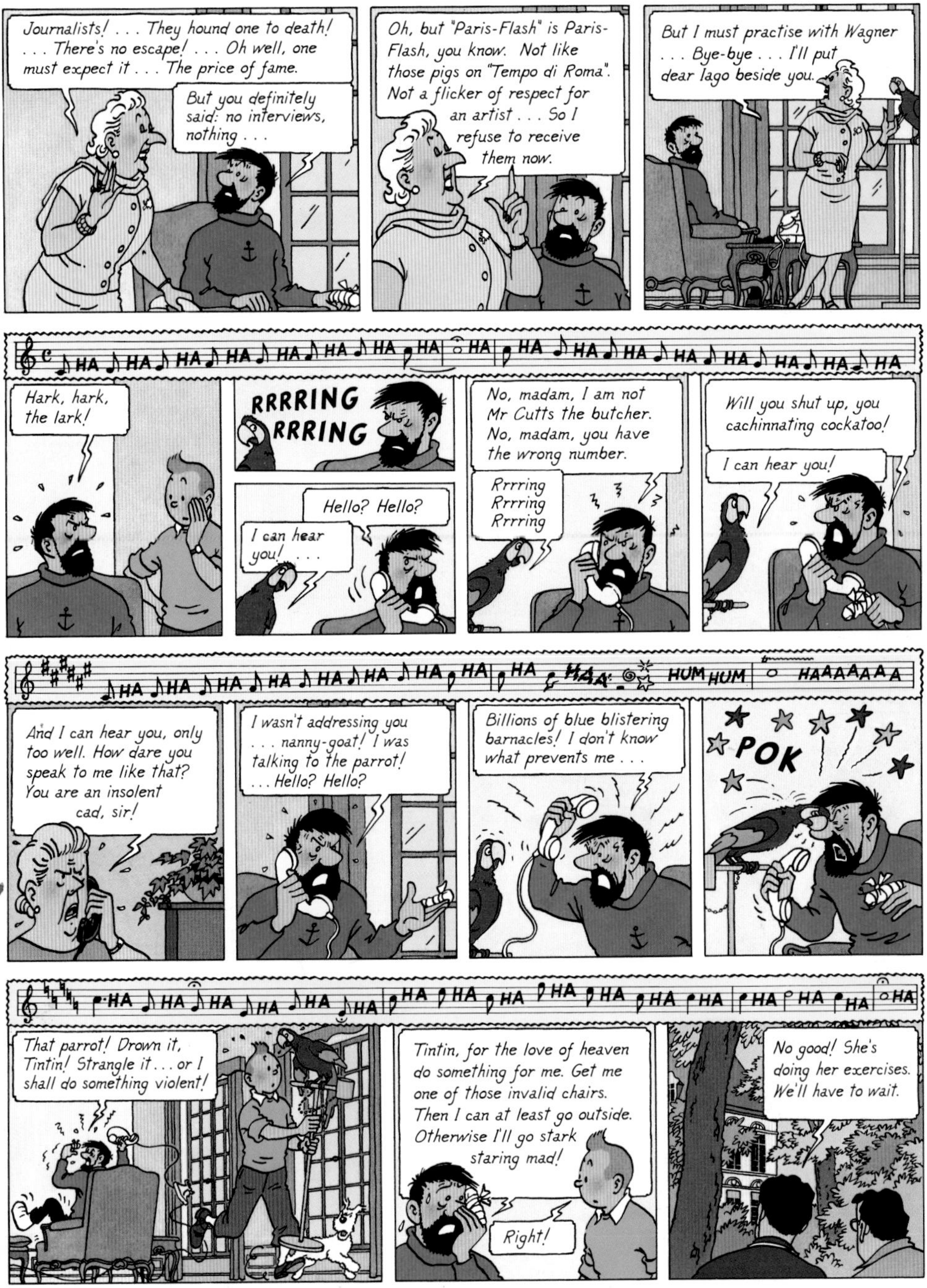
Journalists! . . . They hound one to death! . . . There's no escape! . . . Oh well, one must expect it . . . The price of fame.
But you definitely said: no interviews, nothing . . .
Oh, but "Paris-Flash" is Paris-Flash, you know. Not like those pigs on "Tempo di Roma". Not a flicker of respect for an artist . . . So I refuse to receive them now.
But I must practise with Wagner . . . Bye-bye . . . I'll put dear Iago beside you.
HA HA HA HA HA HA HA HA HA HA HA HA HA HA HA HA HA HA HA HA
Hark, hark, the lark!
RRRRING RRRING
Hello? Hello?
I can hear you! . . .
No, madam, I am not Mr Cutts the butcher. No, madam, you have the wrong number.
Rrrring Rrrring Rrrring
Will you shut up, you cachinnating cockatoo!
I can hear you!
HA HA HA HA HA HA HA HA HA HA HAA HUM HUM HAAAAAAA
And I can hear you, only too well. How dare you speak to me like that? You are an insolent cad, sir!
I wasn't addressing you . . . nanny-goat! I was talking to the parrot! . . . Hello? Hello?
Billions of blue blistering barnacles! I don't know what prevents me . . .
POK
HA HA HA HA HA HA HA HA HA HA HA HA HA HA HA HA HA HA
That parrot! Drown it, Tintin! Strangle it . . . or I shall do something violent!
Tintin, for the love of heaven do something for me. Get me one of those invalid chairs. Then I can at least go outside. Otherwise I'll go stark staring mad!
Right!
No good! She's doing her exercises. We'll have to wait.

Yes, I know . . . I couldn't help it. I had to finish a tombstone: it was urgent. What? Yours is urgent too: yes, I know . . . Look I'll be there first thing tomorrow morning . . . Yes, without fail.

If he's not here tomorrow I'll get someone else, and that's flat.

Captain! Captain!

?

Here's your new racing car.

?

♪HA ♪HA ♪HA ♪

Hooray! I'm free!

Wooah! Wooah!

♪HA ♪HA ♪HA ♪HA ♪HA ♪

Peace at last . . . And there's old Cuthbert, pruning his roses . . . .

Meanwhile . . .

Ah, Paris-Flash! Come in gentlemen. I will inform the signora.

Hello, Cuthbert. Working already this morning?

Very well, thank you. And you? . . . How's the foot?

Oh, not so bad! . . . Anyway, I might have broken my leg . . . Then I really should have looked a fool.

Cool? In the shade perhaps, but in the sun it's really quite hot.

Great news, Captain - but this is strictly between ourselves - I have succeeded in raising a completely new variety of rose.

Well done! Splendid! . . . Better than building rockets and chasing off into the blue.

No, no, white! . . . But such a white! . . . Pearly, sparkling, immaculate! . . . And the shape - perfect! . . . And what perfume - exquisite!

Well, Professor, I congratulate you.

OW!

?

And the name? Aha! You will never guess . . .

What was that? Who shouted?

I've had an idea – I think I may say an inspiration.

Hi! . . . Stop, whoever you are!

Idiot! Did you have to put your great feet into a wasps' nest?

As I told you, the rose I have created is white. Now, what is white in Italian?

Bianca, of course . . . Bianca! You follow me?

Bianca! Bianca! . . . Who were those ectoplasms, bolting like rabbits? That's what interests me!

Yes, Bianca, like our delightful guest. This rose shall be called "Bianca Castafiore". A charming compliment, don't you think?

The scoundrels! I'll bet they were up to no good!

But the world must wait . . . You mustn't breathe a word, I implore you. It must be a complete surprise.

What? . . . Which? . . . A surprise? . . . For whom?

That's agreed, isn't it? . . . I can count on you . . . This is strictly between ourselves.

Strangers in the park . . . What's it all about?

Hello, who's that on the seat? Oh, it's . . .

IRMAAA!

IRMAAA!

Yes, madame.

Where are you, Irma?

Here, madame. I'm coming.

Take cover!

Have you seen Captain Hammock? I simply must find him!

If you see him, tell him we've finished. These gentlemen from "Paris-Flash" have concluded their interview and would so like to meet him.

Yes, madame.

Disaster! They're coming this way. I'm caught like a rat in a trap!

You know, he's just a dear old sea-dog, a bit crusty at first, but . . .

. . . beneath a rough exterior he hides the simple heart of a big, lovable child.

There he is asleep, and in the shade, too.

Zzzz . . .
Zzzz . . .

Captain Paddock! Oh, you naughty man, look at you, asleep in the shade! You'll catch your death of cold!

What? . . . Oh, I must have been asleep.

Look, I've brought your coat. It's chilly out here . . . Now, now, now!

But I'm not cold!

I see I must scold you for something else, too . . . That jersey, it really won't do on a man of your age!

But . . .

It's like your hair! . . . When will you learn to do it properly, and stop looking like a scruffy little schoolboy?

But . . .

Let me introduce Christopher Willoughby-Drupe and Marco Rizotto of "Paris-Flash".

Hello!

'Morning.

Well, gentlemen, now that you've all met, I will release you. Roam about in the grounds as you please. Captain Hassock and I will expect you to lunch.

Now, my dear, let us have a little chat.

Well, what do you make of it?

The same as you, chum! This is a sensation . . . But we must be sure . . .

True or not, Marco my boy, it'll sell!

I can just see the cover!

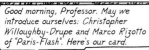
Look, a gardener. Come on, we'll try to pump him.

OK!

But . . . it isn't the gardener . . . It's Professor Calculus, who went to the moon with Tintin. He should be in the know.

Let's go!

Good morning, Professor. May we introduce ourselves: Christopher Willoughby-Drupe and Marco Rizotto of "Paris-Flash". Here's our card.

From the Yard?

Reporters! . . . So that's it! The Captain had to tell someone. He's already tattled to the papers about my new rose, the old gossip!

Tell me, Professor, off the record, isn't there something in the wind between La Castafiore and Captain Haddock? . . . Plans for a wedding? . . . Am I right?

It was the Captain who told you, wasn't it?

Well . . . yes and no . . . You know how it is . . . we reporters . . . flair, you understand . . . So it's true?

Great sunspots! And he promised to say nothing! It was to have been a surprise . . .

I quite understand . . . How soon will it be?

It all depends on the weather . . . But it could happen any day now.

Aha! So it's imminent, then! And . . . how long has this been fixed? Can you give any little snippets about them . . . How they first met, for example?

Precisely! . . . It was two years ago . . .

. . . at the Chelsea Flower Show. But ssh! Here she comes . . . Signora Bianca, with the Captain. Not a word about this!

Right!

Er . . . the Professor was telling us . . . er . . . about his roses. How magnificent they are!

Exquisite. I was just saying so to Captain Havoc.

Meanwhile . . .

Got that? Sugarplum . . . Oriana . . . Semiramis . . .

That's right . . . Exactly . . . No, no, I'll ring you myself . . . OK then . . . Till tomorrow.

Oh, how I adore flowers! They bring them in armfuls, but I never get tired of them!

Dear lady, allow me to offer you this modest "Crimson Glory" . . . until . . . er . . . something better comes along . . . Ha! ha!

Oh, Professor!

MMMM! What a sweet scent!

Smell, Captain! . . . Inhale the fragrance . . . Exquisite, isn't it?

YEOW!

Billions of blistering barnacles! I've been stung by a bee!

My poor boy, how did you manage to do that? And what a terrible fuss! You frightened me to death! Wait, I'll help you. First remove the sting . . . There! Then apply crushed rose petals to the spot.

Th-e-re! Better already, aren't we?

Now, my friends, I'll leave you. I must change for lunch . . . Ciao!

Trala laaa ♪ ♪ ♪ ♪

You're looking for Captain Maggot, I'm sure. You'll find him in the rose garden. The poor darling, he's been stung on the nose by a bee.

Oh!

A bee-sting on the nose . . . Poor Captain: that could be horribly painful.

E-E-EEK! MY NECKLACE!

26

IRMA-A-A! Yes, madame.
IRMA-A-A!

Oh, it's you! . . . Something frightful has happened: I've just broken my necklace!

Don't worry, signora. I'm sure we'll find all the beads.

There you are at last! I've been calling you for hours. You should have been here to pick up my necklace.

I am so grateful, my young friend. It's not that this necklace is particularly valuable: it's only fashion jewellery. But it's from Tristan Bior. And say what you like, Bior is still Bior!

Er . . . obviously!

Now let's see about the Captain's nose.

Don't think I'm angry with you, Captain, but why did you tell them about my rose?

What? Your rose?

Your rose! Will you shut up about your rose! Blistering barnacles, if I hadn't had one shoved in my face, I shouldn't have a nose like an overgrown strawberry!

Oh no, white!

Excuse me, madame, have you seen my embroidery scissors . . . you know, the little gold ones . . .

Why should I have seen them, girl? It's not my job to look after your things.

I didn't say that, madame . . . It's strange, I had them earlier, when you called me the first time; when I returned to my seat I couldn't find them.

Well, have a good look, my child . . . No one's going to steal a pair of scissors, are they?

No, madame.

Meanwhile . . .

Little scissors made of gold . . . Aren't they pretty, Uncle Mike?

Very nice!

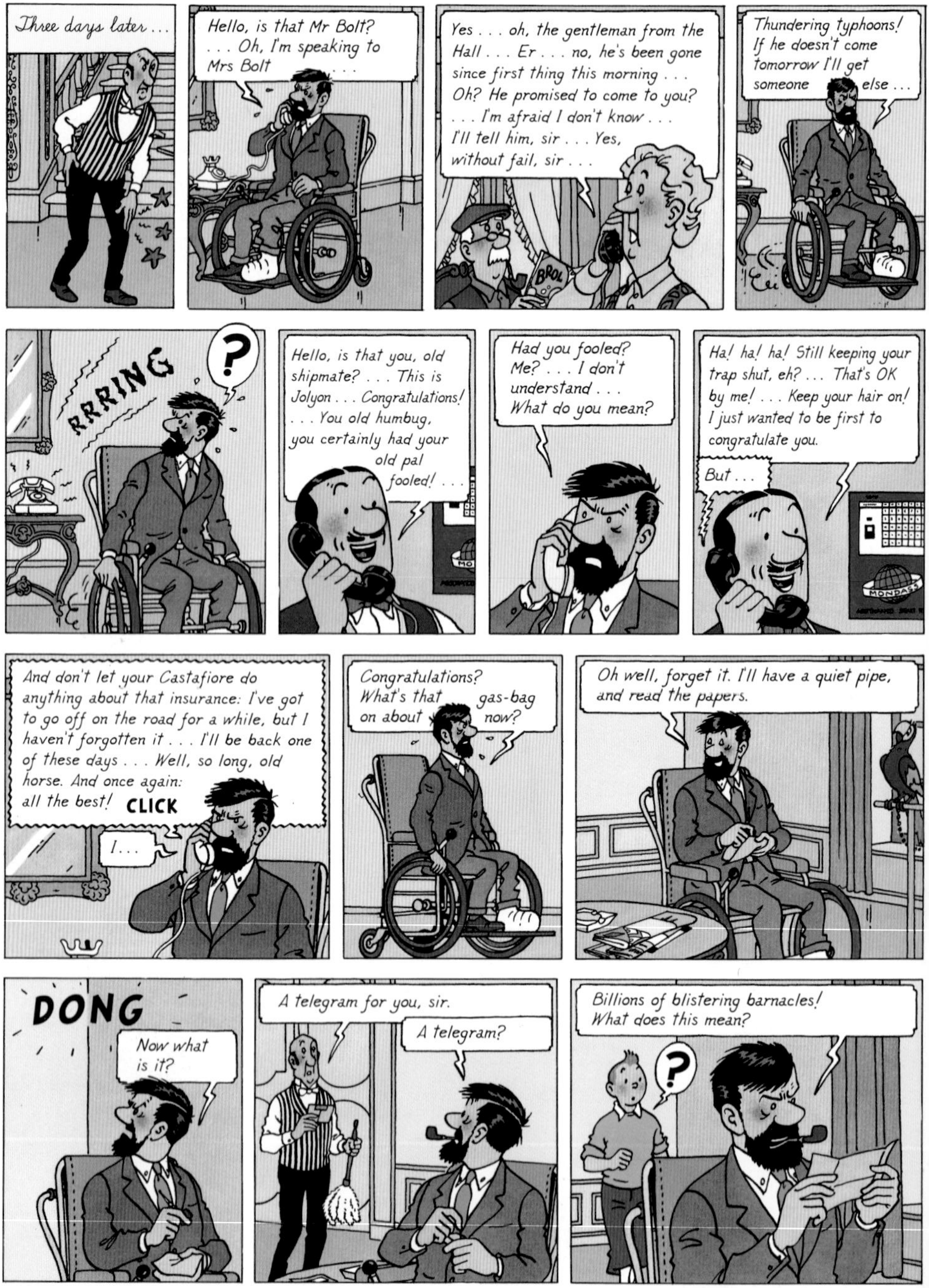
Three days later . . .
Hello, is that Mr Bolt? . . . Oh, I'm speaking to Mrs Bolt . . .
Yes . . . oh, the gentleman from the Hall . . . Er . . . no, he's been gone since first thing this morning . . . Oh? He promised to come to you? . . . I'm afraid I don't know . . . I'll tell him, sir . . . Yes, without fail, sir . . .
BROL
Thundering typhoons! If he doesn't come tomorrow I'll get someone else . . .
RRRING
?
Hello, is that you, old shipmate? . . . This is Jolyon . . . Congratulations! . . . You old humbug, you certainly had your old pal fooled! . . .
Had you fooled? Me? . . . I don't understand . . . What do you mean?
Ha! ha! ha! Still keeping your trap shut, eh? . . . That's OK by me! . . . Keep your hair on! I just wanted to be first to congratulate you.
But . . .
MONDASS
And don't let your Castafiore do anything about that insurance: I've got to go off on the road for a while, but I haven't forgotten it . . . I'll be back one of these days . . . Well, so long, old horse. And once again: all the best!
CLICK
I . . .
Congratulations? What's that gas-bag on about now?
Oh well, forget it. I'll have a quiet pipe, and read the papers.
DONG
Now what is it?
A telegram for you, sir.
A telegram?
Billions of blistering barnacles! What does this mean?
?

Read that and tell me if it conveys anything to you. And that idiot Wagg has just rung up to congratulate me.

Oh!

Heartiest congratulations, Captain Chester...

Doesn't make sense, does it?

WHAT?

PARIS FLASH
INTERNATIONAL

SCOOP!

MILANESE **NIGHTINGALE** BIANCA CASTAFIORE **WILL MARRY OLD SEA LION**

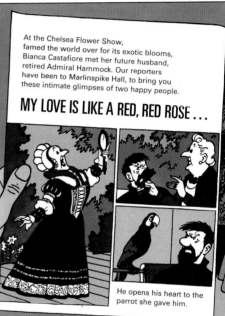

At the Chelsea Flower Show, famed the world over for its exotic blooms, Bianca Castafiore met her future husband, retired Admiral Hammock. Our reporters have been to Marlinspike Hall, to bring you these intimate glimpses of two happy people.

MY LOVE IS LIKE A RED, RED ROSE...

He opens his heart to the parrot she gave him.

...Loneliness banished, he never tires of hearing the golden voice, singing for him the famous Jewel Song from "Faust"...!!???!!

Blistering barnacles! Wait till I get my hands on the miserable molecule of mildew who dreamed up this   balderdash!

Hello-o-o! I can hear you!

CRO!

29

Buon giorno, Tintin! Buon giorno, Captain Bootblack!

Have you seen the marvellous article about me in "Paris-Flash"?

Yes, I have seen it, madame! . . . You call it marvellous? . . . Announcing our marriage!

Oh, yes, priceless, isn't it?

But it doesn't mean a thing. The newspapers have already engaged me to the Maharajah of Gopal, to Baron Halmaszout, the Lord Chamberlain of Syldavia, to Colonel Sponsz, to the Marquis di Gorgonzola, and goodness knows who. So you see, I'm quite used to it . . .

Well I'm not, madame, and I . . .

RRRING

HELLO!

This is Thompson and Thomson, with a 'p' and without . . . Our west bishes . . . er . . . our wet dishes . . . I mean, many congratulations, Captain. We've just seen "Paris-Flash".

KOUA KOUAKOUIN KOUIN-KOUIN KOUA KOUIN KOUA . . . BANG!

Nitwitted ninepins!

How very odd: not a word about my rose.

But . . . but . . . oh, goodness! . . . Goodness gracious! . . . Goodness gracious me!

My dear friend! . . . My dear old friend! Most hearty congratulations! . . . How happy I am to hear the news! But why didn't you tell me before?

A few telegrams, sir. And may I be allowed, sir, to offer my most respectful felicitations.

Good wishes, Cutts the butcher . . . Congratulations, Mr and Mrs Bolt . . . Sincere greetings, Doctor Patella . . . My most delighted good wishes, Oliveira da Figeira . . .

RRRING

Hello? . . . Yes . . . yes . . . Supavision . . . One moment, please . . .

It's a television company, sir . . . They want . . . Now television!!

Oh no! Leave me alone! I refuse to behave like a performing seal in front of a camera!

But sir . . .

There's no but about it . . . I've had enough of reporters! . . . Tell them I'm out!

But sir, it's Signora Castafiore they wish to speak to.

To me? But my good man, why didn't you say so before?

Hello-o-o! . . . Yes, I can hear you! . . . Supavision? . . . Yes . . . I'd adore to . . . When? . . . Tomorrow . . . Lovely . . . yes . . . I shall look forward to seeing you!

What a bore they are! . . . But what can one do? . . . They'll be here tomorrow afternoon.

Someone here must have given all this to the reporters. I wonder who it was?

Oh, what a charming idea! An aubade!

MARLINSPIKE PRIZE BAND

Your ladyship, Captain, sir . . .

Sssh!

But . . .

On behalf of the Marlinspike Prize Band Supporters' Club I have the honour to present to you with due deference the respectful congratulations of all our members on this felicitous event, which has brought . . .

. . . a light to every throat and a lump in every eye . . .

You must offer them champagne . . .

What? . . . Champagne? . . . Never!

Several glasses later . . .

The following afternoon . . .

Forgive us for being so late, signora. On our way out of town we were caught in a traffic jam. Then we wasted time trying to find the way. And to crown it all we had a breakdown!

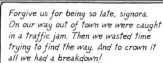

Did you? How priceless!

Thundering typhoons! This is a full-scale invasion!

Oh, sorry!

The television boys! . . . Now or never, Gino! . . . In you go, mix with all that crowd . . . and get to work!

I'll wait in the car just down the road . . . OK?

OK I'll take my gear and chance it . . .

Panel 1 (top):

I'm inside, anyway . . .

With that flood you can light the ceiling.

I'd better explain . . . It's a telerecording and we're also putting it on film.

Panel 2:

Ah, I see . . . Perhaps we can talk more easily sitting down.

Panel 3:

Right . . . I shall appear in the first sequence and say a few words of introduction. Then I put the first question, and the cameras focus on you. From then on I shall only be heard 'off'.

Ah!

Panel 4:

At the end of that sequence I shall ask if you'll be kind enough to sing . . . something specially for the viewers.

Naturally, with pleasure.

Panel 5:

Thank you. For the second sequence, you cross slowly to the piano, where your accompanist will be waiting, and you sing . . . What will you sing, signora?

I . . . er . . . well . . . what about the Jewel Song from "Faust", for instance?

Panel 6:

Excellent . . . Afterwards, I close the interview with a few words of thanks.

Just so!

Panel 7:

We're ready, Andy . . . what about you?

All OK I'd just like to do a voice test, and we're all set.

Panel 8:

Take up the mike, Jim. It's in the picture . . .

Don't mind me, lady. This is only a light meter.

Panel 9:

Good . . . How's that for balance? . . . Silence! . . . Sound on!

Vision on!

Panel 10:

Good evening, viewers. Tonight is rather a special occasion. We are visiting the eminent singer, Bianca Castafiore . . . All right like that?

So far everything's going like clockwork!

OK for sound!

Good. Now, signora, just a few words from you please.

Er... My turn now?... Just a few words?... Well... I... I... I'm happy... so very... happy... Well, I don't really know how to put it... Ah! ha! ha!

OK for sound!

Right. Stand by! Silence now, boys and girls.

Sound on!

Vision on!

OK... Let's roll!

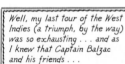

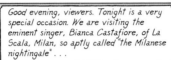

Good evening, viewers. Tonight is a very special occasion. We are visiting the eminent singer, Bianca Castafiore, of La Scala, Milan, so aptly called "the Milanese nightingale"...

Tell me, signora... is it indiscreet to ask the reason for your presence at Marlinspike?

Well, my last tour of the West Indies (a triumph, by the way) was so exhausting... and as I knew that Captain Balzac and his friends...

...would welcome me with open arms, I had no hesitation in inviting myself to stay.

Why, you've installed television! ... Three sets at once!! ... And you never even told me?!?

Ssh!

Oh! look... that's... that's Signora Castafiore! ... Yes, I assure you it is! ... Good gracious! Someone must tell her at once!

She must see it, the dear lady. She simply must!

Professor! Professor! Don't go in there. They're shooting!

E-E-EEK!

Stars above! What is the meaning of all this masquerade?

... A wedding is arranged, and I'm the last to hear about it! ... You install television, but you don't tell me! ... They're shooting a film here, and no one says a word! ... It's a conspiracy! Everyone's plotting to keep me in the dark!

... And poor Signora Castafiore is appearing on television, and no one thinks of telling her! ... It's monstrous!

Come with me, Professor. It's all a misunderstanding.

Come, Professor, let me explain . . .

Pained?! . . . Me? . . . Pained?! Certainly not, but . . .

We'll pick up from the last question . . . Stand by! . . . Sound on!

May I ask, signora, whether you have any plans?

Yes, a series of recitals in the United States, where I shall stay for two months: they are longing to hear me.

Poor Americans! What have they done to deserve it?

Then to South America to conquer the capitals . . .

And reduce them to ruins as well!

And . . . tell me, signora: which works will you perform on your tour . . . or should I say, your triumphal progress?

How well you put it! . . . Yes, as usual, I shall be singing Rossini, Puccini, Verdi, Gouni . . . Oh, silly me! Gounod!

Ah, Gounod? Wasn't it in Gounod that you achieved your greatest success . . . made your name, in fact?

Yes, the Jewel Song from "Faust" swept me to the pinnacle of fame. They say I'm divine . . .

Please, signora, I know our viewers would be overcome if you would sing that great aria for them . . .

Of course!

Emergency! . . . Take cover! She's going to sing!

Hello-o-o! I can hear you!

Come on, let's press on. It's getting late.

Vision on!

Stand by!
...Sound on!

AAAAH ♫ ♪ ♪
My beauty . . .

. . . past compare ♪ ♫
these jewels bright ♫
♫ ♪ I wear ♪ ♪ ♪

AAAH! ♪ ♫ ♫
♪ My beauty ♫ ♪

In you go!

I CAN HEAR YOU!

Sacrilege! Who dares to interrupt?

Cut!

Madamina! . . . It's Iago; he's escaped from his perch!

How clever animals are! And what a true instinct they have for art! Look at darling Iago; obviously he couldn't resist my voice! . . . But come, my pet, I must take you back. Excuse me, I won't be a moment.

Oh, there you are, Captain Bedsock. Just imagine, Iago got free from his perch all by himself, just to come and hear me!

Hmm! . . . Amazing!

Meanwhile...

Quick as you can, now . . . All ready? . . . Quiet studio please!

Tell me, ♪ ♫ ♫ ♪
♫ ♪ was I ever
♫ ♪ Marga . . .

. . . RITA . . . ?!

Damn! A blackout!

This is the last straw!

The fuses, I expect . . .

Anyone got a match?

☆HELP!

MERCY! MY **JEWELS!**

Mind the cables!

IRMAA-AA! MY JEWELS! Upstairs! Run!

Yes, madame!

Here, Snowy, stay close to me, otherwise you'll get trodden on.

WOOAH!

OH!

OOH!

YI! YI! YI!

MERCY! MY JEWELS!

What's the idea, running around in the dark? . . . Where are you off to?

PLOK PLOK PLOK PLOK

SLAM

That's the front door! . . . Come on, Snowy! Let's see!

WOOAH!

Down the drive! . . . Someone running away! . . . Great snakes, it's the photographer!

Too late to catch him now!

WOOAH! WOOAH!

AAAH!

AAAH!

Ah, there are the lights.

What was it, Nestor?

Only the fuses, Mr Tintin.

Meanwhile . . .

This'll please the boss!

Oh, madame! Madame!

THUMP

That cursed step again!

Your je . . . je . . . je . . . jewels . . .

Well, Irrmaaa?

Your je . . . madame, your jew-jew . . . your jewels!

In heaven's name, speak, girl!

Gone, madame! . . . All gone! . . . BOO-HOO-OO!

MORTE!!

AAAAAA

AAAAAA

Quick! Quick!

AAAAAA **?**

Over there! On the sofa!

Hey! . . . Here's another out cold!

We must ring the police at once.

Smelling salts . . . She needs smelling salts!

A fine carry-on!

I knew it would happen! . . . Boo-hoo-hoo! . . . I knew it would!

I may as well tell you, your photographer skedaddled off under the cover of darkness . . . I saw him making a dash for it.

Our photographer? . . . Who? . . . The photographer who was here just now? He was nothing to do with us.

But I thought he belonged to your outfit.

And I thought he was a private photographer engaged by Signora Castafiore.

Hello? . . . Marlinspike police? . . . This is Captain . . . What?

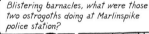

I said: wrong number, sir. This is Cutts the butcher . . . Not at all sir . . .

Hello? . . . Marlinspike police? . . . Oh, good . . . This is Captain Haddock.

Good evening, Inspector . . . Can you send someone along here at once? . . . There's been a serious robbery . . . What?! . . . A stroke of luck?!

What? . . . Who? . . . No?! . . . They were with you? Good heavens! . . . On their way? They'll be here any minute now? . . . But what were they doing . . . Yes . . . I see . . . All right, I'll wait till they arrive . . . Goodbye, Inspector.

Blistering barnacles, what were those two ostrogoths doing at Marlinspike police station?

So the photographer did it . . . That's odd . . . very odd indeed!

I know that look: it means trouble!

Oh, there you are, Tintin . . . We have visitors coming; you'll never guess who!

Oh? . . .

BOANG **GLING** **ZZING** **BING-GLING** **DING** **CLING**

Hello-o-o! I can hear you!

? **!?**

Visitors, you said? . . . I bet it's the Thompsons!

Quite right!

You poor, poor things! . . . What happened?

I . . . er . . . I think I must have braked a little late . . .

To be precise: I think you didn't brake at all!

You're not hurt, I hope?

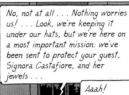

No, not at all . . . Nothing worries us! . . . Look, we're keeping it under our hats, but we're here on a most important mission: we've been sent to protect your guest, Signora Castafiore, and her jewels . . .

Aaah!

You dunder-headed Ethelreds! . . . I suppose you've come to shut the stable door, eh?

Good-evening, Captain!

The stable door? . . . No . . . We came by car . . .

The Captain means that the horse has gone: someone's just stolen the Castafiore jewels.

No?

Who?

That's what we've got to find out. But come in, and we'll put you in the picture.

A few minutes later . . .

Those are the facts . . . Everything seems to point to the mysterious photographer and yet . . .

Yet what? It's the classic crime: an accomplice cuts off the current while . . .

Out of the question . . . The current wasn't cut off: the fuses went.

A fuse, a power failure, it's all the same to me, young man. It was dark, and that was what the thief wanted.

Maybe . . . But he couldn't tell when the fuses were going to blow, or even that they'd blow at all . . . It was pure chance.

Hmm!

Just what I'd have said!

Well, since you're so keen to dot the 'i's and cross the 't's, I'd be interested to hear your answer to another little question which I might ask you . . .

You say the fuses blew . . . All right . . . But did you discover that for yourself? . . .

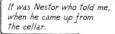

It was Nestor who told me, when he came up from the cellar.

Nestor? . . . The butler? . . . Aha!

Aha!

Nestor, who once worked for those crooks the Bird brothers . . . A good testimonial!

You know perfectly well, when those gangsters were tried the evidence proved that Nestor knew nothing of their activities. Anyway . . .

Anyway, blistering barnacles, Nestor is absolutely honest, and I forbid you to suspect him!

We shall see, we shall see! . . . Meanwhile, we'll proceed with the routine questioning.

Very well. Follow me.

Look out, there are cables all over the place.

Yes . . . We know!

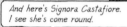

Thompson and Thomson, certified detectives.

No one is to leave!

And here's Signora Castafiore. I see she's come round.

Ah, Signora Nightingale, the Milanese Castafiore . . .

Signora!

Charmed!

Madam, we are here to set light to . . . er, to throw light on the circumstances surrounding your terrible loss . . .

To be precise . . . er . . .

Go on, gentlemen.

Just to clear up one point, madam: where were the jewels usually hocked . . . I mean locked?

In a drawer in my room, upstairs . . . Oh my jewels! . . . My beautiful jewels! . . .

Dead or alive, we shall find them, madam. Leave no stone unturned, that is our policy . . . Which reminds me: I presume your jewels are fully insured?

Alas, no, gentlemen . . .

Mr Swag promised to fix the whole thing up for me . . .

Swag? Fix it up? . . . Fix what? . . . Madame, is this some sort of conspiracy? . . .

No, no gentlemen. Mr Swag represents an insurance company.

Ah, that's all right . . . Otherwise . . .

Yes, otherwise . . .

Now, your jewels were in a drawer upstairs . . . Good . . . Was the drawer locked?

Yes, and the key was hidden in a vase. I fetched it from there earlier on, when I took the case out of the drawer.

The case? . . . What case was that, madame? . . .

Why, my jewel-case of course, the one I . . .

I . . . Mamma mia! . . . I remember now!

I was sitting here . . .

There! . . . There! . . . What did I tell you?

My jewels! Look! The little darlings! . . . All here? . . . Yes! . . . Oh, I could weep for joy, I'm so pleased to see them!

I really am a feather-brain! . . . I completely forgot; I'd come downstairs with my jewel-case, when these nice people from television arrived. How too, too hilarious! Ahaha! . . . What a good laugh! . . . Don't you agree, gentlemen?

Laugh, madam? . . . Us, madam? . . . We are not amused, madame! . . . Good night!

Quite so; we are not amusing!

What is wrong? . . . Oh dear, what have I done? . . . Why are they so cross?

Here, your hats! . . . And mind the cables!

Thank you, we can manage . . . We've told you before: we're not children!

BANG CLING

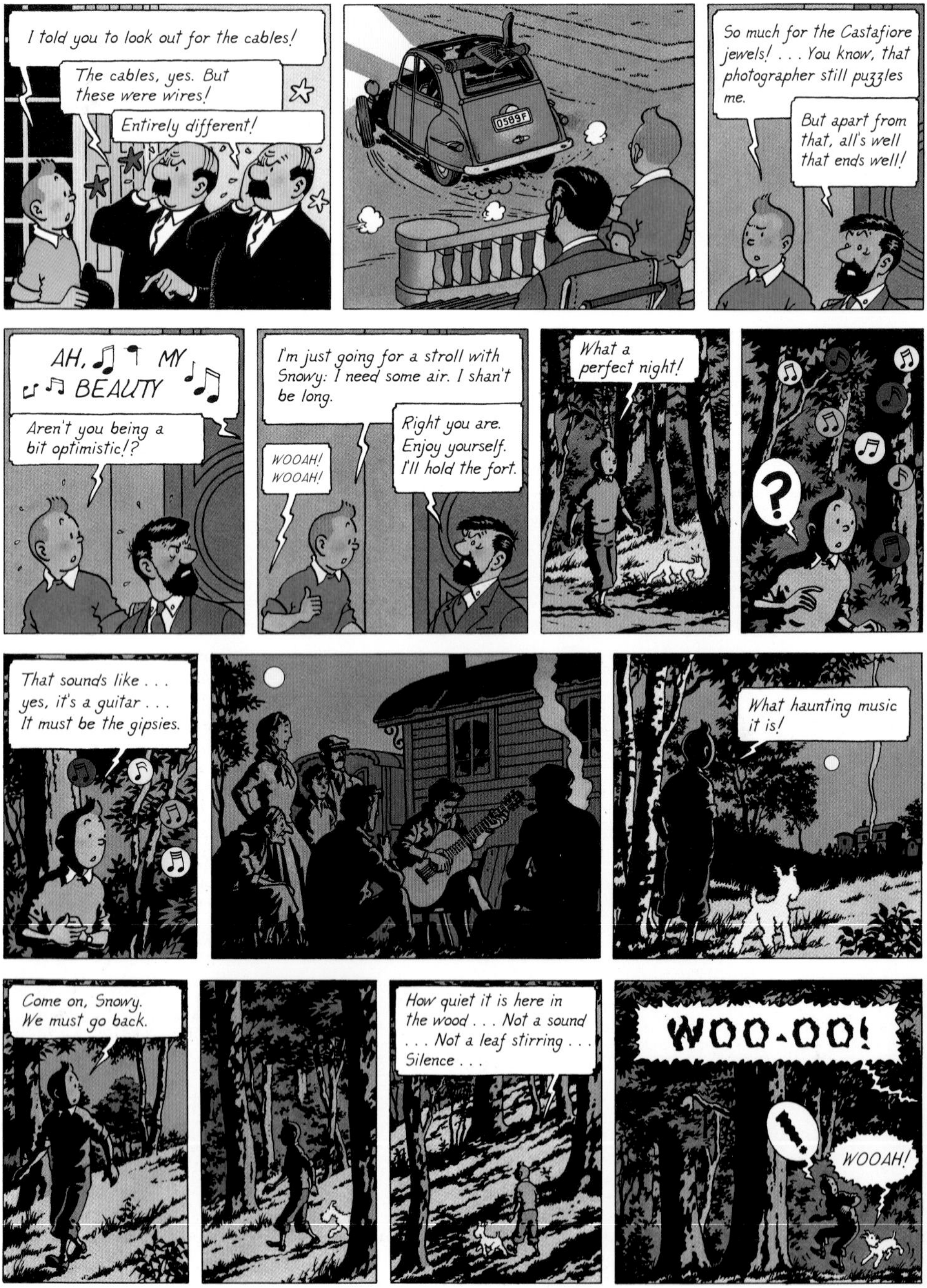
I told you to look out for the cables!
The cables, yes. But these were wires!
Entirely different!
0589F
So much for the Castafiore jewels! . . . You know, that photographer still puzzles me.
But apart from that, all's well that ends well!
AH, MY BEAUTY
Aren't you being a bit optimistic!?
I'm just going for a stroll with Snowy: I need some air. I shan't be long.
WOOAH! WOOAH!
Right you are. Enjoy yourself. I'll hold the fort.
What a perfect night!
?
That sounds like . . . yes, it's a guitar . . . It must be the gipsies.
What haunting music it is!
Come on, Snowy. We must go back.
How quiet it is here in the wood . . . Not a sound . . . Not a leaf stirring . . . Silence . . .
WOO-OO!
!
WOOAH!

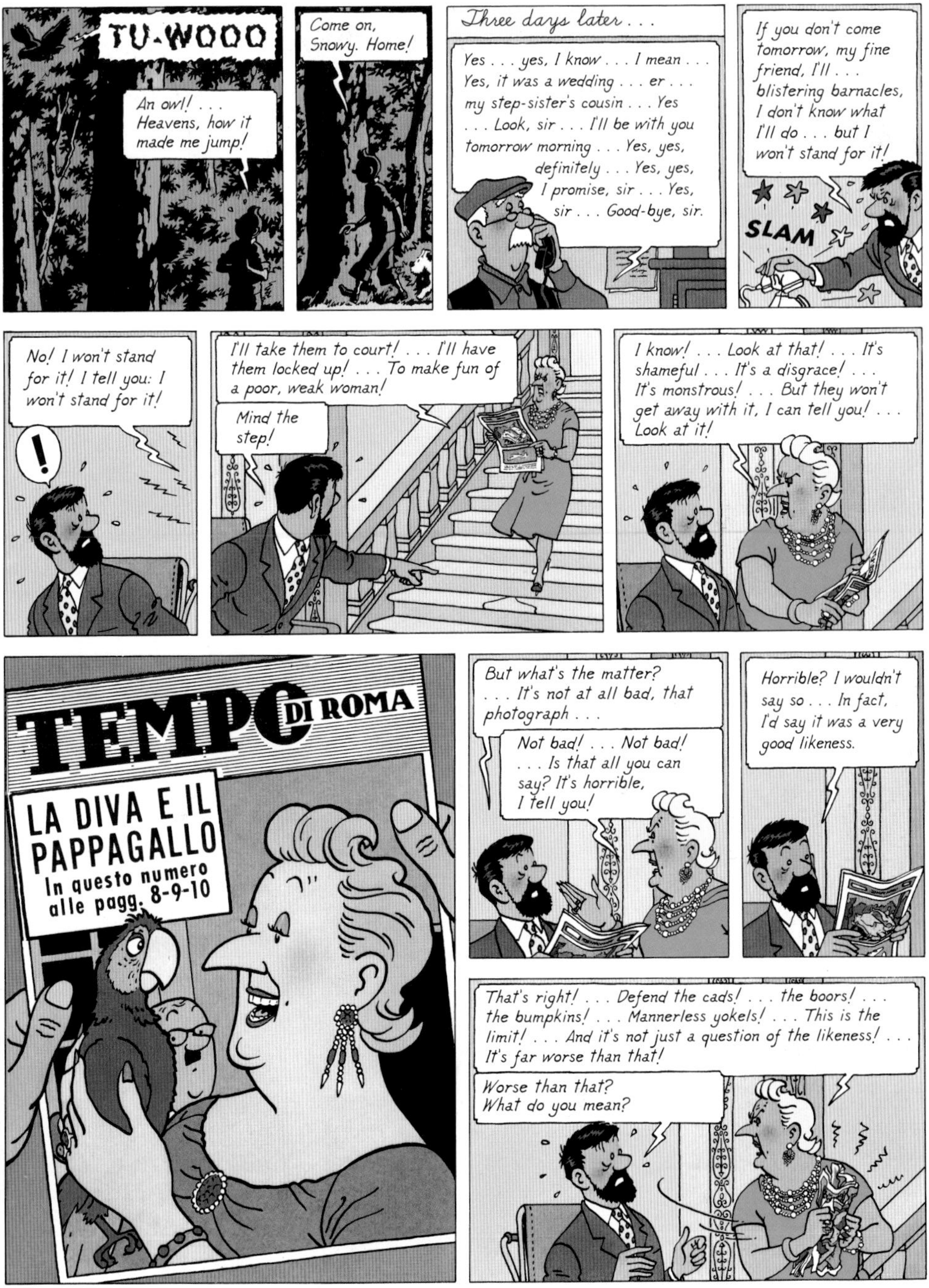
TU-WOOO
An owl! . . . Heavens, how it made me jump!
Come on, Snowy. Home!
Three days later . . .
Yes . . . yes, I know . . . I mean . . . Yes, it was a wedding . . . er . . . my step-sister's cousin . . . Yes . . . Look, sir . . . I'll be with you tomorrow morning . . . Yes, yes, definitely . . . Yes, yes, I promise, sir . . . Yes, sir . . . Good-bye, sir.
If you don't come tomorrow, my fine friend, I'll . . . blistering barnacles, I don't know what I'll do . . . but I won't stand for it!
SLAM
No! I won't stand for it! I tell you: I won't stand for it!
!
I'll take them to court! . . . I'll have them locked up! . . . To make fun of a poor, weak woman!
Mind the step!
I know! . . . Look at that! . . . It's shameful . . . It's a disgrace! . . . It's monstrous! . . . But they won't get away with it, I can tell you! . . . Look at it!
TEMPO DI ROMA
LA DIVA E IL PAPPAGALLO
In questo numero alle pagg. 8-9-10
But what's the matter? . . . It's not at all bad, that photograph . . .
Not bad! . . . Not bad! . . . Is that all you can say? It's horrible, I tell you!
Horrible? I wouldn't say so . . . In fact, I'd say it was a very good likeness.
That's right! . . . Defend the cads! . . . the boors! . . . the bumpkins! . . . Mannerless yokels! . . . This is the limit! . . . And it's not just a question of the likeness! . . . It's far worse than that!
Worse than that? What do you mean?

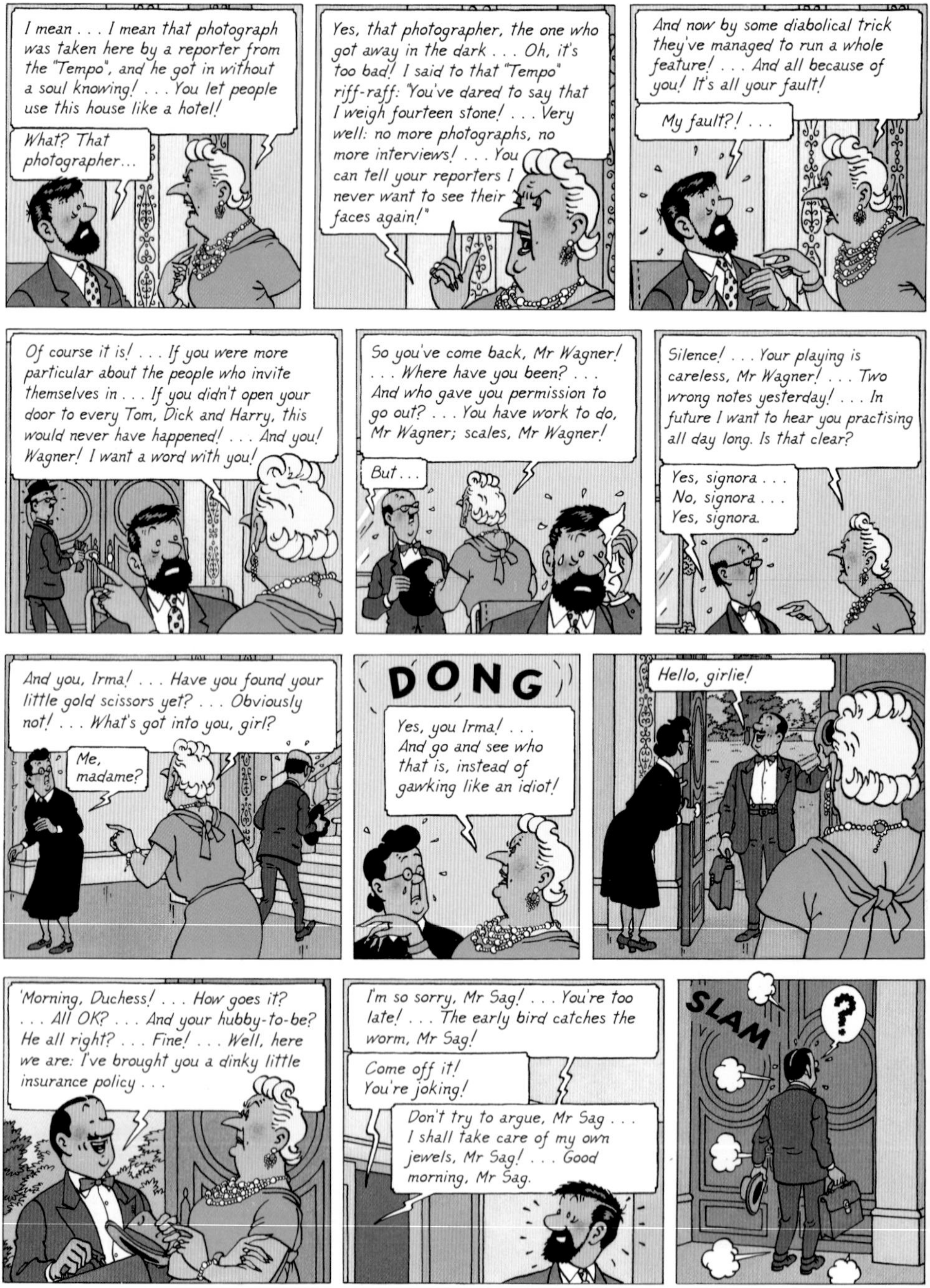
I mean . . . I mean that photograph was taken here by a reporter from the "Tempo", and he got in without a soul knowing! . . . You let people use this house like a hotel!
What? That photographer...
Yes, that photographer, the one who got away in the dark . . . Oh, it's too bad! I said to that "Tempo" riff-raff: "You've dared to say that I weigh fourteen stone! . . . Very well: no more photographs, no more interviews! . . . You can tell your reporters I never want to see their faces again!"
And now by some diabolical trick they've managed to run a whole feature! . . . And all because of you! It's all your fault!
My fault?! . . .
Of course it is! . . . If you were more particular about the people who invite themselves in . . . If you didn't open your door to every Tom, Dick and Harry, this would never have happened! . . . And you! Wagner! I want a word with you!
So you've come back, Mr Wagner! . . . Where have you been? . . . And who gave you permission to go out? . . . You have work to do, Mr Wagner; scales, Mr Wagner!
But . . .
Silence! . . . Your playing is careless, Mr Wagner! . . . Two wrong notes yesterday! . . . In future I want to hear you practising all day long. Is that clear?
Yes, signora . . .
No, signora . . .
Yes, signora.
And you, Irma! . . . Have you found your little gold scissors yet? . . . Obviously not! . . . What's got into you, girl?
Me, madame?
DONG
Yes, you Irma! . . . And go and see who that is, instead of gawking like an idiot!
Hello, girlie!
'Morning, Duchess! . . . How goes it? . . . All OK? . . . And your hubby-to-be? He all right? . . . Fine! . . . Well, here we are: I've brought you a dinky little insurance policy . . .
I'm so sorry, Mr Sag! . . . You're too late! . . . The early bird catches the worm, Mr Sag!
Come off it! You're joking!
Don't try to argue, Mr Sag . . . I shall take care of my own jewels, Mr Sag! . . . Good morning, Mr Sag.
SLAM
?

This is the end!

Ah, dear lady. It's quite extraordinary; I just found this magazine on the floor . . . And guess whose charming likeness adorns the cover . . . Look!

I know, Professor Candyfloss! I know! . . . And kindly refrain from calling it a likeness!

Isn't it? . . . A most striking resemblance . . . As for the parrot . . .

. . . he looks as if he's enjoying the joke . . . But wait . . .

That isn't all . . . Wait, there are some more pages inside. Now let me see . . .

Ah, Chester!

So you deign to come? It's ten minutes since the bell rang! I suppose you think I'm here to answer the door for you!

Let's see now . . .

But . . .

One moment, dear lady . . . I think I've got it . . . Yes, here we are . . .

!?

Look . . . ?!

But I could have sworn . . .

The days go by . . .

Scales! scales! scales! scales!

. . . until one morning

Scales! scales!

MERCY! MY JEWELS!

There she goes! . . . She's lost her geegaws again.

!?

MURDER!

You hear?

Yes, yes . . . don't worry: she'll find them in a minute or two.

MY EMERALD!

THUMP

Someone's missed that step again!

?

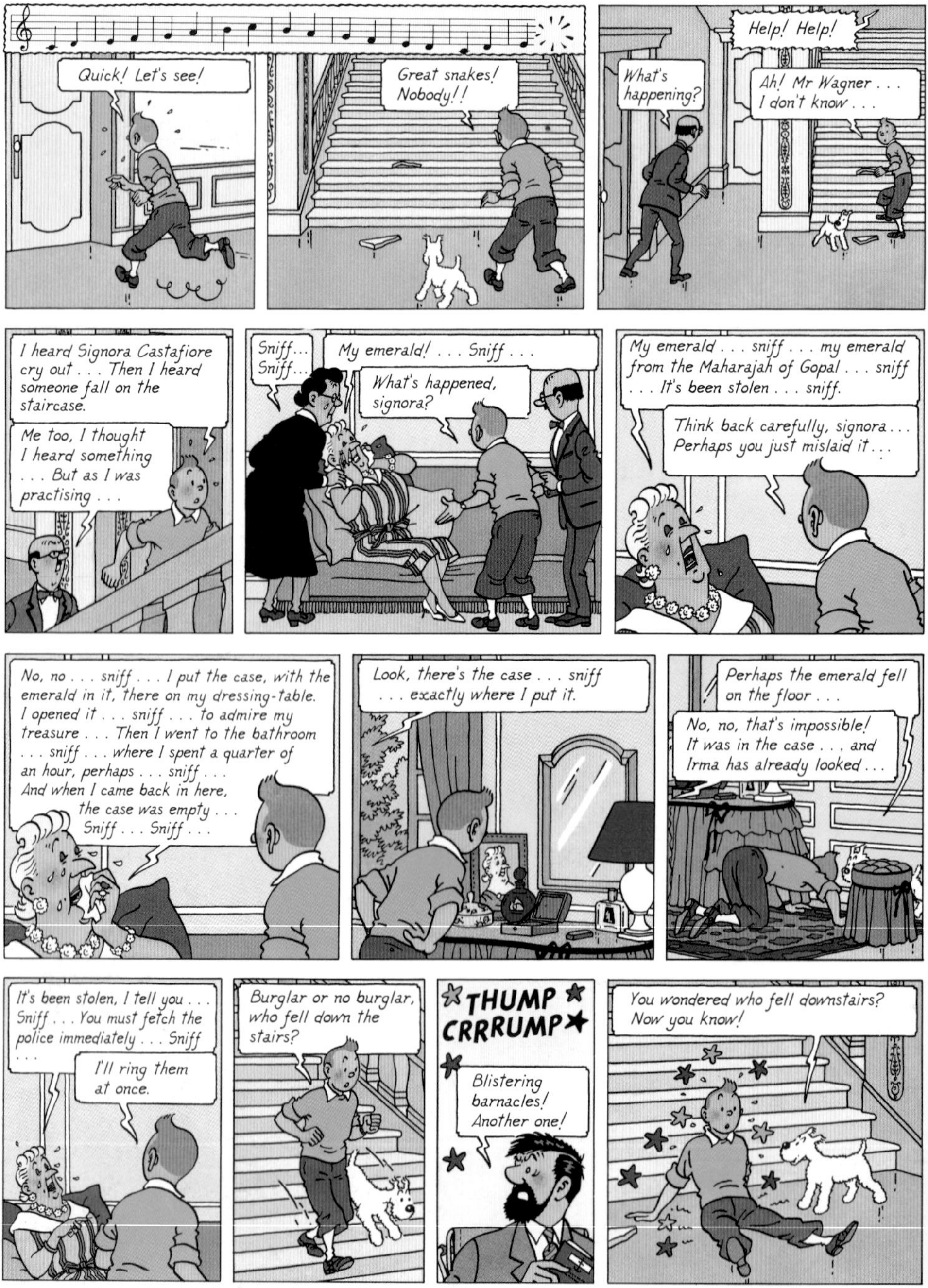

Quick! Let's see!
Great snakes! Nobody!!
Help! Help!
What's happening?
Ah! Mr Wagner . . . I don't know . . .
I heard Signora Castafiore cry out . . . Then I heard someone fall on the staircase.
Me too, I thought I heard something . . . But as I was practising . . .
Sniff... Sniff...
My emerald! . . . Sniff . . .
What's happened, signora?
My emerald . . . sniff . . . my emerald from the Maharajah of Gopal . . . sniff . . . It's been stolen . . . sniff.
Think back carefully, signora . . . Perhaps you just mislaid it . . .
No, no . . . sniff . . . I put the case, with the emerald in it, there on my dressing-table. I opened it . . . sniff . . . to admire my treasure . . . Then I went to the bathroom . . . sniff . . . where I spent a quarter of an hour, perhaps . . . sniff . . . And when I came back in here, the case was empty . . . Sniff . . . Sniff . . .
Look, there's the case . . . sniff . . . exactly where I put it.
Perhaps the emerald fell on the floor . . .
No, no, that's impossible! It was in the case . . . and Irma has already looked . . .
It's been stolen, I tell you . . . Sniff . . . You must fetch the police immediately . . . Sniff . . .
I'll ring them at once.
Burglar or no burglar, who fell down the stairs?
THUMP CRRRUMP
Blistering barnacles! Another one!
You wondered who fell downstairs? Now you know!

Unless I'm very much mistaken, it was the thief who fell on the stairs just now.

Hello? Yes, this is me . . . Yes, with a 'p', as in Philadelphia . . . Good mor . . . What . . . A robbery?! . . . An emerald!?! But . . . I . . . Look . . . Signora Castafiore . . . She's quite sure, isn't she; it really has been stolen this time?

A good question.

Yes, I'm afraid it has.

Good . . . That's lucky for her. I don't mind telling you, if she'd got us up to Marlinspike on another wild goose chase we wouldn't have come.

Definitely not!

Half an hour later . . .

In a nutshell . . . If the theft was committed by someone in the house, then there are only six suspects: Irma, Wagner, Nestor, Calculus, Tintin, and of course you yourself, Captain.

Are you suggesting . . . !?

Wait! . . . Three on our list can be ruled straight out: you, because you couldn't have gone upstairs in your wheelchair; Tintin, who was with you; and Wagner: he was playing the piano in the maritime gallery.

If you can call it playing . . .

That leaves Irma, Nestor, and the Professor.

One of those three a criminal? . . . You must be crazy!

And so, with your permission, we will question each of them separately, in private.

All right. I'll send Nestor in . . . But you're wasting your time.

Where was I? . . . In the garden, near Professor Calculus who was pruning his roses . . . I was watering the begonias when I heard Signora Castafiore shouting . . . I looked up at the windows . . .

Oho! You admit you could see the windows from where you were?

Certainly, sir . . . Then, as the cries continued, I dropped my watering can and hastened towards the house . . .

You were in a hurry to reach the house, eh? . . . That is all. Please ask the Captain to send in Irma.

Sniff . . . I was busy sewing in my room . . . sniff . . . Suddenly . . . sniff . . . I heard madame calling out . . . sniff . . . I ran to her room . . . sniff . . . just in time . . . sniff . . . to catch her in my arms . . . sniff . . . as she fainted . . . sniff . . .

Aha!

Your mistress has told us she spent about a quarter of an hour in the bathroom. In short, knowing her habits, you would have had an opportunity to enter her room, without any noise, and slip out with the emerald . . . or drop it from the window to an accomplice . . . To Nestor, for instance! . . . Come on! Confess!

EEEEEEEEEK!

Help!

Tintin! Save me!

Beasts!

OW!

YEOW!

?!

Beasts! Beasts! Beasts!

Irma! Irma! What's the matter? ... Stop!

They ... sniff ... they accused me ... sniff ... of stealing ... sniff ... madame's emerald ... I ... sniff ... who have never ... sniff ... taken a pin ... sniff ... which didn't belong to me ... sniff ... In fact ... sniff ... It was I ... sniff ... who had my little scissors stolen ... sniff ... and my beautiful silver thimble ... And they dare accuse me ... sniff ... Those wicked men!

BOO-HOO-HOOO!

Is that true? Did you really accuse her?

Er ... well ... I ... sort of ... You see, it's a trick that comes off sometimes.

Just a slight mishap. An occupational hazard ... Will you send in Calculus?

Certainly. But if I were you, I'd try some other method.

Professor, is it true that Nestor was near you when Signora Castafiore first cried out?

Not at all! It's not in the least inconvenient. I've been told about the theft, and I am heartbroken for the dear lady, heartbroken.

Yes ... well ... er ... To get back to my question, Professor ...

I thought of that at once, of course ... And I'd already come to certain conclusions before you sent for me.

No! no! no! I won't stand for it!

Of course, it's only a matter of simple direction finding; watch my pendulum.

Oh, so there you are!

It's swinging to the south-east. In fact it's pointing ...

What is this I hear? ... You had the effrontery to accuse Irma? ... My honest Irma! ... I won't stand for it! To attack a poor, weak woman! I shall complain to the United Nations!

... in the direction of the gipsy camp.

And if Irma gives in her notice, as she may well after such an insult, will you find me a new maid? . . . And what about the higher wages the new girl will want: will you pay those? . . . I tell you, if you don't apologize to Irma . . .

. . . I leave this house immediately. I shall tell the Captain!

You see? It points south-east.

Now . . . where were we? . . .

You understand, I'm not accusing anyone. It's simply that my pendulum indicates the direction of their camp.

A camp? What are you talking about?

Excuse me! I must stop you there! . . . They are real gipsies. I've seen them as clearly as I see you!

I say, your friend Calculus, is he a bit . . . er, you know? He keeps on talking about a gipsy encampment.

Yes, that's right. There's a Romany camp quite close.

Is that true? . . . Why didn't you say so before? . . . They're the villains, without a shadow of doubt!

But look here, what proof have you?

Proof? We shall find it! . . . Those sort of people are always thieving! There's no time to be lost: take us to their camp.

All right, I will. But you've no right to suspect them just because they're gipsies.

I'll be surprised if they're still there. Having done the job, they'll have bolted.

I don't think so!

Where's the camp?

OH!

Well?

They . . . they've gone! . . . But I saw them only last night . . .

What did I tell you? They've done a bunk.

They won't have got far.

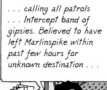

. . . calling all patrols . . . Intercept band of gipsies. Believed to have left Marlinspike within past few hours for unknown destination . . .

Two days later . . .
"Investigation into the theft of the Castafiore emerald continues" . . . etc etc . . . Ah! "The gipsies who were camping near Marlinspike at the time of the robbery have been assisting the police in their inquiries. A headquarters spokesman refused to comment on the affair." . . . There!
BROL
Those poor things . . . And I'm absolutely certain they are innocent.
Me too, I'd stake my life on it . . . but . . .
Tintin! Captain! My dear friends! . . . A sensational discovery! . . . Sen-sa-tion-al! . . . I've just invented a television set!
You old pioneer!
Colour television, of course! The other day, looking at all those sets, I thought to myself: what a pity the pictures are only in black and white!
You know, someone has already . . .
Not at all, it's just a question of know-how. Now listen carefully . . . The people you see on the little screen are in black and white, aren't they? But in the studio? . . . What about that?
The studio?
Er . . .
I don't need to tell you . . . In the studio the subjects are all in colour . . . Well, the purpose of my apparatus is to restore those colours! . . . How? . . . How? . . . Well, roughly speaking, by colour filters inserted between an ordinary television set and a special screen. I call it "Super-Calcacolor".
But that's brilliant!
You think so? . . . In all modesty I must say my own comment would be: brilliant! But you shall judge my invention for yourselves. Tonight they have that famous programme "Scanorama" . . . Will you join me?
That evening . . .
Now my friends, hold your breath! . . . This is an historic moment!
Tonight . . . BING . . . Scanorama . . . BONG . . . your look at life . . . DONG
. . . brings the big news of three continents to your fireside. Our roving cameras give you a close-up of . . .
. . . the 21st Taschist Party Congress at Szohôd, the secret life of the Abominable Snowman, and the jewel robbery at Marlinspike . . .
Well, I'll be . . .
What a coincidence!
How very strange!

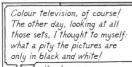

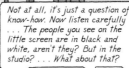

At the 21st Taschist Party Congress at Szohôd, Marshal Kûrvi-Tasch, in an exceptionally violent speech . . .

The picture isn't absolutely clear, but I can adjust it . . .

DIGADOG DAGADIGADUG DOGODOGDOG DAGODAGODAGODUG DIGADIGDUG

That's better, isn't it?

It's the sound, now!

All right, eh?

The sound! . . . Thundering typhoons, adjust the sound!

CRACK

?

Oh dear! . . . A valve has gone! . . . It won't take long to replace . . .

Ten minutes later . . .

There! That's done it!

. . . summary of the facts. As you know, the famous Italian singer Bianca Castafiore is staying in this country . . .

Ah, ♫ ♪ my beauty ♪♫ past ♫ compare ♪ ♪

Is that me? Oh, how horrible!

At historic Marlinspike Hall, the prima donna was the victim of a daring robbery. A magnificent emerald vanished . . . mysteriously!

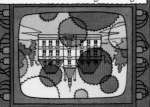

Today a Scanorama reporter went down to Marlinspike and spoke to the officers in charge of the case. Over to Thompson and Thomson . . .

No, our lips are sealed. We can't tell you whom we suspect, but it isn't anyone in the house. Mum's the word, you know.

Yes, dumb's the word, that's our motto. So we're not allowed to tell you about the gipsies, though we suspected them from the start . . .

Especially after they cleft their lamp . . . er . . . left their camp, the morning after the robbery. But we soon ran them to earth, and then when we searched their caravans we made a startling discovery!

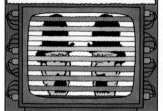

Not only did we discover a pair of scissors belonging to Signora Castafiore's maid, but in one of their caravans . . .

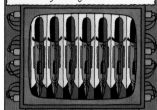

. . . we found a messed-up flunkey . . . er . . . a dressed-up monkey. Obviously, the emerald could only have been stolen by a man climbing the wall: in fact, a man of remarkable agility . . . And that man has been found: the monkey! Of course the whole bunch . . .

. . . denied it furiously. The scissors had been 'found' by a little girl. As for the monkey, he'd never been out of his cage.

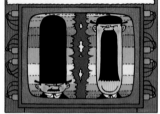

So that's how things stand . . . but we're keeping it under our hats, of course. All we have to do now is recover the emerald . . .

And for a couple of master-minds like you, gentlemen, that will be child's play . . . Thank you for putting us so clearly in the picture.

Now we turn from the excitement and suspense of a police investigation to another burning topic that is hitting today's headlines . . .

Oh no! That's enough!

Stop! My eyes are simply streaming!

Enough! Enough!

Naturally, it isn't entirely perfect   yet, but . . .

My eyeballs are doing the shimmy!

I'm seeing six of everything!

Me too!

The next morning . . .

Poor gipsies! . . . I'm still convinced they're innocent . . . I've had another look at the wall: even a monkey climbing would have left some trace, but there wasn't a sign. What then?

Hello! There's Mr Wagner going into the village, on Nestor's old bike.

He must have got permission to leave his piano. Now's our chance, Snowy . . .

We'll go back indoors . . . and we'll be spared that piano for a change!

Surely I didn't imagine it ... I just saw Mr Wagner going off on his bike ... So who can be playing the piano?

What have you found, Snowy?

Wooah! Wooah!

Oho! Someone's hidden a ladder down here ... Better and better! ... Well, since it's here we'll make use of it.

He won't be back yet ... Up we go!

!?

?

Great snakes!

A battery tape-recorder! It's a playback of his own scales! But what's it all in aid of? ...

Why? Why? ... Well, Mr Wagner, we're going to find out! First, I must be quick and put the ladder back.

There!

Hide yourself somewhere, Snowy, and don't make a sound.

Wooah!

And now, maestro, I'm ready for you!

No one about: I'll risk it ...

Can I give you a hand, Mr Wagner?

No thanks, I can manage.

H-h-how did you get in here?

The same way as you, Mr Wagner . . . But do put down the ladder . . .

I . . . er . . . I do it to get a little exercise . . . Original, don't you think?

Very! And the tape-recorder . . . for the same purpose, eh?

Oh, yes, the tape-recorder . . . Look, you must promise not to tell Signora Castafiore. I worked out a plan so I could get some fresh air from time to time . . . She keeps me at the piano all day long, you know, and . . .

Fresh air? Village air, I believe, Mr Wagner.

Oh, so you know! Then I'd better tell you everything . . .

IRMAA! . . . Oh, have you seen Irma?

Now I'm in for it! I forgot to lock the door!

Irma? No signora.

Thank you . . . But . . . Well, Mr Wagner, what about your scales?

My s-s-scales, s-s-signora? . . .

But he's playing them, signora . . . as you can hear.

Of course . . . So he is . . . I wasn't thinking, forgive me!

Silly me! . . . So absent-minded!

Thanks . . . But why did you save me from her?

I wanted to get you alone . . . Now, sit down at the piano: it's safer . . . Then talk!

All right . . . I'll tell you everything. It's the horses . . . I'm a gambler, you see. I go to the village every day to telephone my bets . . .

Hmmm!

Is that so? . . . Still, you weren't in the village when the emerald was stolen . . . when some unknown person fell down the stairs . . . It was you wasn't it?

Yes, it was I.

I'd been up to the attic . . . and on my way down I heard Signora Castafiore cry out . . . I hurried to get back to my piano, and missed the step.

Why were you in the attic?

Well, on a number of evenings I thought I heard someone walking about up there . . . at dusk . . . like the signora did on the night we arrived. In the end I decided to get to the bottom of it . . .

Why didn't you simply ask us?

I didn't want to make a fool of myself, if it was only a false alarm . . . Anyway, I didn't find anything.

One last point, Mr Wagner. The day after you came, I found your footprints under Signora Castafiore's window . . .

Golly, how some people do love to talk!

Yes . . . it's quite possible. After that incident during the night I went round there, to make sure no one could have climbed the ivy.

Good . . . That's all the explanation I need.

No, I don't think Wagner stole the emerald: he seems to be telling the truth . . . Well, now I've got to find the real culprit!

In any case, I'll visit the attic tonight. We must follow every lead . . . Coming, Snowy?

Ah . . . at last!

At nightfall . . .

Ssh!

I say, Tintin, how long must we stay here?

Ssh, Snowy! Listen . . .

CRACK

Pooh! It's only a rat, or a mouse. Shall I catch it?

Ssh!

POK POK POK

Oh! . . . Look over there! . . . An old owl; he must roost up here!

POK POK POK

There's the "monster" who paces the attic, and frightened Signora Castafiore when he looked in her window!

TU·WHOOO

We can go down now, Snowy. There's nothing more up here

Just another false trail.

Why, Captain! You're better! How wonderful!

Yes, the doctor's just gone: he's taken off the plaster.

You've no idea how good it feels to be standing on my own two feet again!

Careful! Don't lean . . .

. . . on that!

See you soon, doctor!

Great snakes! What's going to happen?

One day I really must turn out the clutter in this car!

What was it? . . . What happened?

What happened? What was it? . . .

My dear Captain Padlock . . . Why, you're up! . . . I'm so glad.

Thanks!

It grieves me to cloud your happiness, but I have sad news for you: I must leave you tomorrow.

No! . . . Not really? It can't be true!

Alas, dear friend! They are clamouring for me at La Scala in Milan: a farewell performance in Rossini before I leave for the States.

I'm terribly upset . . . I'm shattered . . . You won't change your mind?

You're an angel, trying to keep me here, but I already have my tickets.

Ah!

She's going! She's going!

She's go-go-go-going away ♩♩ Hip hip hip hooray! This is my lucky day!

She's go . . . guo . . . gug! . . . Ta-ra-ra-er . . . um . . . yes . . . H'mm.

. . . *This is my lucky day! . . . My wheelchair's going away!*

The big baby!

Come along in. A drink will soon put you right.

The moment of departure comes . . .

Goodbye, signora . . . Bon voyage!

Goodbye, dear Captain Hatbox! Thank you again for your charming hospitality . . . It grieves me so to leave you, but I give you my promise: I'll be back!

I . . . I'm sure you will!

As for my emerald . . . sniff . . . sniff . . . the moment you have any news . . .

Yes, yes, I'll let you know at once, never fear . . .

Dear lady, I beg you to accept these humble roses, the first of a new variety I have created . . . I have ventured to give them your beautiful name, "Bianca"!

What a sweet idea!

They are exquisite! . . . Ex-x-x-quisite! And what perfume! Smell them, Captain Stockpot!

No, thank you!

Dear Professor, let me embrace you!

SMACK

Now I simply must go . . .

Yes . . . yes, you really must . . . Goodbye!

Arrivederci! Take care of Iago!

Don't you worry!

Goodbye, dear lady . . .

Come back soon!!

MERCY, MY JEWELS!

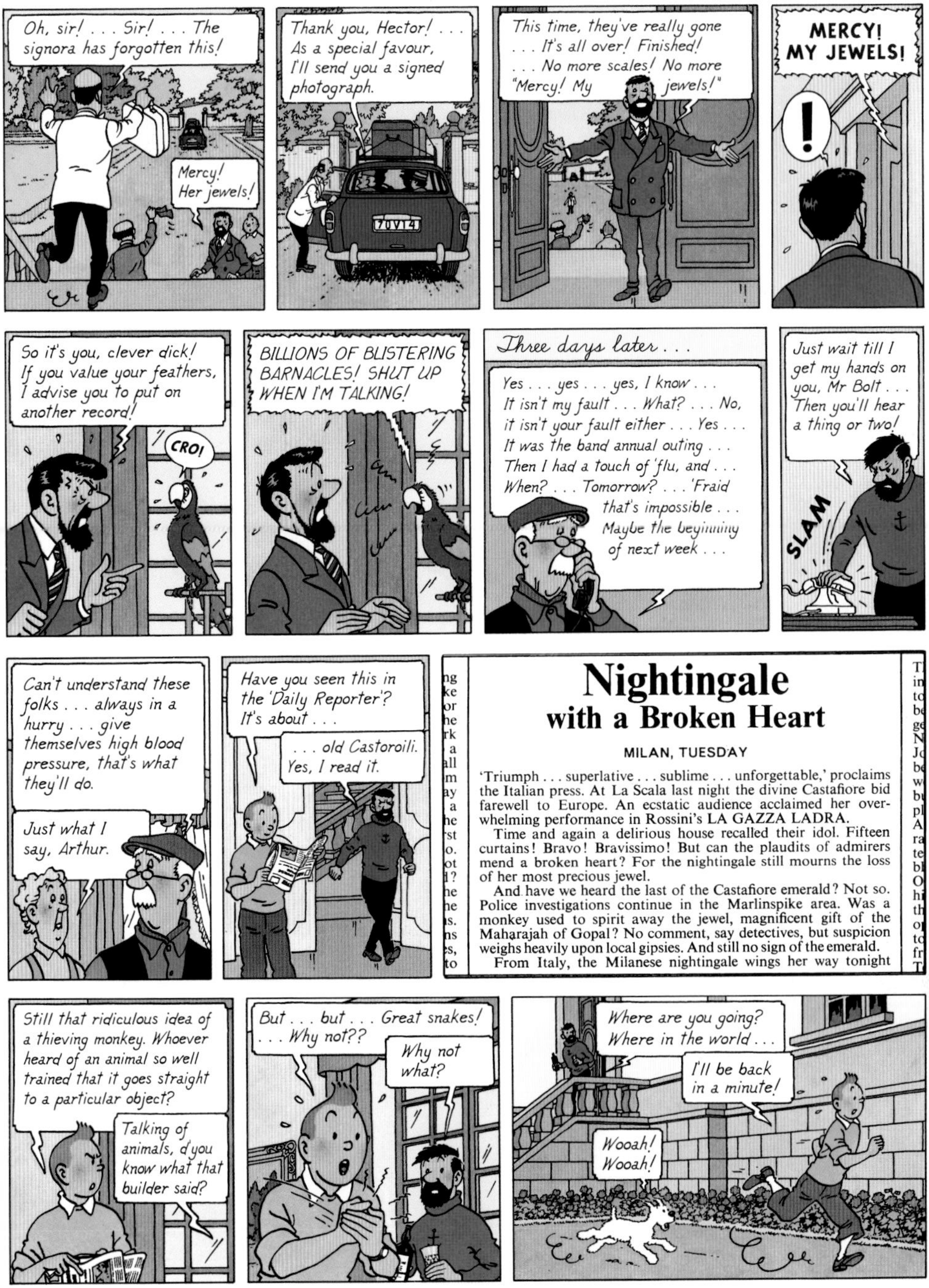
Oh, sir! . . . Sir! . . . The signora has forgotten this!
Mercy! Her jewels!
Thank you, Hector! . . . As a special favour, I'll send you a signed photograph.
70V14
This time, they've really gone . . . It's all over! Finished! . . . No more scales! No more "Mercy! My jewels!"
MERCY! MY JEWELS!
!
So it's you, clever dick! If you value your feathers, I advise you to put on another record!
CRO!
BILLIONS OF BLISTERING BARNACLES! SHUT UP WHEN I'M TALKING!
Three days later . . .
Yes . . . yes . . . yes, I know . . . It isn't my fault . . . What? . . . No, it isn't your fault either . . . Yes . . . It was the band annual outing . . . Then I had a touch of 'flu, and . . . When? . . . Tomorrow? . . . 'Fraid that's impossible . . . Maybe the beginning of next week . . .
Just wait till I get my hands on you, Mr Bolt . . . Then you'll hear a thing or two!
SLAM
Can't understand these folks . . . always in a hurry . . . give themselves high blood pressure, that's what they'll do.
Just what I say, Arthur.
Have you seen this in the 'Daily Reporter'? It's about . . .
. . . old Castoroili. Yes, I read it.
Nightingale with a Broken Heart
MILAN, TUESDAY
'Triumph . . . superlative . . . sublime . . . unforgettable,' proclaims the Italian press. At La Scala last night the divine Castafiore bid farewell to Europe. An ecstatic audience acclaimed her overwhelming performance in Rossini's LA GAZZA LADRA.
Time and again a delirious house recalled their idol. Fifteen curtains! Bravo! Bravissimo! But can the plaudits of admirers mend a broken heart? For the nightingale still mourns the loss of her most precious jewel.
And have we heard the last of the Castafiore emerald? Not so. Police investigations continue in the Marlinspike area. Was a monkey used to spirit away the jewel, magnificent gift of the Maharajah of Gopal? No comment, say detectives, but suspicion weighs heavily upon local gipsies. And still no sign of the emerald.
From Italy, the Milanese nightingale wings her way tonight
Still that ridiculous idea of a thieving monkey. Whoever heard of an animal so well trained that it goes straight to a particular object?
Talking of animals, d'you know what that builder said?
But . . . but . . . Great snakes! . . . Why not??
Why not what?
Where are you going? Where in the world . . .
I'll be back in a minute!
Wooah! Wooah!

I wonder what's got into him?

Tell me, Captain, is there any message you'd like to send to Signora Castafiore?

A message? . . . Me? . . . For Castafiore?

No, a message! . . . I forgot to tell you, I'm leaving today for Milan: I'm going there to demonstrate my Super-Calcacolor to the International Television Congress. Naturally, I shall call upon our charming friend.

Oh? Well, tell her whatever you like: but for pity's sake, don't invite her back to Marlinspike!

That's very kind: I'll tell her. She'll certainly be touched by your invitation . . .

Captain! Captain!

Now what? . . . Has he set the house on fire?

Is there a woodman anywhere near?

A woodman? . . . Yes, Charlie Sawyer, in the village . . . But why?

Thanks! . . . Oh, I almost forgot . . . Ring up the Thompsons . . . Tell them to come here as soon as possible: about the emerald.

About the emerald? . . . What? . . .

Later! . . . And remember to telephone, won't you?

But Tintin, look here . . .

Half an hour later . . .

We've only come as a special flavour . . . er, savour . . . er, well, so far as we're concerned, there's absolutely nothing Tintin can add to the case. Once and for all, the job was done by the gipsies, with the help of their monkey.

It's as clear as day to us, eh Thompson?

To be precise: dear as clay. That's my opinion and I'm stuck with it!

There's only one thing Tintin can tell us: where the emerald is hidden.

And if you'll come with me, gentlemen, I will do precisely that!

You?! No?! Yes?!

You've discovered where the gipsies have hidden the emerald?

The gipsies haven't hidden anything.

Look up there . . . That's where you'll find the key to the whole mystery!

There?

Up where?

Yes, where up there?

Up there, in that poplar . . .

That poplar? . . . All I can see is a nest.

Yes, but it's a magpie's nest, Captain.

What? You mean to say . . .

?

That a magpie stole the emerald: yes, I'd bet my life on it.

Thundering typhoons! And you borrowed that kit from old man Sawyer to climb up to the nest . . .

Exactly!

For heaven's sake be careful, Tintin!

I will!

CHAK-CHAK!

Tintin! Do please watch your step!

Don't worry, I'm . . .

CRACK

!

61

Look out for the dead branch!

CRACK

No damage done! ... What about you? Have you found anything?

Yes, and how! I've got Irma's thimble ...

AND THE EMERALD! HERE'S THE EMERALD!!

Some bits of glass ... a marble ... and a monocle ... That's the lot ... I'm coming down.

Chak-chak

Thief!

Wonderful! ... Tintin, you're a genius! ... But what on earth suddenly made you think of a magpie?

Do you remember the name of the opera they mentioned in the paper?

I don't know ... "Pizza" or "Ragazza" ... or something ...

"La Gazza Ladra" ... in other words, The Thieving Magpie! Then the light dawned!

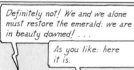

I thought to myself: "There's a 'gazza ladra' somewhere around ... But where? ... What about the spot where Miarka found the scissors? They must have fallen from the robber's hiding-place." ... So I ran to look, and there was the nest! ... Well, that clears the gipsies!

Just our luck! The one time we manage to catch the culprits they turn out to be innocent! It's really too bad of them!

You'd think they'd done it on purpose!

Anyway, thanks to us, the emerald has turned up. And all we have to do is to return it to Signora Castafiore.

You know, Cuthbert Calculus is just leaving for Milan. Couldn't we give him the jewel?

Definitely not! We and we alone must restore the emerald: we are in beauty downed! ...

As you like: here it is.

You know, what pleases me is the relief for the gipsies. They'll be completely cleared of suspicion now.

It's a sight for sore eyes ...

To be precise, I'd say ...

? ? OH!

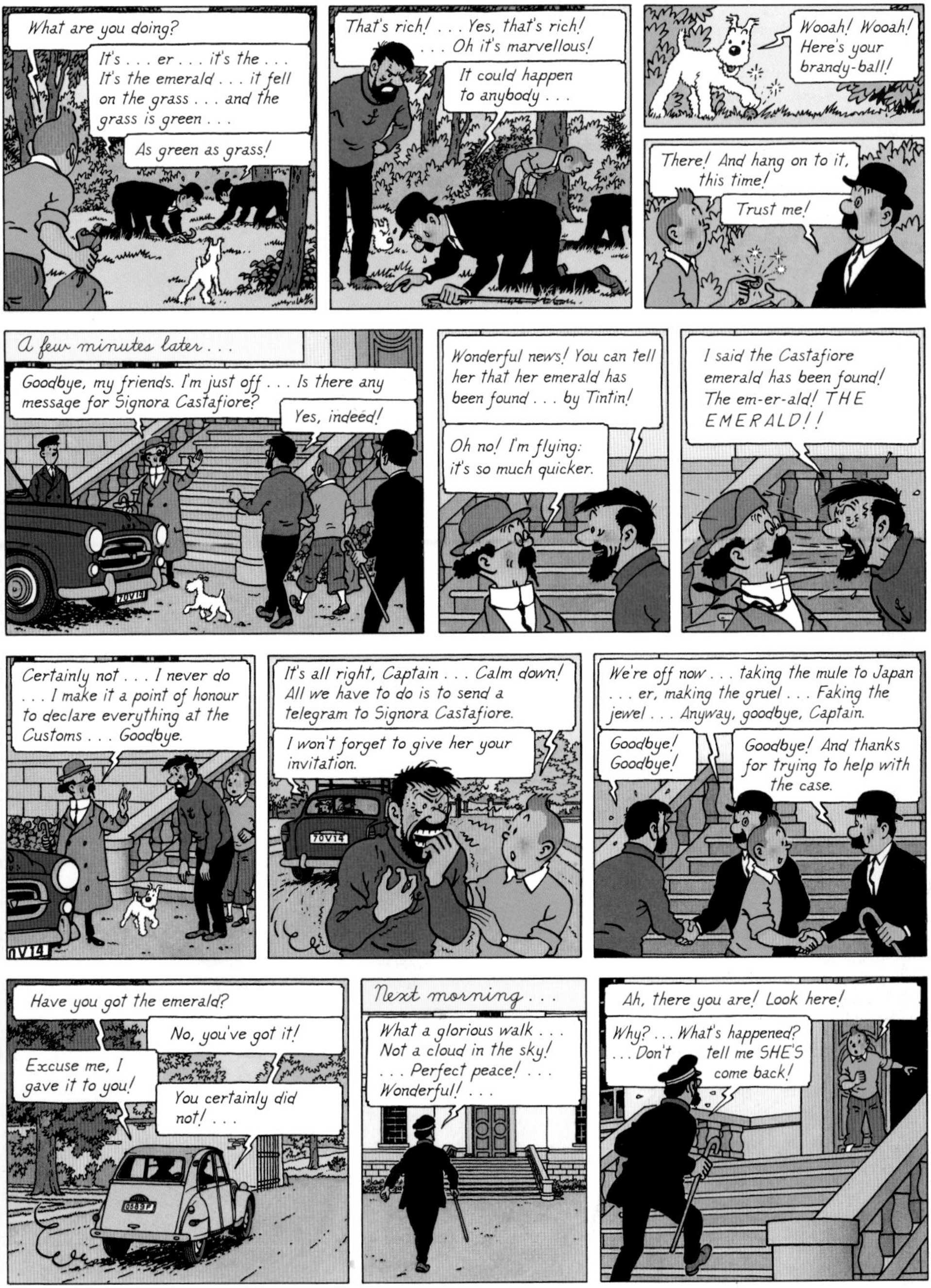
What are you doing?
It's . . . er . . . it's the . . . It's the emerald . . . it fell on the grass . . . and the grass is green . . .
As green as grass!
That's rich! . . . Yes, that's rich! . . . Oh it's marvellous!
It could happen to anybody . . .
Wooah! Wooah! Here's your brandy-ball!
There! And hang on to it, this time!
Trust me!
A few minutes later . . .
Goodbye, my friends. I'm just off . . . Is there any message for Signora Castafiore?
Yes, indeed!
Wonderful news! You can tell her that her emerald has been found . . . by Tintin!
Oh no! I'm flying: it's so much quicker.
I said the Castafiore emerald has been found! The em-er-ald! THE EMERALD!!
Certainly not . . . I never do . . . I make it a point of honour to declare everything at the Customs . . . Goodbye.
It's all right, Captain . . . Calm down! All we have to do is to send a telegram to Signora Castafiore.
I won't forget to give her your invitation.
We're off now . . . taking the mule to Japan . . . er, making the gruel . . . Faking the jewel . . . Anyway, goodbye, Captain.
Goodbye! Goodbye!
Goodbye! And thanks for trying to help with the case.
Have you got the emerald?
No, you've got it!
Excuse me, I gave it to you!
You certainly did not! . . .
Next morning . . .
What a glorious walk . . . Not a cloud in the sky! . . . Perfect peace! . . . Wonderful! . . .
Ah, there you are! Look here!
Why? . . . What's happened? . . . Don't tell me SHE'S come back!

Look! Mr Bolt has been to mend the step.

That's wonderful! . . . Ah, he's put a board across it: to give the mortar time to set. I expect he warned you.

No, he didn't. But it's quite obvious . . .

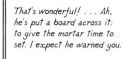

Maybe, but I'm just mentioning it for your own good. You can't be too careful . . . For heaven's sake, remember, don't put your foot on that step!

Right, Captain.

Indeed, sir.

For the next few days you must step over . . . like tha-a-t! You understand?

Yes, Captain.

Very good, sir.

You see? It's perfectly easy. You just have to think what you're doing . . .

DONG

Hello . . . Who's that?

It's me again . . . I forgot to tell you . . .

Ah, Mr Bolt! It was nice of you to come . . .

TU-WHOO

That's a real shame! I just popped back to say, wait a day or two before using that step . . . Too bad: a lovely bit of marble, that was!

Chak-chak

Blistering barnacles, that's the end!

HERGÉ

64

HERGÉ
★
THE ADVENTURES OF
TINTIN
★

FLIGHT 714
TO SYDNEY

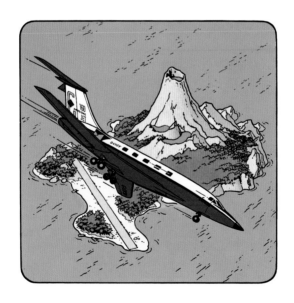

LITTLE, BROWN AND COMPANY
New York Boston

FLIGHT 714 TO SYDNEY

A Qantas Boeing 707 touches down at Kemajoran airport, Djakarta. Flight 714 from London arrives in Java, last stop before Sydney, Australia . . .

I keep telling you. We're in Java! . . . Djakarta!

How very strange. I'd have sworn it was Djakarta.

This IS Djakarta, ten thousand thundering typhoons!

Rangoon? You must be joking.

Blistering barnacles! Djakarta! Djakarta!!DJAKARTA!!! Can't you listen to what I say?

Botany Bay? . . . Then why didn't you say we'd arrived?

No, Professor, we're not in Australia yet. It's Djakarta.

Yes, I know. But I thought at first it was Djakarta.

Welcome to Java! Transit passengers this way, please . . .

Transit passengers . . . that means us.

This is more like it. I'm no Skye terrier . . . I prefer my feet on the ground!

I say, Tintin, what about a little drink?

Good idea. Why not?

There's the bar, look . . .

Fine!

Hey! . . . Stop! . . . Are you trying to make a fool of me?

BAR RESTAURANT

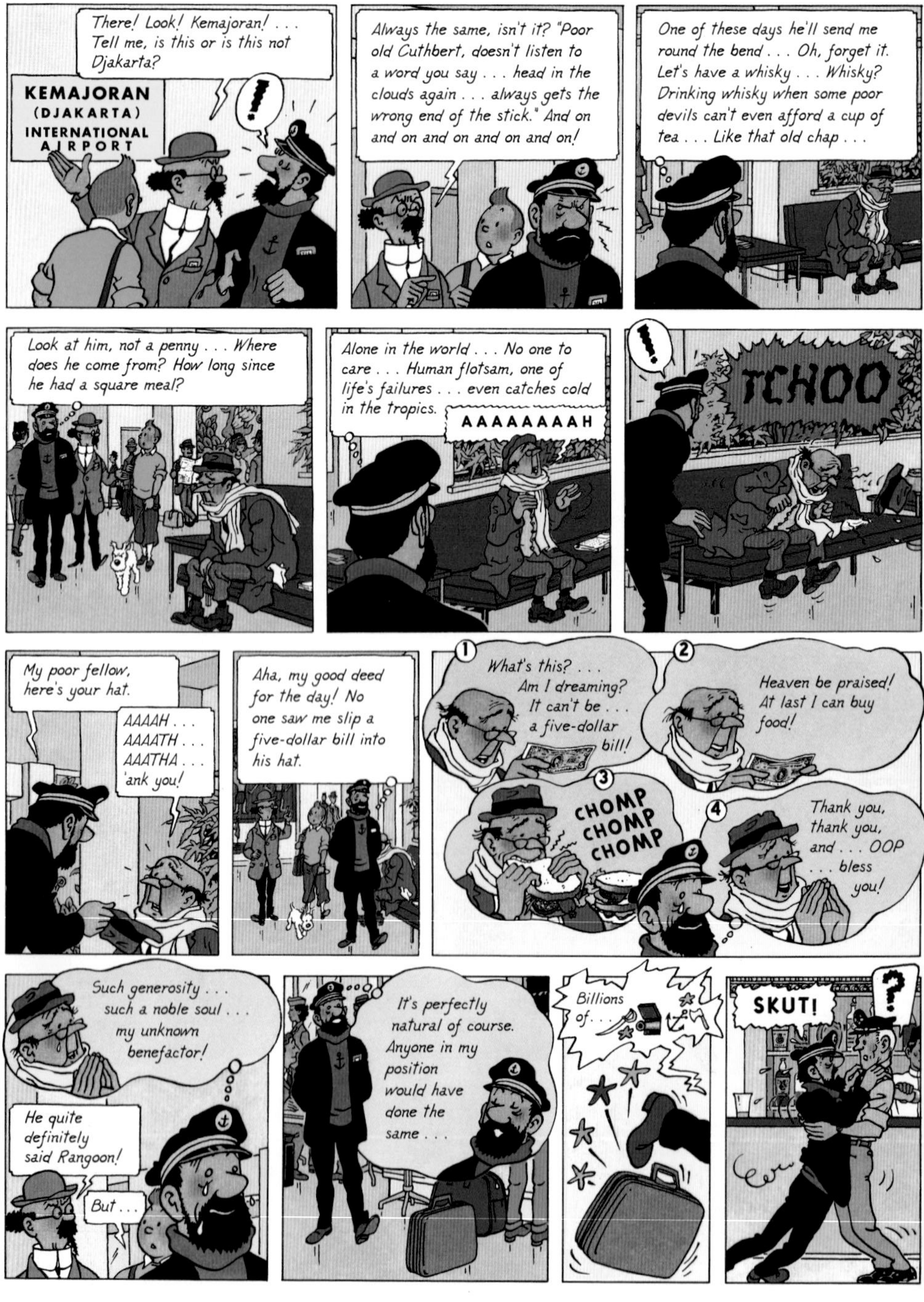
There! Look! Kemajoran! . . . Tell me, is this or is this not Djakarta?
KEMAJORAN
(DJAKARTA)
INTERNATIONAL AIRPORT
Always the same, isn't it? "Poor old Cuthbert, doesn't listen to a word you say . . . head in the clouds again . . . always gets the wrong end of the stick." And on and on and on and on and on!
One of these days he'll send me round the bend . . . Oh, forget it. Let's have a whisky . . . Whisky? Drinking whisky when some poor devils can't even afford a cup of tea . . . Like that old chap . . .
Look at him, not a penny . . . Where does he come from? How long since he had a square meal?
Alone in the world . . . No one to care . . . Human flotsam, one of life's failures . . . even catches cold in the tropics.
AAAAAAAAH
TCHOO
My poor fellow, here's your hat.
AAAAH . . . AAAATH . . . AAATHA . . . 'ank you!
Aha, my good deed for the day! No one saw me slip a five-dollar bill into his hat.
What's this? . . . Am I dreaming? It can't be . . . a five-dollar bill!
Heaven be praised! At last I can buy food!
CHOMP CHOMP CHOMP
Thank you, thank you, and . . . OOP . . . bless you!
Such generosity . . . such a noble soul . . . my unknown benefactor!
He quite definitely said Rangoon!
But . . .
It's perfectly natural of course. Anyone in my position would have done the same . . .
Billions of . . .
SKUT!

SKUT!! . . . Our old friend Skut, the Estonian pilot . . . What a wonderful surprise!

Captain Haddock! . . . Tintin! I glad to see you again!

And this is Professor Calculus. I'm sure you've heard about him.

Yes, yes. I proud to meet you Professor.

No, Calculus.

Skut, you Baltic bandit! We haven't seen you since that Red Sea scrimmage. What are you doing here?

I pilot private aeroplane. You know famous tycoon Laszlo Carreidas? . . . OK, him my boss.

Laszlo Carreidas? The aircraft manufacturer? "The millionaire who never laughs"?

That him. Carreidas aircraft, Carreidas cloth, Carreidas oil . . . stores, newspapers, Sani-Cola . . . all him. We fly to Sydney to International Astronautical Congress.

Well I'm . . . ! That's where we're going. We've been invited to the Congress . . . guests of honour, you know . . . the first men on the moon . . .

Bravo! I thought you go on new adventure . . .

No, by thunder! Adventures are out . . . right out, for good! This is a pleasure trip, an ordinary flight. No fuss, no upsets, no commotion . . .

WOOAH

Blasted mongrel, skulking down there! Almost broke my neck! . . . Telex for you, skipper, here's the flight plan.

Oaf!

Thank you. I introduce: Paolo Colombani, co-pilot with me . . . My friends: Captain Haddock, Professor Calculus, Tintin.

'Morning!

Hi!

Any trouble, Colombani?

No, skipper. Pressure constant, light wind from the south-east, low cloud base . . . everything OK . . . See you later.

He is new navigator. Regular navigator fall ill on way, in Teheran . . . Suddenly to hospital . . . Colombani fill place.

Not the nicest I've met!

Clod!

Ah, here come my boss. Mr Carreidas happy to meet first men to land on moon.

"The millionaire who never laughs" . . . Him?

Still, he must be kind-hearted; he's taken that little emigrant under his wing. Good for him!
Mr Carreidas, I please introduce my friends to you: Captain Haddock, Professor Calculus, Tintin. They went in rocket and were first men on moon. You remember? . . .
I . . .
How d'you do, Mr Carreidas.
?
?!
Er . . . No . . . Excuse . . . this Mr Spalding, secretary of Mr Carreidas . . . Here is Mr Carreidas.
It can't be!
I never shake hands: it is extremely unhygienic . . . I do vaguely remember some expedition, but the details escape me . . . As I recall, it didn't affect the stock market.
Hello? . . .
?
There seems to be . . . Allow me . . .
Presto!
My hat! . . . You're a trespi . . . no, I mean . . . presti . . . prestigidi . . . prestidigita . . . ta . . . ta . . .
TAAAH . . . AAAH . . .
HA HA HA
HA HA HA . . . prestidigitator!
HEE HEE OH HO HO HAAA
I . . . ha! ha! . . . I . . . it's incredible . . . incredible . . . ha! ha! It's quite incredible!
Spalding!
Yes, Mr Carreidas.
You heard, Spalding?
Yes, Mr Carreidas.
It hasn't happened for years.
As you say, Mr Carreidas.
This is an occasion!
Yes, Mr Carreidas.
Drinks, Spalding!
At once, Mr Carreidas.

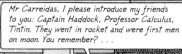

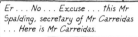

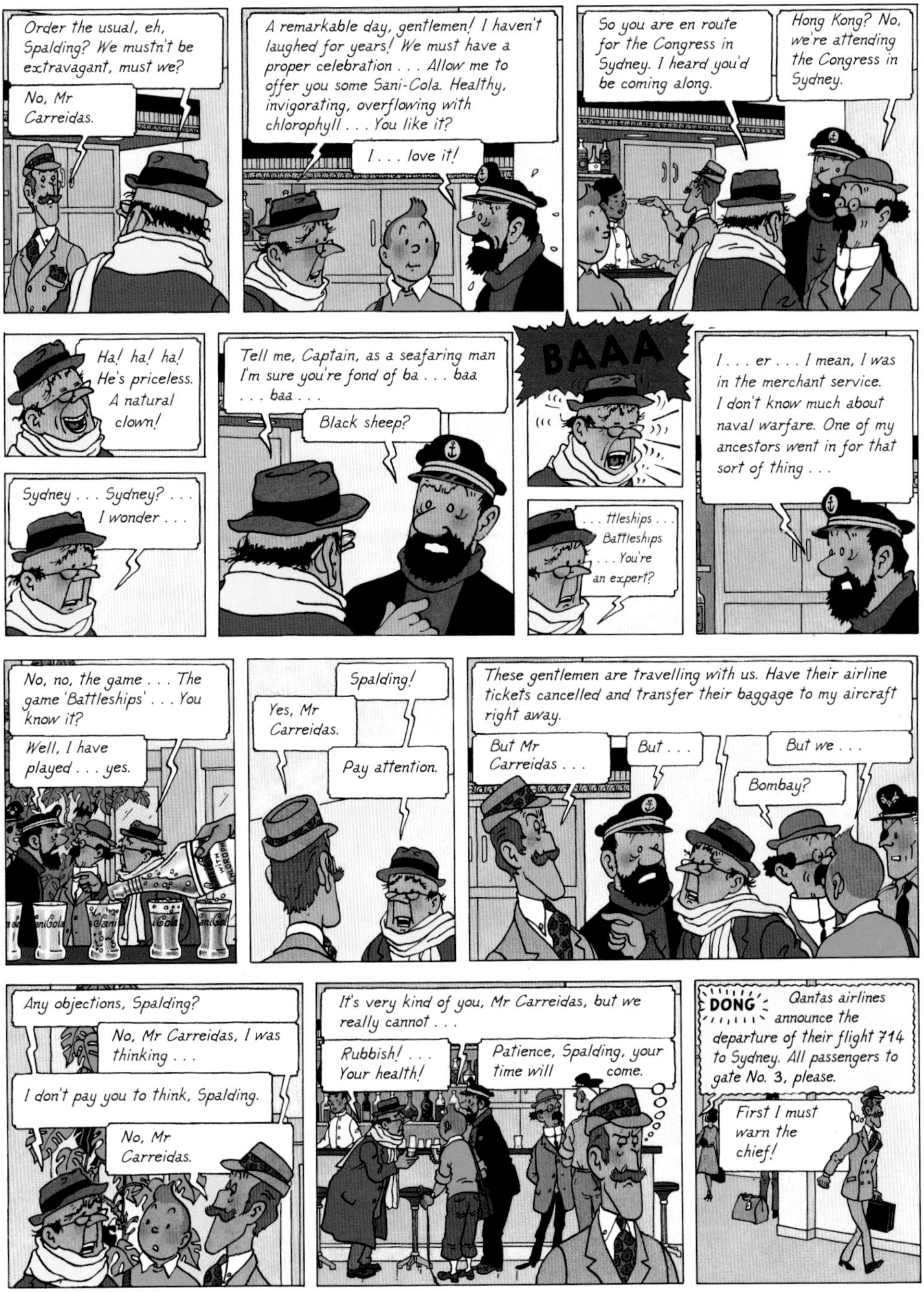

Order the usual, eh, Spalding? We mustn't be extravagant, must we?
No, Mr Carreidas.
A remarkable day, gentlemen! I haven't laughed for years! We must have a proper celebration . . . Allow me to offer you some Sani-Cola. Healthy, invigorating, overflowing with chlorophyll . . . You like it?
I . . . love it!
So you are en route for the Congress in Sydney. I heard you'd be coming along.
Hong Kong? No, we're attending the Congress in Sydney.
Ha! ha! ha! He's priceless. A natural clown!
Sydney . . . Sydney? . . . I wonder . . .
Tell me, Captain, as a seafaring man I'm sure you're fond of ba . . . baa . . . baa . . .
Black sheep?
BAAA
. . . ttleships . . . Battleships . . . You're an expert?
I . . . er . . . I mean, I was in the merchant service. I don't know much about naval warfare. One of my ancestors went in for that sort of thing . . .
No, no, the game . . . The game 'Battleships' . . . You know it?
Well, I have played . . . yes.
Spalding!
Yes, Mr Carreidas.
Pay attention.
These gentlemen are travelling with us. Have their airline tickets cancelled and transfer their baggage to my aircraft right away.
But Mr Carreidas . . .
But . . .
But we . . .
Bombay?
Any objections, Spalding?
No, Mr Carreidas, I was thinking . . .
I don't pay you to think, Spalding.
No, Mr Carreidas.
It's very kind of you, Mr Carreidas, but we really cannot . . .
Rubbish! . . . Your health!
Patience, Spalding, your time will come.
DONG
Qantas airlines announce the departure of their flight 714 to Sydney. All passengers to gate No. 3, please.
First I must warn the chief!

But Mr Carreidas . . . our baggage . . . and our reservations . . .

Don't give it a thought. Spalding will arrange everything.

But there's Snowy . . . he's such a fidgety traveller, and . . .

Snowy . . . fidgety . . . Great snakes!

SNOWY

He's gone! He's escaped from his lead! Look, he's chewed it through and slipped off somewhere. Excuse me . . . I must go after him!

Now where's that rapscallion?

Meanwhile . . .

Is that you, Walter? . . . Spalding here . . . Quick . . . Listen . . . You must contact the chief: old Sneezewort has invited three people to travel with us . . . friends of the pilot . . . met them accidentally . . . So it's all off . . . Understand?

Too late, Spalding: everything's fixed. Anyway, you don't really imagine the chief's going to change his plans for three stray hangers-on? . . . You have your orders; do as you're told.

But Walter, with three extra passengers the whole thing could be wrecked, and if . . .

So there you are, rascal! Come here!

Nicked! Back on that dratted lead!

Walter, you must listen . . .

CLICK

I know you hate this but you have to wear it . . . You'll land me in all sorts of trouble . . .

?

!

I . . . I didn't see you there . . . I was . . . er . . . telephoning . . . A distant cousin who . . . er . . . lives in Djakarta . . . Now I must see about your luggage and cancel your reservations . . .

I'm sorry to be a nuisance . . .

Not at all. Delighted to be of service.

See you later.

DONG

This is the last call for Qantas airlines Flight 714 to Sydney. All passengers please go immediately to gate No. 3.

He was spying on me!

A cousin, indeed! That's a tall story!

And you, Professor. You enjoy Battleships?

Battledore? I used to be very good . . . And not only battledore. I've been an all-round sportsman in my time, though you may not think so now.

Tennis, swimming, rugger, soccer, fencing, skating . . . I did them all in my young days. Not forgetting the ring, too: wrestling, boxing, and even savate . . .

Savate? . . .

No, no, no! I said savate, French boxing . . . Stars above! They make me laugh nowadays with their judo and their karate. Savate! That was real fighting! . . .

Using your feet as well as your fists . . . I was a champion . . . unbeatable . . . just you watch this . . .

HUP!

THUMP

Perhaps I'm a little out of practice. It'd soon come back if I went into training.

Isn't it time you stopped acting the goat?

Ha! ha! ha! He's a remarkable fellow!

I beg your . . .?

Er . . . I . . . er . . . was saying you . . . must stop tiring yourself out.

Everything is settled, Mr Carreidas. We can go now.

And about time too, Spalding!

?

Are you coming, Captain?

Yes . . . straight away.

Spalding was right. Sneezewort has collected three passengers . . . that's their bad luck! . . . But . . . but . . .

I must be seeing things! . . . It's Tintin!!

73

This is my newest brain-child: the Carreidas 160. A triple-jet executive aircraft, with a crew of four, and six passengers. At 40,000 feet the cruising speed is Mach 2, or about 1,250 m.p.h. The Rolls-Royce-Turbomeca turbojets deliver in total 18,500 lbs of thrust . . .

It's magnificent!

WOOAH

The most advanced feature lies in the aerodynamics of the . . .

Ah, there's Gino, my steward . . . A Neapolitan. I wonder . . .

Telefono from New York for il signor Commendatore.

That'll be Goldberg.

Hold the line, please.

Please board the aircraft, gentlemen. Gino, look after my guests.

Si, signor Commendatore.

Hello . . . Yes . . . Of course: the Parke-Bennet sale . . . Well? . . . Three Picassos, two Braques and a Renoir . . . Junk! . . . Anyway, I haven't an inch of space to hang them.

What's that? . . . Onassis after them? . . . Then buy! . . . Get them all! . . . What? . . . I don't care how much, buy!

You met navigator Colombani . . . This is new radio operator, Hans Boehm.

Hello!

Captain!

Well, well . . .

More new crew?

Si . . . no fortuna we have on this viaggio . . . Other radio operator in accidente at airport in Singapore . . . with petrol tanker . . .

But presto presto il Signor Spalding find new radio operator . . . Il Signor Spalding is molto intelligente . . . Il Signor Spalding . . .

THUMP

? ?

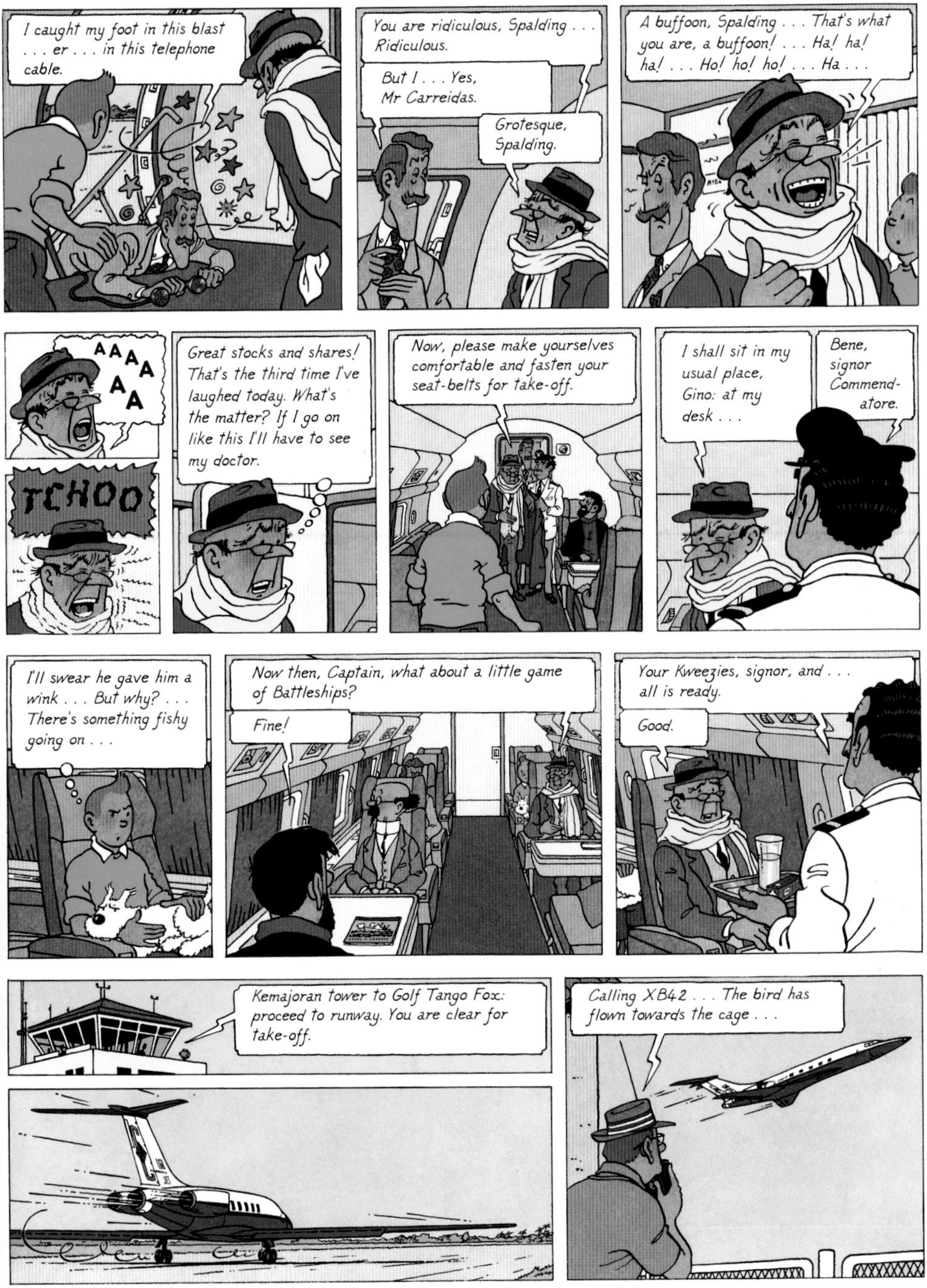

I caught my foot in this blast . . . er . . . in this telephone cable.
You are ridiculous, Spalding . . . Ridiculous.
But I . . . Yes, Mr Carreidas.
Grotesque, Spalding.
A buffoon, Spalding . . . That's what you are, a buffoon! . . . Ha! ha! ha! . . . Ho! ho! ho! . . . Ha . . .
AAAAA
TCHOO
Great stocks and shares! That's the third time I've laughed today. What's the matter? If I go on like this I'll have to see my doctor.
Now, please make yourselves comfortable and fasten your seat-belts for take-off.
I shall sit in my usual place, Gino: at my desk . . .
Bene, signor Commend-atore.
I'll swear he gave him a wink . . . But why? . . . There's something fishy going on . . .
Now then, Captain, what about a little game of Battleships?
Fine!
Your Kweezies, signor, and . . . all is ready.
Good.
Kemajoran tower to Golf Tango Fox: proceed to runway. You are clear for take-off.
Calling XB42 . . . The bird has flown towards the cage . . .

C4, D4, E4? Not a bad start, Captain. You've sunk a submarine, but the other two shots went into the water.

Aha!

This is going to be good! . . . Now for my pipe. Oh, I hope the smoke won't bother you?

Smoking is strictly prohibited, Captain. Even the smell of tobacco upsets me.

!

My turn now. Let me see . . . A4, B4 . . . and . . . er . . . C2.

Good shot, Mr Carreidas! . . . A destroyer sunk with two shells, and a hit on another destroyer.

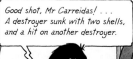

Now I'll have a go. I must fight back! . . . C5, D5, E5.

Bad luck, Captain! All three shots into the sea . . . I think I'll try A8, B8, C8.

Blue blistering barnacles!

A cruiser sunk: three direct hits! . . . You're psychic! . . . Still, what do you say to C6, D6, E6, eh?

All missed, I'm afraid . . . What bad luck! . . . I haven't got second-sight, you know . . . just natural talent, that's all. Now I must concentrate . . .

Anyone'd think he could see my board . . . And what's more, he won't let me smoke!

Hello, that's odd . . . I'd swear . . . I must be dreaming . . .

For my third salvo: G1, G2, G3.

THE WING!

The wing! What about the wing?

What about the wing? ...Nothing, except it's come loose!

A goose? ... Really? Where?

"It's come loose"! Ha! ha! ha! Oh! ho! ho! AHAHAA!

I beg your pardon, but I don't see what's so amusing about being in an aeroplane that starts shedding its wings in mid-air!

What a pity! I didn't see the goose ... but modern aeroplanes move so fast.

There's no danger to the aircraft, Captain. It's just the swing-wing in operation.

Very funny! "Just the swing-wing". What might that mean?

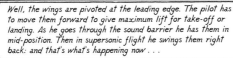

Well, the wings are pivoted at the leading edge. The pilot has to move them forward to give maximum lift for take-off or landing. As he goes through the sound barrier he has them in mid-position. Then in supersonic flight he swings them right back: and that's what's happening now ...

But let's get back to our game. See what you think of my next broadside, Captain. G1, G2, G3.

Ten thousand thundering typhoons! Three direct hits on my battleship! You're incredibly lucky!

Just a matter of skill, Captain. Skill and logic ... Your turn.

Now why is Spalding getting so agitated?

He keeps looking at his watch, too   ... Very odd!

E1, E2, E3.

He's getting up ... Why?

All three into the water!

I'll just go along to the pilot's cabin, Mr Carreidas ... to see   everything's all right.

Do you have to keep disturbing me, Spalding? Can't you see I'm busy?

It's my turn to fire, Captain.

I don't think I trust our friend Spalding ...

Mr Carreidas sent me along: he wants to know our position.

We've just passed the radio-beacon at Mataram on the island of Lombok. We're heading now for Sumbawa, Flores and Timor.

Good.

By the way, skipper. Mr Carreidas would like a word with you.

Me? . . . Then I'll come at once.

You take over the controls, Colombani.

OK

You go. I'll be along.

G6, H6, I6.

The old man cheating again.

Thundering typhoons! Still bang on target! It's fantastic!

A cruiser sunk! Holed three times! . . . Now I'll try . . . er . . . F1, F2, F3.

A destroyer hit once, and two shots wide . . . Well, what is it?

You send for me, Mr Carreidas?

Me? . . . No? . . . Why?

But Mr Spalding just come and say to me . . .

Spalding? That half-witted . . .

Is it not true, Mr Spalding, you say . . .

Hand's up! Come on, all of you!

SPALDING!?!

78

And what is the meaning of this stupid joke, Spalding?

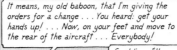

It means, my old baboon, that I'm giving the orders for a change . . . You heard: get your hands up! . . . Now, on your feet and move to the rear of the aircraft . . . Everybody!

Spalding, I'll . . .

Everybody? . . . Just a minute . . . Isn't someone missing?

That's it, young what's-your-name . . . Tintin. Good for you! Take away his gun!

?

!!!!

A brave try, my clever friend. But it didn't come off! Now get with the others and cut the funny business. I've got my eye on you!

Bravo, Spalding!

Ah, it's you, Hans. Help me lock them up.

Spalding! It . . . I . . . You . . . You're sa-sa-sa- . . .

Is this a television film?

Mamma mia!

ATCHOOO

You're sacked, Spalding!

Spalding, I'm giving you notice, d'you hear? You have totally betrayed the trust I placed in you! . . .

And you're such a trustworthy character yourself, aren't you, Sneezewort? You low-down cheat, you even used closed-circuit television to win a game of Battleships!

Ssh, Spalding! I forbid you! . . . Silence!

Come on, now. All of you into the kitchenette! One false move and . . . Understand? . . . Move!

Spalding, you are discharged!

That's them in the cooler. Now for stage two . . .

Open the door, Spalding! ... Otherwise I'll ... er ... I'll ... Spalding!

Fraud!

A few more seconds and I'd have fixed him, but you saw ...

Mamma mia!

Spalding is two-faced crook!

Are you addressing me?

Now call up the control tower at Macassar. Pitch some yarn or other to keep them quiet.

Spalding! ... Spald-i-ing! I didn't mean to be cross! ... Now come along, be a good boy, Spalding, open up!

Macassar tower? This is Golf Tango Fox. We are just passing over Sumbawa. Nothing to report. We'll call you again before we reach the Darwin control zone. Over and out.

OK. Now straight down to sea level.

Going down? ... Where shall we be landing?

You ask hi-jackers up front!

My ears are singing like Castafiore in full spate!

Swallow and it goes.

Swallow what?

Swallow, that's what!

We still descending. They want to fly low, they escape from radar.

Swallow?

I suppose so.

Swallow?

GLUG

Ah, my ears have popped. She's gone!

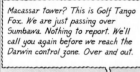

We'll soon be in the clear ...

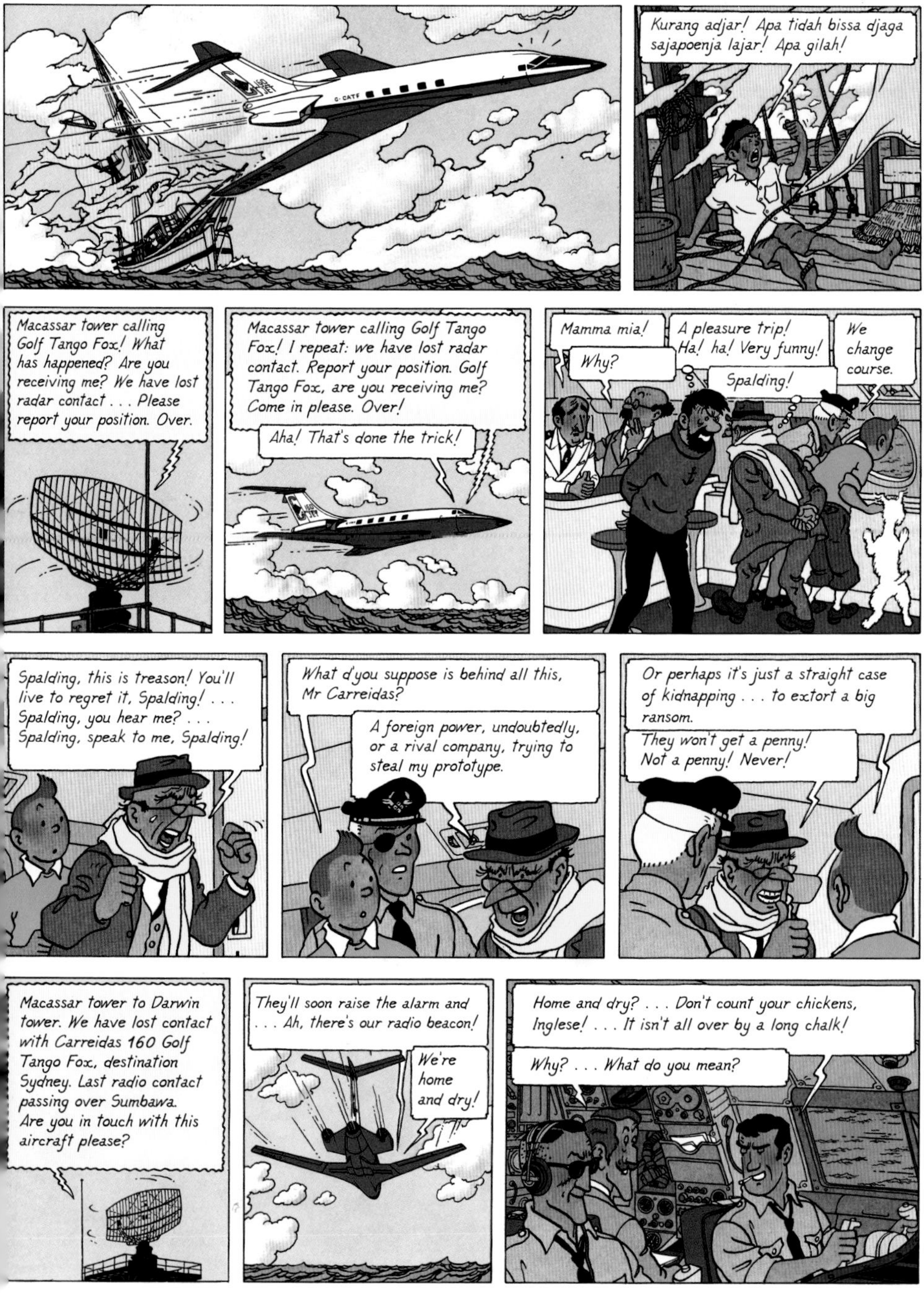
Kurang adjar! Apa tidah bissa djaga sajapoenja lajar! Apa gilah!
Macassar tower calling Golf Tango Fox! What has happened? Are you receiving me? We have lost radar contact . . . Please report your position. Over.
Macassar tower calling Golf Tango Fox! I repeat: we have lost radar contact. Report your position. Golf Tango Fox, are you receiving me? Come in please. Over!
Aha! That's done the trick!
Mamma mia!
Why?
A pleasure trip! Ha! ha! Very funny!
Spalding!
We change course.
Spalding, this is treason! You'll live to regret it, Spalding! . . . Spalding, you hear me? . . . Spalding, speak to me, Spalding!
What d'you suppose is behind all this, Mr Carreidas?
A foreign power, undoubtedly, or a rival company, trying to steal my prototype.
Or perhaps it's just a straight case of kidnapping . . . to extort a big ransom.
They won't get a penny! Not a penny! Never!
Macassar tower to Darwin tower. We have lost contact with Carreidas 160 Golf Tango Fox, destination Sydney. Last radio contact passing over Sumbawa. Are you in touch with this aircraft please?
They'll soon raise the alarm and . . . Ah, there's our radio beacon!
We're home and dry!
Home and dry? . . . Don't count your chickens, Inglese! . . . It isn't all over by a long chalk!
Why? . . . What do you mean?

What do I mean? . . . Just this: the runway we're going to land on is about a quarter the length we need for a bus like this! . . . So, you can reckon it's ten to one we'll break our silly necks!

Ten minutes later . . .

There's our rendezvous: the island of Pulau-pulau Bompa.

Right. We'll regain height to 1000 ft, reduce speed, set the wings for landing, empty the tanks. And in we go!

They climb again. I think prepare to land . . . Yes, there is island . . . And there is runway . . . But . . . crazy! Is crazy! Runway much too short!

They're ready for us.

Yes, I saw.

Ah, the wheels are down, they're coming in.

Flaps down, Hans!

Can't you stop rolling us around, you pock-marked pin-headed pirate of a pilot!

They put down flaps.

All sit with back against forward partition, hands behind head!

Now, Colombani boy, it's all or nothing!

Quick, the parachute!

WHAP

WOOOAAAH
Mamma mia!
Hands behind head, Captain!

CRACK

The parachute's burst!
Reverse the engines!

WOO-OW!
Thundering typhoons! Some people travel for fun!

WOW-OW-OW
Brakes! . . . Brakes!
They're full on!

BANG

The nose-wheel's burst!
I can't hold her!

We're going too fast! We're done for!

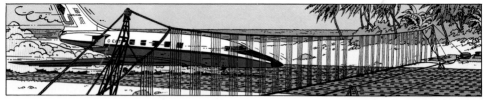

Bashi-bazouks!

Mamma mia!

WOOAAAH

Saved!

Aha! Operation Carreidas successfully accomplished!

Sure!

What a beastly experience! But we're alive, that's all that matters!

We'd better get busy with the prisoners.

Never have I had such a rough landing. You're fired!

Get moving, or I'll be doing the firing! Someone's waiting for you!

WOW-OW-WOO-OW

Keep that animal quiet!

He's absolutely terrified.

Mamma mia!

You wanted me?

Snowy, Snowy, quiet now, Snowy!

WOOAAH

SNOWY!

WOOAAH

Snowy! Here, Snowy! SNOWY!

Fire! Go on, shoot! Kill the tyke. It's gone mad!

WOOAAAH

RRRRR

WOOOOAAAAH

RRRRR

RRRRRR RRRRRR

Murderers! Devils! Let me go! Let me go, I tell you!

Bungling fools! You'd miss an elephant at five yards! Get after that infernal mongrel, and make sure you wipe it out!

That voice!?

RASTAPOPOU... LOS

Himself, dear boy!

Welcome to my island paradise!

Your surprise is charming to see! . . . You thought Papa Rastapopoulos was eaten by the Red Sea sharks, eh? Ha! ha! ha! ha!

Now the boot is on the other foot! I have you trapped in my little tropical garden. And you walked in all by yourselves! . . . You should have minded your own business, my dear friends, and stayed on Flight 714.

Get rid of my cigar? But of course. Your wish is my command, Mr Carreidas!

We knew you were a swine, Rastapopoulos. Now we know you're a dirty swine at that!

Well said!

Get rid of that cigar! No one smokes in the presence of Laszlo Carreidas!

Insolent puppy! You dare to defy me? When I have you here in my power? . . . And I've got you all right, you little fool!

I've got you. I've got you all, and I shall crush you like . . . like . . .

. . . like I crush an insignificant spider!

Diavolo!

MDJRK

... I ... er ... you ...
Anyway, this island will be
your grave!

Get everything fixed right
away, Allan.

OK, boss.

You see?

In a couple of hours every trace
of you and your plane will have
vanished. And your money, Mr
Carreidas, your lovely, lovely
loot, will be mine!

You're
mad!

It's a bore, you know, to stop being
a millionaire ... When I went bust,
I couldn't face the sweat of making
another fortune for myself. So I
decided it'd be easier, and quicker,
to take yours!

You're   mad!

No, just well informed, that's all.
I know, for example, that you
have on deposit in a Swiss bank -
under a false name, of course,
you always were a cheat - a quite
fantastic sum of money ...

I know the name of the bank: I know the
name in which you hold the account; I have
some magnificent examples of the false
signature you use ... In fact, the only thing
I don't know is the number of the account,
and that you are now going to give me!

Never!

Never say "never", my dear
Carreidas ... Wouldn't you agree
with me, Doctor Krollspell?

He! he!

You can torture me! Pull out
my nails, roast me over a slow
fire ... even tickle the soles
of my feet ... I won't talk!

RRRRRR   RRRRR

SNOWY!

Ah, getting rid of the
dog, I expect.

Cowardly brute!

Hold your tongue! I am talking with my friend Carreidas, not you!

Who mentioned torture, my dear Laszlo? Whatever do you take us for? . . . Savages? . . . Shame on you! How vulgar! . . . We aren't going to hurt you. Kind Doctor Krollspell has just perfected an excellent variety of truth-drug. It's a painless cure for obstinate people who have little secrets to conceal.

A truth-drug? . . . Villain! . . . Blackguard! . . . Bully! . . . A . . . aa . . . aaa . . .

AAAA

TCHOO

Stop! My hat! . . .

Whoops!

Take him with you, Doctor Krollspell. Get your little black bag ready. I'll join you in a minute.

My hat! . . . My hat! . . .

Come along!

Give the poor chap his hat, you son of a sea-gherkin! He could get sunstroke!

My hat! . . .

Sunstroke, eh? But what about you? You aren't wearing a hat either . . .

Don't worry about me.

But I do. I want you wrapped up!

?!

Ten thousand . . .

Ha! ha!

Ha! ha!

Tramps! . . . Terrapins! . . . Two-timing troglodytes!

Enough fooling: take them to the cooler.

OK

Come on, get going! . . . The old boozer's had a drop too much. Can't see the end of his nose. Tintin, you're in charge of the steering. Now then, on your way!

He who laughs last laughs longest. Remember that, pockmark!

We're going uphill. Get in single file. Don't forget, Tintin, you're in charge of bluebeard!

Left, Captain . . .

Right . . . A little more to the right . . . That's it . . .

Now keep to the left . . .

Straight ahead . . .

Careful! Keep left now . . .

GRMBLLL

Left, Captain, left . . .

LEFT!!

LEFT!!!

RIGHT left, Cap . . .

DOINNG

Ten thousand thundering typhoons! . . . Just you wait, Allan! When I get my hands on you I'll stuff your cap right down your throat, badge and all!

Ha! ha! ha!

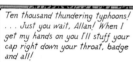

Come on, keep moving. Not much further.

Will you step into my parlour, gentlemen?

Home sweet home: an old Japanese bunker. And here you stay till Carreidas talks. So make yourselves comfortable.

What happens to us afterwards?

I'm not supposed to tell you yet; boss's orders. But I'd hate to keep a secret from old shipmates like you . . . You'll go back on board the aeroplane, which will then be towed out to sea . . . and sunk. With you inside, of course! . . . Ha! ha! ha!

CLANGGG

Scorpion!

Baboon! . . . Orang-utan! . . .

Ha! ha! ha!

Bandit! . . . Bootlegger! . . . Bashi-bazouk! . . . Breathalyser! Brigand!

Keep your hair on, Captain . . . I mean . . . Come and let me try to get that hat off!

'ull 'ard, 'a'ain! . . . 'ull! 'ull!

Can I be of any assistance to you?

'ooray

Billions of blue blistering barnacles. I . . . Oh, sorry! . . .

HA! HA! HA! HA! It suits you! You look fabulous!

It's disgraceful! . . . Yes, disgraceful! . . . I said disgraceful!

Ssh! . . . Quiet! . . .

Why? What's the matter?

I suppose you think it's funny!

No, it's nothing . . . I thought for a minute I could hear Snowy barking.

Of course. Poor old Snowy!

Disgraceful! That's what I call it!

Don't you worry, Tintin . . . If we get out of this alive we'll make the butchers pay. I'll . . .

Thanks, Captain. Whatever we do, it won't bring poor Snowy back to life.

I . . . er . . . well . . . yes . . . hm . . . er . . .

Anyway, remember our own death sentence is only suspended, until Carreidas talks . . . But I wonder, will he talk?

He'll talk, Mister Rastapopoulos, he'll talk all right.

I hope so for your sake, doctor!

Never! . . . And anyway, I want my hat!

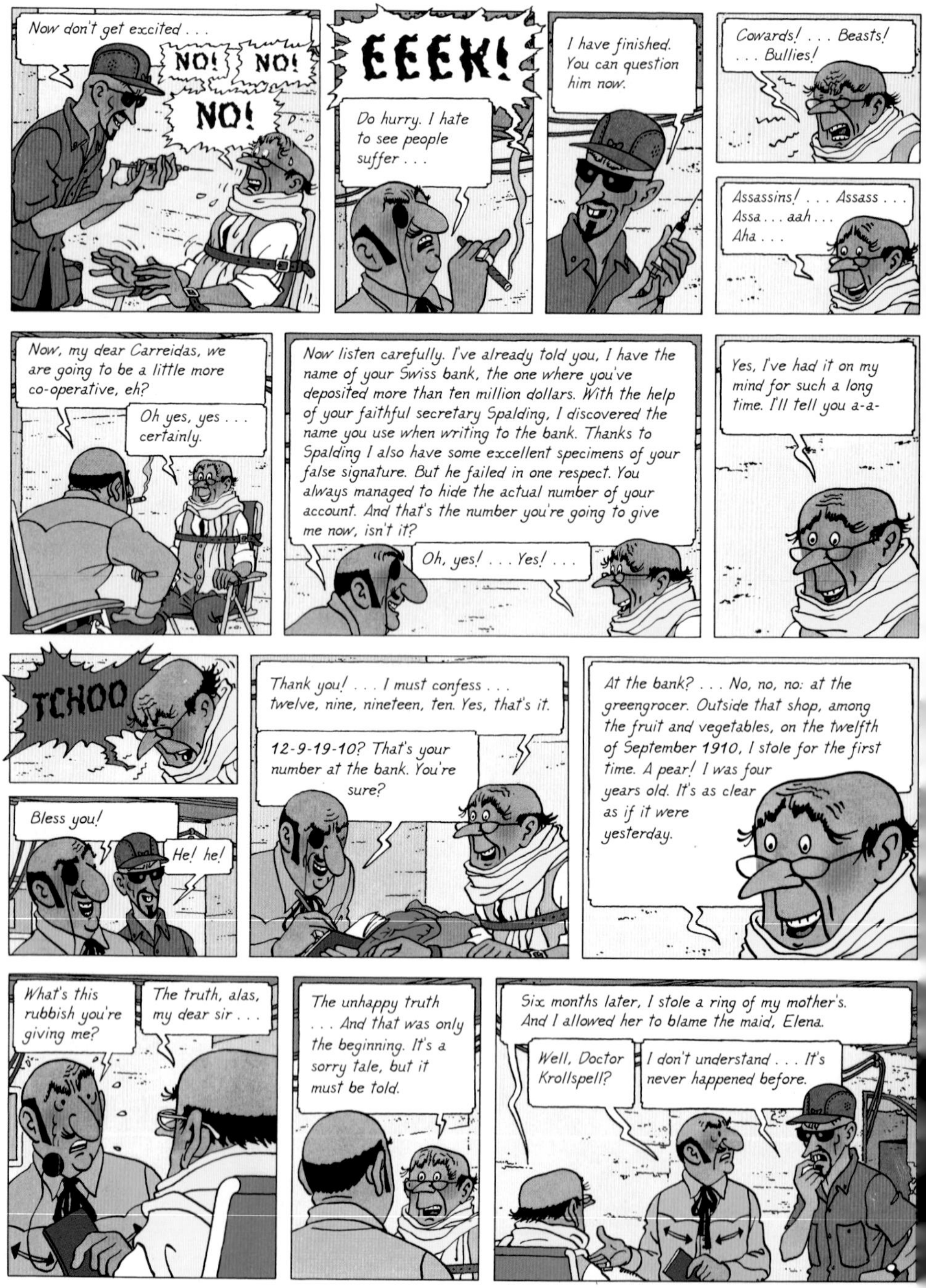
Now don't get excited . . .
NO! NO!
NO!
EEEK!
Do hurry. I hate to see people suffer . . .
I have finished. You can question him now.
Cowards! . . . Beasts! . . . Bullies!
Assassins! . . . Assass . . . Assa . . . aah . . . Aha . . .
Now, my dear Carreidas, we are going to be a little more co-operative, eh?
Oh yes, yes . . . certainly.
Now listen carefully. I've already told you, I have the name of your Swiss bank, the one where you've deposited more than ten million dollars. With the help of your faithful secretary Spalding, I discovered the name you use when writing to the bank. Thanks to Spalding I also have some excellent specimens of your false signature. But he failed in one respect. You always managed to hide the actual number of your account. And that's the number you're going to give me now, isn't it?
Oh, yes! . . . Yes! . . .
Yes, I've had it on my mind for such a long time. I'll tell you a-a-
TCHOO
Bless you!
He! he!
Thank you! . . . I must confess . . . twelve, nine, nineteen, ten. Yes, that's it.
12-9-19-10? That's your number at the bank. You're sure?
At the bank? . . . No, no, no: at the greengrocer. Outside that shop, among the fruit and vegetables, on the twelfth of September 1910, I stole for the first time. A pear! I was four years old. It's as clear as if it were yesterday.
What's this rubbish you're giving me?
The truth, alas, my dear sir . . .
The unhappy truth . . . And that was only the beginning. It's a sorry tale, but it must be told.
Six months later, I stole a ring of my mother's. And I allowed her to blame the maid, Elena.
Well, Doctor Krollspell?
I don't understand . . . It's never happened before.

Poor Elena! How she protested her innocence. But they threw her into the street . . . And I nearly died of laughing! Even then I was the devil incarnate!

The dose can't have been strong enough. I'll give him another shot.

Very well.

I was only a child. From my tenderest years I have never ceased to do my neighbours down. Amazing, isn't it?

Th-ere!

Now who's going to give his account number to his old friend, Rastapopoulos, eh?

Me! . . . Me! . . . I am!

2. 17. 6 . . .

2. 17. 6? Excellent my dear Carreidas. That's all I wanted to know.

Yes, 2. 17. 6. That was it. The exact amount. I sneaked it one morning, some years later, from my elder sister's handbag.

? You dare to joke with me?

Believe me, it is no joking matter. I am rotten, rotten to the core.

Your account number! Tell me! I order you to tell me!

I'm so mean that I even cheat at games in my aeroplane. Imagine, I installed closed-circuit television to let me see my opponent's fleet . . . Dreadful, isn't it, at my age?

I don't care! I don't care! I don't care!

But you should care. There are lessons to be learned from the life of a dishonest . . . of a . . . dishon . . . dis . . . ZZZ-ZZZ-ZZZ

He's gone to sleep! . . . Your serum is a success, Doctor Krollspell! A brilliant success!

Meanwhile . . .

If we get out of this mess alive I swear I'll never touch whisky again . . .

. . . for a hundred . . . no, fifty . . . er, say ten . . . well, three days . . . That's a promise!

Ssh! . . . Quiet! . . . Listen!

I didn't say anything!

It's Snowy! . . . I'm sure it's Snowy! . . . Listen!

Nnn! Nnn!

It's Snowy! He's alive! . . . Snowy!

Ssh! Keep quiet!

Nnn! Nnn!

Quiet, by thunder! . . . You'll bring the guards in!

Nnn! Nnn!

You hear dog? . . . I tink . . .

I hear 'um.

Calm down, Snowy, calm down.

Nnn! Nnn!

Ssh-h-h-h.

Nnn! Nnn!

Golly, what's the matter? He's tied up.

Go on, Snowy! Go on!

SCRUNCH

SCRUNCH

SCRUNCH

He's done it! I can free my hands. Thanks, Snowy!

Wonderful! Three cheers for Snowy.

HIP HIP

NO!

HOOOOOO

. . . RAY!?

What's the matter?

Blistering barnacles, what have I done . . .

Someone's coming . . .

Which man cry?

Let's hope Snowy understands what to do . . .

I don't care what anyone says, it's a thoroughly stupid joke!

Which man 'e go cry? . . . You tell!

He's there . . . He understood.

OUCH

?

YEOW

Now for it! One, two, three!

WHAM

WHAM! . . . Well done!

Fine left hook!

WHAM

Fine right, uppercut for other one!

And again! Bravo!

First, let's take that hat off poor Calculus.

A neat job, eh, boys?

Ma professore, it was not uno joke.

I don't deny it. It was just a stupid joke, that's all.

Now we must try to rescue poor Mr Carreidas.

Poor? . . . Him? . . . Risk our lives for that cheat?

How'd we find him, anyway, miserable old Midas?

By using his hat.

Using his hat?

Yes. Where is it? . . . Ah, on the floor.

Get the scent, Snowy.

Sniff, sniff . . . That reminds me of someone . . .

Find him, Snowy!

Seek him out!

I . . . er . . . it will work this time, Mister Rastapopoulos. I've doubled the dose . . . I . . . I shall succeed . . .

I strongly advise you to, doctor!

ZZZZ

ZZZZ

ZZZZ

You were wearing this hat, Captain. That's why Snowy made a mistake.

Anyway, thanks to Snowy at least we're free, and can look for Mr Carreidas.

I know, but rescuing him is another matter.

I've got a suggestion. The Captain and I go in search of Carreidas. You, Skut, take the Professor, Gino and the prisoners, and hide somewhere near the bunker. Keep out of sight, and wait till we come back. Is that all right?

Is good plan, Tintin. I prefer to go with you and Captain. But I stay with other friends and prisoners.

Thanks, Skut. Now, let's go.

Ready, Professor?

Extraordinary! I've never seen that before.

You must hurry: there's no time . . .

So you've noticed it too? . . . I've never seen my pendulum oscillate so fast . . . Never in my life!

It's incredible . . . Look! It's absolutely incredible . . . I've never seen anything like it!

A few minutes later . . .

This is an ideal place for you to hide. Be sure you don't make any noise. Keep a sharp eye on the prisoners. If all goes well, we'll come straight back here.

Goodbye, Tintin. Goodbye, and good luck!

Good luck to you, Skut.

Why did I ever leave Marlinspike?

Let anyone mention travel to me again and I'll tell him . . .

CRCCH

?

CAPTAIN? . . .

CAPTAIN? . . .

WHERE ARE YOU?!

Billions of blistering barnacles!

W-where are you?

Here!

How on earth did you get in there?

I don't know. I went to step over some roots and whoosh! I shot down between them.

I fell on a sort of smooth slab . . . like a flagstone. Let's investigate. There's something funny about this place . . . a weird atmosphere.

I can feel it too . . . But we must push on. We'll look later, if we get time.

Not so fast, Snowy.

Oh! Come and look . . . quietly . . .

?

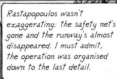

Rastapopoulos wasn't exaggerating: the safety net's gone and the runway's almost disappeared. I must admit, the operation was organised down to the last detail.

I didn't see the plane: must have been camouflaged.

I expect so.

We must be getting near: look at Snowy. He's on to something.

Crumbs! Another bunker, with two guards outside. That'll be where they're holding Carreidas.

Th-th-there! . . . He . . . he . . . he's w-w-waking up . . . He . . . he . . . he . . . he'll t-t-t- . . . he'll t-t-talk.

95

They aren't paying much attention. All the better for us.

Kita di rumah biassa tambah sedikit sambal ulek.

Itu bukan djelek, tentu lebih enak tetapi . . .

Ssh-h-h-h! . . . Or bang-bang . . . Understand?

Understand? Quiet, or else . . .

Disarm them first, Captain . . . Good . . . Now, tie them up, quick as you can. Better gag them too. You can use their own shirts.

Sorry, old man, but you know how a sailor has a passion for knots!

Now, you moth-eaten monkey, how's that, eh?

Have you decided? Will you co-operate, or do I use stronger measures? Are you going to talk, you little reptile?

A little reptile . . . that's what I am. It can't be said too often. There's no excuse, either. Think of all the good examples I had when I was a boy. My grandfather, for instance. Think of my grandfather . . .

. . . my maternal grandfather . . . just a humble confectioner, a maker of Turkish delight in Erzerum. A simple, honest man. "Laszlo", he used to say, "Laszlo, remember: an ill-gotten camel gathers no gain . . ."

It's all your fault, charlatan! You'll pay for this!

YEOW

Clumsy quack! . . . You jabbed me with your needle, curse you!

I . . . I'm t-terribly sorry . . .

The . . . the syringe . . . it . . . it was empty? Doctor! It was empty, wasn't it? . . . Tell me!

I . . . er . . . y-y-yes . . .

. . . it was . . . er . . . empty . . . er . . . almost . . . You . . . you aren't feeling bad . . .

Me? Bad? . . . Bad? Me? . . . Bad?

Me? Bad? Of course I'm bad! I'm the devil incarnate . . . that's what I am. And let's hear anyone try to deny it!

I beg your pardon! I am the devil incarnate . . . and I'm richer than you are, too!

So what? Listen to this! I ruined my three brothers and two sisters, and dragged my parents into the gutter. What d'you say to that, eh?

Peanuts! Kid's stuff! My great-aunt was so ashamed of me she lay down and died! Beat that!

Amateur! You're not in my class. Think of my scheme to kidnap you . . . that took a man of real cunning, a man without a shred of decency . . . a fiend!

You, doctor, I promised you forty thousand dollars to help me get the account number out of Carreidas. And all the time I'd made a plan to eliminate you when the job was done . . . Diabolical, wasn't it? . . . Don't you agree?

And the Sondonesian nationalists . . . poor deluded fools. I lured them into this. I said I'd help them in their fight for independence. Ha! ha! ha! If only they knew what lies in store for them!

Their junks are mined already. They'll be blown sky-high, long before they see their homeland.

He's a monster!

The same goes for the others . . . Spalding, and the aircrew. Rich men, that's what they think they'll be, with the money I flashed under their noses. But they'll be disposed of when I'm ready. Ha! ha! ha! The Devil himself couldn't do better!

Pooh! You aren't out of the nursery!

Now let's get this straight. Yes or no! Do you or do you not admit that I'm wickeder than you?

Never! . . . Never, d'you hear? . . . I'd sooner die!

All right, if that's what you want! Die!

Quick! Time we intervened!

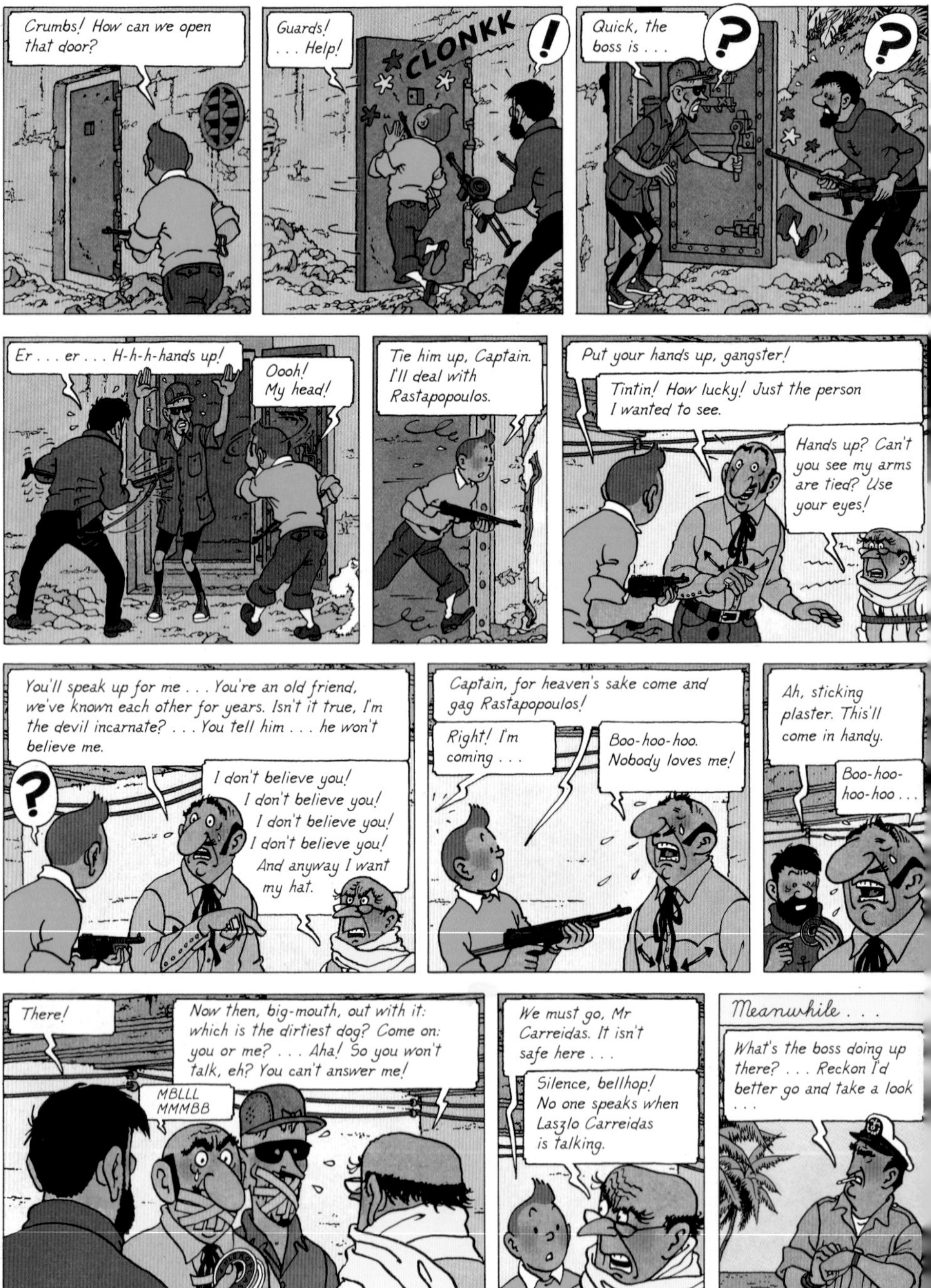
Crumbs! How can we open that door?
Guards! . . . Help!
CLONKK
!
Quick, the boss is . . .
?
?
Er . . . er . . . H-h-h-hands up!
Oooh! My head!
Tie him up, Captain. I'll deal with Rastapopoulos.
Put your hands up, gangster!
Tintin! How lucky! Just the person I wanted to see.
Hands up? Can't you see my arms are tied? Use your eyes!
You'll speak up for me . . . You're an old friend, we've known each other for years. Isn't it true, I'm the devil incarnate? . . . You tell him . . . he won't believe me.
?
I don't believe you! I don't believe you! I don't believe you! I don't believe you! And anyway I want my hat.
Captain, for heaven's sake come and gag Rastapopoulos!
Right! I'm coming . . .
Boo-hoo-hoo. Nobody loves me!
Ah, sticking plaster. This'll come in handy.
Boo-hoo-hoo-hoo . . .
There!
Now then, big-mouth, out with it: which is the dirtiest dog? Come on: you or me? . . . Aha! So you won't talk, eh? You can't answer me!
MBLLL MMMBB
We must go, Mr Carreidas. It isn't safe here . . .
Silence, bellhop! No one speaks when Laszlo Carreidas is talking.
Meanwhile . . .
What's the boss doing up there? . . . Reckon I'd better go and take a look . . .

If you set yourself up as the devil incarnate, my good sir, you answer back. You shut people's mouths . . . You . . .

MBLLL For goodness sake, Mr Carreidas, we're in danger . . .

Who gave you permission to interrupt me, pipsqueak? . . . Get this into your head: nothing, and nobody, stops Laszlo Carreidas from speaking!

Is that so?!

MBLL MMBBB MMBLL BBMLBBLL

Nothing, and nobody, eh?

Ah, his hat. Thanks, Snowy. Perhaps that'll help restore his temper . . .

If you'd only be reasonable we shouldn't have to do this, Mr Carreidas.

MBLLL

We've wasted enough time. Let's go. I'll see if the coast's clear.

Yes, yes, do that. I'm coming.

OK. No one about. You can bring them.

Coming . . . coming . . .

Captain! Captain! Do hurry up!

I'm coming . . . coming . . .

Coming, coming! When are you coming? Now, or next week?

I'm sorry . . . I . . . I had a spot of bother with some sticking plaster. You know what I mean. I managed to get rid of it in the end . . .

Good. But hurry now.

We must leave the two Sondonesians. We'll have our hands full with those three comedians. So, off we go!

Right!

Let's hope we don't run into any more trouble.

?   ?

-BANG-

WHIUIUIUW

!

RATATATATAT

Stop! Don't waste our ammunition. I'm afraid we're going to need it soon enough!

Bandit!

We'll have the whole gang on our backs in less than ten minutes. Quick, we must rejoin the others.

OK, I'm with you.

MMBLLL

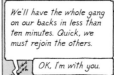
U?∪
??

What am I doing, bound and gagged? . . . Who dared . . . I . . . Diavolo! I've been taken prisoner!

BLMMBL

What . . . what's going on? . . . Where am I . . . What's happened?

WHEEEET   WHEEEET

Blasts on a whistle. That'll be Allan summoning his men. They're on our trail.

Allan's after them. We aren't finished yet . . .

Faster, Captain, faster . . .

I must delay them . . . That shouldn't be too difficult . . .

? ?

He went down like a ninepin. Crumbs! He's passed out.

Thundering typhoons!

What shall we do, Captain? We can't leave him: he's too valuable as a hostage.

I know . . .

But if we have to carry him they'll catch us up in no time.

Wait . . . maybe there's another solution.

Just what I'm looking for.

What are you doing?

SNAP

?

I only want to make sure he really is unconscious.

What, with that thorn?

?????...

NNNN!

You see? A well-chosen spot . . . one little prick, and . . . . whoops-a-daisy!

We must be close to where we left the others . . .

CRACK

?

What on earth's that?

A monitor!

What's it doing here, pestilential pachyderm? . . . Looks as if it escaped from the Ice Age!

MMMMMMMM

MMMMMMMM

MMM   MM

MMMMMMMM

MMBBL   MMMMM

I'll catch Carreidas. The Captain will soon pick up Rastapopoulos.

Foiled! He's after me already!

You won't get far, my beauty!

Where's Rastapopoulos!

Don't know . . . pfpf . . . My gun . . . pfpf . . . got hooked up . . . pfpf . . . dratted tree . . . Terribly sorry . . .

Not your fault, Captain. A pity, all the same . . . Still, let's move on. No use chasing after him: he'll be miles away by now.

About ten yards . . . pfpf . . . at the most . . . pfpf . . . idiots!

All right, Tintin. Let me just collect my gun.

Cunning devil . . . he's escaped!

MBLLL

GRRRR

I left Snowy to guard Carreidas, but I think Krollspell would do it just as well.

Hmm.

Quiet! . . . Ssh! . . . Listen! . . . They can't be far . . .

102

?!

HEY! BOSS!

? Allan!... Saved!

BOING

Meanwhile...

I'm not too happy about Krollspell ... I think you trust him too far.

I agree it's risky...

BLMMBM... MBMMBL...

...but he knows now that his worthy employer had him booked for a sticky end. So the doctor's as keen as we are to keep out of his clutches. You saw how he helped us?

Yes...I know...but...

YEEEK!

!

!

W-what a horrible shriek... It's... bloodcurdling...

Ugh! Enough to make your hair stand on end...

YOWK!

Cheer up, boss: that's the last.

YEOW!

I wonder... It sounded like Rastapopoulos...

Whoever it is, he isn't very happy.

What are you hanging around for? Get after them! And don't forget, I want Carreidas and Krollspell alive! Just...

...crack 'em on the nut, eh?

Idiot!... Must you keep reminding me?!

Follow me, boys!... Death to the enemies of the Sondonesian revolution!

There! . . . Careful! . . . Don't make any noise . . . They mustn't . . .

Wooah! wooah! wooah! wooah!

!

There they are! I can see them . . . You press on with the others, Captain.

But I . . .

Go, Captain! I won't take any chances.

Wooah! wooah!

BANG
BANG

WHIUUUW

WHIUUUW

OK. My turn now! . . . A burst on the left . . .

RATATATAT

And another on the right.

RATATATAT

Now beat it fast while they think I'm still there . . .

W-what's the m-matter . . . I feel . . . I feel as if someone's speaking right inside my head . . .

Higher up? To the left? Under a big flat rock . . . Yes . . . yes, I'll do as you say . . .

Now it's my turn to cover you . . .

No, come with me! I know where we shall be safe!

Safe? . . . Safe where? . . . What d'you mean?

I don't know. But there should be a big flat rock higher up. Keep close! This way, quick!

A big flat rock? How on earth can you know that?

Come on! Quick! Hurry!

There! . . . That's it . . . Now, behind those bushes . . .

?

!

In you go, doctor. Be careful, there should be about ten steps . . .

But how do you know?

Yes, I see them.

All right? . . . Good. Here's Carreidas. Hold him tight in case he falls.

MBLLL

You next, Captain. Quickly! We mustn't let them see where we've gone . . . Do hurry!

Tintin, I insist! Tell me where you're taking us!

I don't know. But I'm sure it's our only chance. For goodness sake make up your mind!

All right, I'll come.

?

!

Ugghh! . . . Beastly things! . . . Go away!

Oh, come on, Captain! They're quite harmless. They won't eat you.

For heaven's sake come along, Captain!

And be dive-bombed by vampires? . . . Never! I'm staying here!

BANG

BANG

WHIIIT

WHIIIT

!

BANG

WHIIIT

Ha! ha! Too clever by half! They're cornered!

Tintin! . . . This is Allan . . . Come on out! You'd better be sensible, or I might get impatient . . . and toss a grenade in after you.

No answer? . . . OK, if that's how you want it . . .

Wait while I take the pin out . . .

. . . and here she comes . . . One . . . two . . .

. . . thr . . .

I'm crazy! What am I doing? The boss said he wanted Carreidas and the doctor alive! . . . He'd have my hide for this . . .

B-but w-what shall I do with th-this . . .

Hey! Take cover, you lot! I'm going to throw this grenade as far as I can.

Whew! That really had me sweating!

BOOM

There, that's got me out of trouble . . .

What misbegotten madman had that brilliant idea?! . . . Chucking grenades about!!

So it was you, clodhopper! Dim-witted oaf! Numbskull!

!

Village idiot! What about our prisoners, eh? Where are they?

Th-th-there . . . in the c-c-cave . . .

Th-th-there . . . In the c-c-cave . . . In the c-c-cave! In the c-c-cave! And what's stopping you from getting them out of the c-c-cave; eh? . . . What are you waiting for!

Well? Get on with it! . . . What's stopping you from getting them out, eh? . . . What are you waiting for?

Stop! ... Brenti! ... Brenti la!

Now what? Keep moving, can't you!

Disana ... Diatas batu karang ... Lihatlah tanda dawa 2 terbang ini diatas kereta 2 berapi.

Saja.

Itu betul.

Well, what is it? What's the matter? Are the brave soldiers of the revolution afraid to tackle a drunken sailor, an undersized urchin, and a few bats?!

No, no master. We no 'gree go down dark place. We no be allowed go down dark place, master. Look 'um that sign, master - God's they put 'um dere ... They come from sky in fire lorries. If we go in they punish us proper proper, master.

WHAT?

What are you babbling about? ... What's this nonsense ... Are you disobeying my orders? You'll pay dearly for your cowardice, you dogs!

No, boss! ... We must keep calm. We need them ... And remember how frightened they were last night when we saw that strange light in the sky ... Let me handle this.

All right, now. You there, go back to the beach as fast as you can and tell the two airmen we want them. At once!

I 'gree, master.

Tell them to bring torches, a rope, and their guns, of course.

I 'gree master.

They're to be here before nightfall!

I do, master.

Fine! ... Now, it's you I'm talking to, Captain Grog-blossom, you and wonderboy! If you don't come out of that rat-hole quietly, with your hands in the air ...

... you'll be carried out feet first!

The crew won't be long . . . then we'll soon crack this . . . er . . . sorry, boss . . . er, have a cigarette?

Shut up!

CRACK

What is that? . . .

Oh! A monkey! . . . A prob . . . a . . . Got it! A proboscis monkey!

Ha! ha! Look, scooting along like a rabbit!

My, what a sight! . . . What a conk! . . . Did ever you see such a conk?

Reminds me of someone . . . Now, who can it . . .

?!+☆ pfff ? hm

Meanwhile . . .

Hello! Here's one of our chaps come back . . .

Big man 'e want you: make you go, chop chop . . .

Now what's the matter?

It should have been finished hours ago, and the plane at the bottom of the sea. We shall end up being spotted here. Ah, here's the news   bulletin.

There is still no trace of the aircraft owned by millionaire Laszlo Carreidas which disappeared between Macassar and Darwin. The search, which has been called off at nightfall, will be resumed at dawn.

Good, that gives us a few hours' respite. Come on, boys.

Not me! I'm not crawling about in the jungle . . .

That'll do, Spalding. Move!

Look here, Tintin, when are you going to explain? Where the blue blistering blazes are you taking us?

I've told you, Captain, I haven't the remotest idea . . . Someone seems to be guiding me. I'm just obeying orders. That's all I can say . . .

And another thing: how is it we can see our way down here? By rights it should be black as the inside of a cow.

I know. It's queer. It reminds me of that strange light in the Temple of the Sun.

But I think we've nearly reached our destination . . . Yes, there's the statue I was told about . . .

His lordship's "voices" have described the statue to his lordship, of course. Perhaps they've also been gracious enough to explain why it's so hellishly hot down here! Like a Turkish bath!

I don't know. Perhaps there's a spring of boiling water nearby . . .

Maybe they serve cups of tea, too!

It could be lava. We are very close to a volcano. Excuse me . . .

The eye . . . Press hard on the eye . . . The right one? . . . I see . . .

A secret passage! . . . It's unbelievable! . . . Pressing on the eye released a catch . . . We must go on.

In there? But . . .

I'll come last, Captain. You go, then I can lower the statue into place.

CRACK

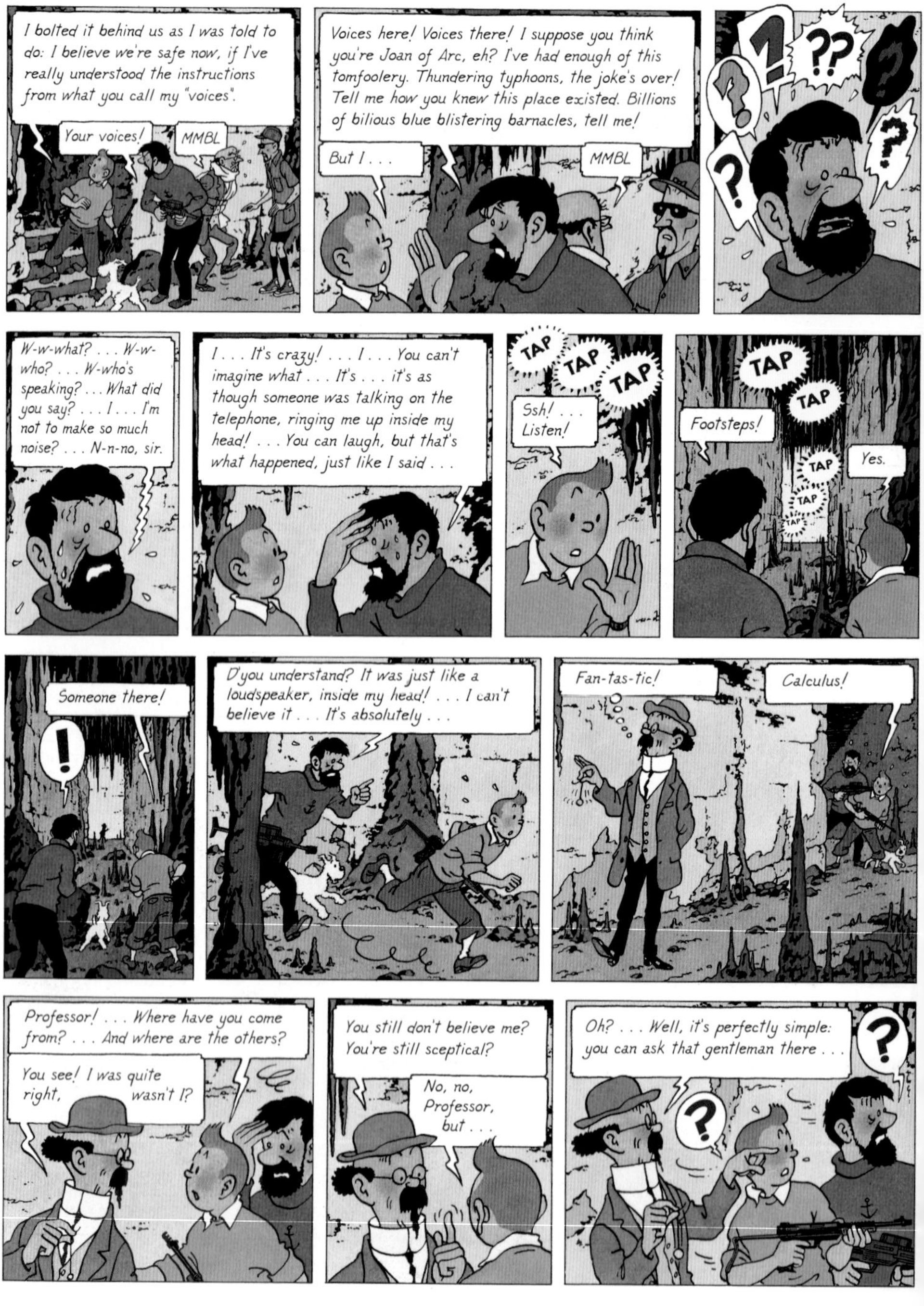

I bolted it behind us as I was told to do: I believe we're safe now, if I've really understood the instructions from what you call my "voices".
Your voices!
MMBL
Voices here! Voices there! I suppose you think you're Joan of Arc, eh? I've had enough of this tomfoolery. Thundering typhoons, the joke's over! Tell me how you knew this place existed. Billions of bilious blue blistering barnacles, tell me!
But I . . .
MMBL
?? ?
W-w-what? . . . W-w-who? . . . W-who's speaking? . . . What did you say? . . . I . . . I'm not to make so much noise? . . . N-n-no, sir.
I . . . It's crazy! . . . I . . . You can't imagine what . . . It's . . . it's as though someone was talking on the telephone, ringing me up inside my head! . . . You can laugh, but that's what happened, just like I said . . .
TAP TAP TAP
Ssh! . . . Listen!
TAP TAP
Footsteps!
TAP TAP TAP
Yes.
Someone there!
!
D'you understand? It was just like a loudspeaker, inside my head! . . . I can't believe it . . . It's absolutely . . .
Fan-tas-tic!
Calculus!
Professor! . . . Where have you come from? . . . And where are the others?
You see! I was quite right, wasn't I?
You still don't believe me? You're still sceptical?
No, no, Professor, but . . .
Oh? . . . Well, it's perfectly simple: you can ask that gentleman there . . .
?
?

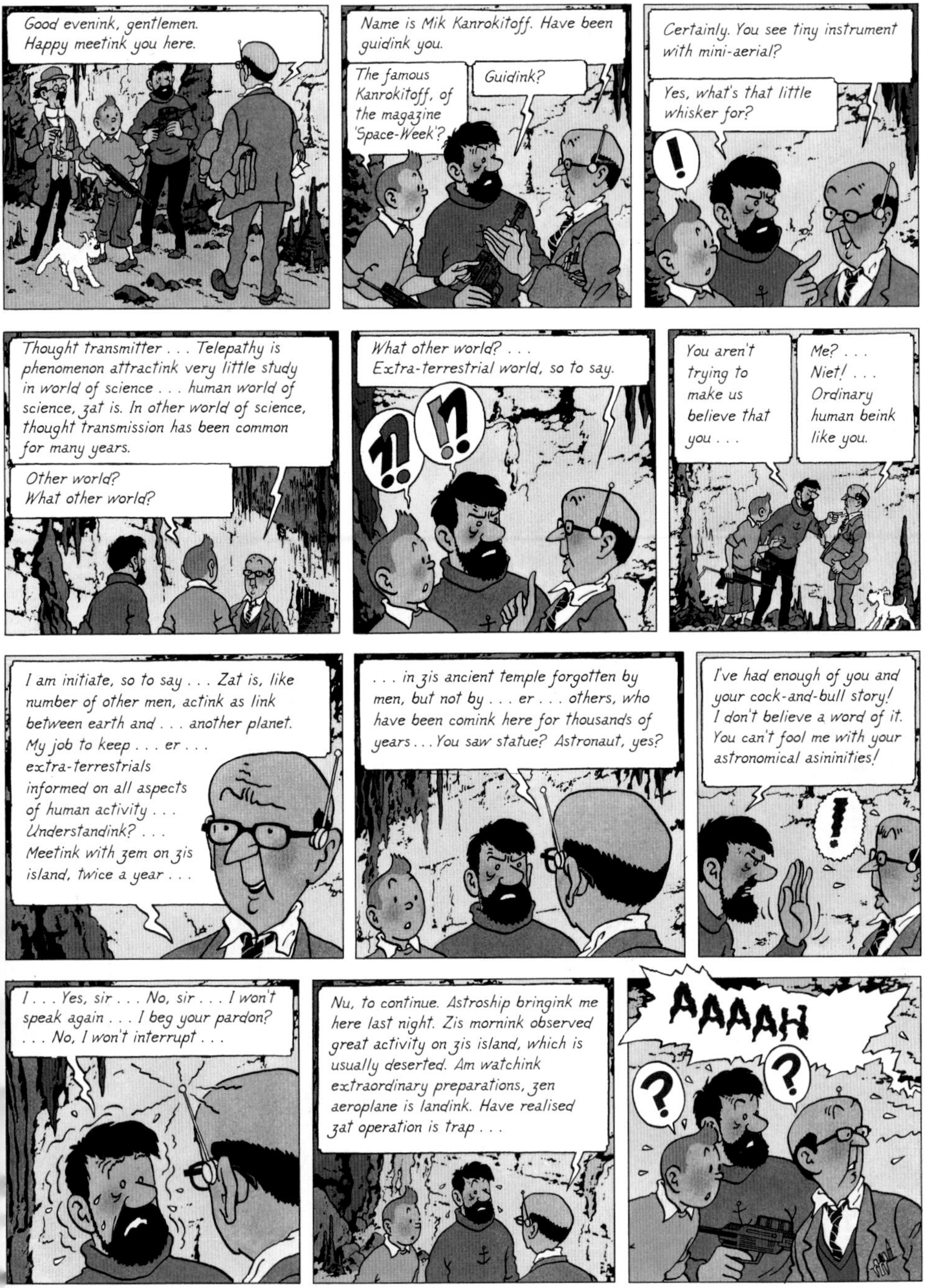

Good evenink, gentlemen. Happy meetink you here.
Name is Mik Kanrokitoff. Have been guidink you.
The famous Kanrokitoff, of the magazine 'Space-Week'?
Guidink?
Certainly. You see tiny instrument with mini-aerial?
Yes, what's that little whisker for?
!
Thought transmitter . . . Telepathy is phenomenon attractink very little study in world of science . . . human world of science, zat is. In other world of science, thought transmission has been common for many years.
Other world? What other world?
What other world? . . . Extra-terrestrial world, so to say.
?!
?!
You aren't trying to make us believe that you . . .
Me? . . . Niet! . . . Ordinary human beink like you.
I am initiate, so to say . . . Zat is, like number of other men, actink as link between earth and . . . another planet. My job to keep . . . er . . . extra-terrestrials informed on all aspects of human activity . . . Understandink? . . . Meetink with zem on zis island, twice a year . . .
. . . in zis ancient temple forgotten by men, but not by . . . er . . . others, who have been comink here for thousands of years . . . You saw statue? Astronaut, yes?
I've had enough of you and your cock-and-bull story! I don't believe a word of it. You can't fool me with your astronomical asininities!
!
I . . . Yes, sir . . . No, sir . . . I won't speak again . . . I beg your pardon? . . . No, I won't interrupt . . .
Nu, to continue. Astroship bringink me here last night. Zis mornink observed great activity on zis island, which is usually deserted. Am watchink extraordinary preparations, zen aeroplane is landink. Have realised zat operation is trap . . .
AAAAH
?
?

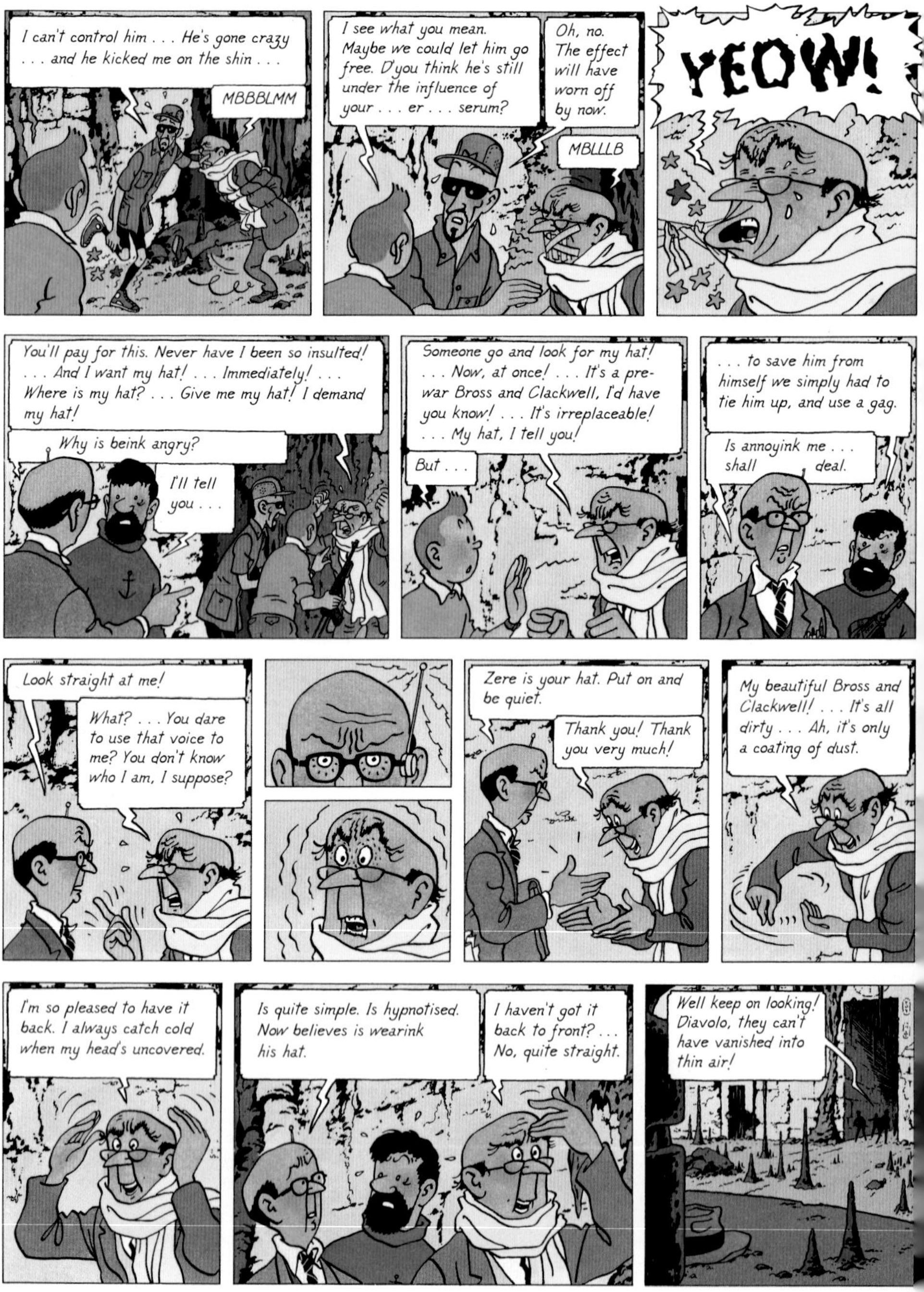

I can't control him . . . He's gone crazy . . . and he kicked me on the shin . . .
MBBBLMM
I see what you mean. Maybe we could let him go free. D'you think he's still under the influence of your . . . er . . . serum?
Oh, no. The effect will have worn off by now.
MBLLLB
YEOW!
You'll pay for this. Never have I been so insulted! . . . And I want my hat! . . . Immediately! . . . Where is my hat? . . . Give me my hat! I demand my hat!
Why is beink angry?
I'll tell you . . .
Someone go and look for my hat! . . . Now, at once! . . . It's a pre-war Bross and Clackwell, I'd have you know! . . . It's irreplaceable! . . . My hat, I tell you!
But . . .
. . . to save him from himself we simply had to tie him up, and use a gag.
Is annoyink me . . . shall deal.
Look straight at me!
What? . . . You dare to use that voice to me? You don't know who I am, I suppose?
Zere is your hat. Put on and be quiet.
Thank you! Thank you very much!
My beautiful Bross and Clackwell! . . . It's all dirty . . . Ah, it's only a coating of dust.
I'm so pleased to have it back. I always catch cold when my head's uncovered.
Is quite simple. Is hypnotised. Now believes is wearink his hat.
I haven't got it back to front? . . . No, quite straight.
Well keep on looking! Diavolo, they can't have vanished into thin air!

So, can continue explainink . . . Aeroplane comink down near here: terrible landink. Am seeink you taken prisoner and led away to old block-house.

Yes, but we managed to escape . . .

Is so. But when you are free am seeink you beink followed by other men. I decidink is time for me to intervene. So, am gettink into telepathic communication with you and guidink you to ʒis temple.

You saved our lives! Without your help who knows . . .

TCHOOO

?

OH?

AH!

Have you lost something?

Can't you see my hat has fallen off?

?

Some people need every single thing spelled out in words of one syllable.

Now extra-terrestrials must be decidink what to do with you. Am expectink astroship very soon . . . You in your world say flyink-saucer.

A flying-saucer?!

So now we've come to flying-saucers! You're going too far: we aren't as gullible as that!

You still doubt? So, look over there, to your right.

See there, on wall. Is certainly machine used by people from . . . er . . . other planet.

Thousands of years ago, men were buildink ʒis temple to worship gods who are comink from sky in fire-chariots. In fact, fire-chariots are astroships, like ʒat one. And gods . . . but you have seen statue: what are you thinkink statue is resemblink?

It looks . . . it looks like an astronaut with a helmet, microphone, earphones . . .

And there, on the left, down by the statue . . . what's that?

?

A HAT! IT'S CARREIDAS'S HAT!

You're sure it's his? See if it has his initials.

Confounded thing, it won't come out . . . it's jammed under the pedestal.

If it slipped under the statue you must be able to get it out, fool! . . . It hasn't been glued to the floor! Pull, you milksop, pull hard! Pull! . . .

HNN! . . .
HNN! . . .

RRCH!

IMBECILE! IMBECILE!

IMBECILE!

Sorry, boss! So sorry!

L.C.: Laszlo Carreidas . . . It's his all right. Look, boss.

So . . . you had to rip the brim to pull it free?

That means the statue was standing on it . . . In which case . . . Of course, it's obvious: there must be a secret passage . . . So start looking! All of you!

Go on! Go on! The statue must be hinged . . .

Ten minutes later . . .
It won't shift, boss . . . If only we had some dynamite.

Dynamite? . . . We can do better than that!

Quick, go back to our junk and bring all the plastic explosive intended for those silly Sondonesians! Hurry!

Aha, my clever friends, you don't know Rastapopoulos . . . I'll get you, if I have to demolish this temple stone by stone!

We were talkink about extra-terrestrials: what ӡey will do with you. Probably beginnink by hypnotisink you.

What? Hypnotising us?

No, no, a thousand times no! You don't really believe we'd let ourselves be hypnotised by your prehistoric saucer-sailing spacemen! Not on your life!

Is all right, is all right, you are comink to no harm. You will be hypnotised and are forgettink all ӡat you have seen and heard here, rememberink only flight as far as Sumbawa in Carreidas aircraft.

But how did you know . . . ?

About flight? How I knowink? . . . Nothink telepathic in ӡat. Your comrades Skut and Gino are tellink me . . .

Oh yes, am summoninink ӡem, too . . . ӡey entered temple by another secret openink at same time as professor. Guards ӡat you tied up, I hypnotise ӡem too and set ӡem free. Zey are runnink back and spreadink panic amonk ӡeir comrades.

Good evening!

?

Young man, mind your manners! I took off my hat to you . . . You could at least raise yours in return!

I wouldn't dream of it!

I wouldn't dream of contradicting you, not for one moment, but I myself consider that the temperature here is a little too high.

UPSTART!

POF

?

BIF ☆ BAF BOF

Crumbs!

FLAP FLOP

SLAP ☆ BAF BOF

Cuthbert!!! Stop!

Professor!

Cuthbert! Calm yourself for heaven's sake!

GNAAR

Meanwhile . . .

That fool Allan! What's he doing now? . . .

He should have been back ages ago. I'll blow their statues sky-high . . . Then we'll see . . . Hello?

The bump on my head . . . it's gone! . . . That's a good omen: it means my luck's changing!

BROMM

AN EARTHQUAKE!

What have I done to deserve all this? Me, who'd never harm a fly! . . . There's no justice!

At the same time . . .

WOO-OOO-AAH

Yes, is over . . . Earthquakes very frequent in ʒiʒ area, but never severe . . . Yet ʒis time am wonderink . . .

This time? . . .

Cuthbert, please!

I beg your pardon: he started it!

Your hat? You have it on your head.

I not know why, but ʒis time I feelink very very uneasy . . .

Oh?

Yes, am sensink somethink strange in air. Must not stay here . . . Come, will rejoin your comrades.

What's been going on?

No, it was him!

Come quickly. Have warnink of danger.

Here are your comrades.

Hello!

Tintin!

Mamma mia!

Ah, Captain, Tintin, is good to see you again.

Mamma mia! Tanto gioia to see again il signor Commendatore!

Skut, you old pirate!

Come, come, must not delay . . .

Meanwhile . . .

There you are at last! About time too! . . . But . . . what's happened?

You fee, boff, vere waf an earfquake . . .

I know that, nitwit! . . . In the name of the devil, stop that baby-talk!

Impoffible, boff: I loft my teef. Confounded Fondonefianf . . . vey did vif to me, boff!

Ven I got vere, vey vere in a panic. Laft night vove ftrange lightf in ve fky. Tonight an earfquake. You felt it here . . . vey all ruffed back to veir junkf and make off into ve darkneff like frightened rabbitf.

And I suppose you didn't lift a finger to stop them!

Yef, yef, boff: I did all I could to ftop vem efcaping. It waf hopeleff . . . like trying to ftop a ftampede. Af it waf, I waf very nearly maffacred.

Doesn't matter . . . there's still the rubber dinghy from the aircraft. Now, blow this up!

We'll have fome flpendid fireworkf, boff: veref enough to fmaff ve Empire Ftate Building to fmivvereenf.

That'f it . . . We've got five minutef to get to fafety.

117

Zis gallery is runnink from temple at one end to crater of extinct volcano at other.

BOOMM

? !

Look here, how many more earthquakes have you got up your sleeve?

Zat was not earthquake. Is somethink else: probably explosion set off by zose gangsters. We must hurry. I sensink great danger very close.

Few more minutes and we are comink out of underground . . .

. . . the main thing is, I found my hat.

Of course.

?

PLOP

Good heavens, it's dripping on my head . . . In that case, what am I wearing?

Wait for me. I won't be a minute. I must find my hat!

!

It's on your head! . . . Come back!

Yes, yes! Your hat's on your head, Mr Carreidas.

No, this one isn't mine! It leaks!

!

Crumbs! Those trails of smoke . . . Where are they coming from?

And what's that awful smell? . . . It's sulphur!

AAAH

?

Help! . . .

IT'S LAVA!

My hat! . . . I want my hat! . . .
My own hat! . . . I want it!

Hurry!
Hurry!

RAT
TAT
TAT

Faster! . . . Faster!

I can't . . . And I want
my hat . . .

Come on, quicker!
Just a little bit
more . . .

I . . .

Fine! . . . That's
splendid! . . . You're
going faster than
me now!

!

PSCHH

Up the steps,
quick . . .

You go
up
first!

Come on,
Carreidas
old man . . .

!

Out of my way!

HEEEE!

CAPTAIN! . . .
THE LAVA! . . .
THE LAVA! . . .

Well done, Captain! A brilliant recovery!

Let yourself slide down now . . .

This way, Captain!

Phew! I thought I was in the frying-pan that time!

Come on quickly! We haven't a moment to lose!

I'm coming, I'm coming. That ectoplasm Carreidas, he'd better watch out! Purple profiteering jellyfish! He'll be steak and kidney pudding if I catch him!

Hurry!

It's like a furnace down here now.

Ah, is good, is good! You safe and sound! Come zis way!

The volcano's come to life.

Alas so. Earthquake probably caused small crack in old feed pipe of volcano. Is not so dangerous. But zen explosion is set off . . .

. . . and is enlargink crack and allowink gas and lava to escape . . . In zat case, eruption of volcano is followink . . . Let us be hopink astroship is comink at rendezvous . . .

The heat is becoming intolerable . . . If this goes on . . .

ATCHOO

Shut the door behind you! Can't you feel the draught? Dreadful!

? ? !

And what about all this smoke? You're doing it on purpose. Me with my sensitive throat! Are you trying to kill me?

Now is comink poisonous gas! Hold handkerchiefs over your mouths!

Come on, keep moving!

Well, well, well? What's happening now?

Let's see, what's this down here?

Zis way, quickly! We are nearly outside . . .

Come on, come on. And hold that over your nose!

Phew! At last! A lovely breath of good fresh air.

Astroship should be comink here, to old crater.

Look over there! The sky's blood red!

Yes, yes, must be lava flowink down side of volcano.

Wait! Wait for me! Allan! Allan! Help! Not so fast! Wait for me!

Ve . . . rubber . . . dinghy! . . . It'f our only . . . meanf . . . of efcape!

Have we got everyone?

Er . . . I think so . . . yes . . .

Cuthbert!! . . . Where is Cuthbert???

The professor! He must have been left behind!

WOOAH! WOOAH!

Tintin! . . . Come back, for heaven's sake! . . . Come back, Tintin!

WOOAAAOOAAAH

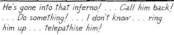

He's gone into that inferno! . . . Call him back! . . . Do something! . . . I don't know . . . ring him up . . . telepathise him!

WOOWOWOWOOW

Come back, my young comrade. Is useless riskink your life.

?

What happened? Did he answer?

Yes, is answerink . . . Is tellink me to go to . . . ! And such polite boy, I thinkink!

Help me! . . . Here . . . help me!

He's back!

Blistering barnacles! Good old Tintin! He's got him!

Quick . . . the kiss of life . . . we must . . . revive him . . .

Hip hip hooray! They're safe!

Yippee! Who's coming for a midnight bathe?

Here, Snowy. Not too far.

Pooh, I can swim, can't I?

Still no sign of astroship . . . Why are zey so late?

How's that, Cuthbert? . . . Better?

Oooh

Look! Look! Water! Lake is emptyink like sink!

RRHOORR RHOR

WOOAAH!

WOOABLUBBLUB

Coming, Snowy! . . . Hang on!

WOOAH WOOAH

Another few seconds and the lake will have vanished! . . . Whatever . . .

RRHOR

BAQUM

How long must I put up with all this dust?

Whew! That's that for the time being! Lucky it was only ash and water vapour, not lava and chunks of rock!

BZZ BZZ BZZ

Astroship! Astroship! . . . Is zere . . . right above us . . . Can hear it!

What, that buzzing like a bee?

BZZ BZZZ BZZ BZZZ

Not a thing to be seen . . .

I take my hat off to them if they land in this murky gloom!

A balloon? . . . Here? . . . Impossible!!

Yes, please be hurryink: zere could be another eruption . . . Yes, be lowerink ladder, please . . .

You are goink aboard astroship. But first, as am explainink, I hypnotise you.

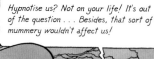
Hypnotise us? Not on your life! It's out of the question . . . Besides, that sort of mummery wouldn't affect us!

Wouldn't affect us . . . wouldn't affect us . . . wouldn't affect us wouldn't . . .

Now, gentlemen, you are at airport at Djakarta. You are boardink Carreidas's aircraft, flyink to Sydney. Zere is ladder. Please go up first, Mr Carreidas.

You followink him, professor, and zen you, Captain Skut.

Gino, please . . . Now you go up, doctor.

You takink Snowy, Tintin . . . And last is goink Captain Haddock.

Excellent . . . You are all in aircraft . . .

You raisink ladder quickly, Chief Pilot! I hearink dangerous rumblinks . . .

Is just in time! . . . Thankink you, Chief Pilot. You excusink me now while I lookink after terrestrial comrades.

You, Mr Carreidas. You playink Battleships with Captain Haddock. You cheatink, naturally.

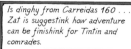
Naturally.

Captain Skut, you are at controls of Carreidas 160. Flight is uneventful. Nothink to report.

Nothink to report. No, nothink at all!

Look zere! . . . Rubber dinghy!

Is dinghy from Carreidas 160 . . . Zat is suggestink how adventure can be finishink for Tintin and comrades.

I fee fomefing in ve fky! What if it?

It's . . . it's a flying-saucer!! It's circling . . . Diavolo! It's coming straight for us! Fire, Allan! . . . FIRE!

You puttink guns down, criminals! ... Game is up! ... You are in my hypnotic power.

All listenink carefully. Zis machine is simply helicopter comink to pick you up ... You climbink aboard!

Yes, sir.
Yes, sir.

Now I speakink to you, Captain Skut, and to your comrades ... You are forgetting everythink zat is happenink since yesterday. You only rememberink zis: after departure from Djakarta for Sydney, unknown causes are forcink you to be ditchink aircraft ...

... and you are havink to board rubber dinghy.

All in boat? ... Skut, Calculus, Gino, Carreidas, Haddock, Tintin, Snowy. Good ... I takink charge of others ... Now sleep, comrades. Zat is my command!

Adieu!

Wooah!
Wooah!

Some hours later ...

Search has been resumed for the passengers and crew of the Carreidas aircraft which disappeared yesterday on a flight to Sydney. Hopes are fading of finding survivors, but aircraft ...

... continue to patrol the area. During the night a volcano thought to be extinct has erupted on the island of Pulau-pulau Bompa in the Celebes Sea. A column of smoke more than thirty thousand feet high is rising from the crater. Observers are keeping watch on the volcano and are studying the eruption from the air.

One more run, Dick. See if we can film the crater.

OK

Hey, Dick! Look down there, at ten o'clock. Look!

Good Lord! A rubber dinghy!

Victor Hotel Bravo calling Macassar tower. We've spotted a rubber dinghy about a mile south of the volcano. Five or six men aboard. We've made several low-level runs over them but there's no sign of life ... except for a little white dog.

Look, Dick! The wind's carrying them towards the island, and there's lava flowing into the sea. They'll be boiled alive like lobsters! We've got to do something. We must save them!

Wooah!
Wooah!

Tonight Scanorama is bringing you a special feature. The brilliant air-sea rescue of six of the men aboard millionaire Carreidas's plane made world headline news. Laszlo Carreidas and five companions were found drifting in a dinghy more than 200 miles off their scheduled route. They were snatched to safety only minutes from death in a lava-heated cauldron, the sea around the volcanic island of Pulau-pulau Bompa. All the survivors were suffering from severe shock. It was several hours before they . . .

. . . recovered consciousness in a Javanese hospital. Our on-the-spot reporter has secured the first interview with the mystery-crash survivors . . . Colin Chattamore in Djakarta.

A put-up job, or I'm not Jolyon Wagg! Bet Carreidas dumped his rotten old crate for the insurance.

Let's begin with the owner of the aircraft . . . This has been a terrible business for you, Mr Carreidas. You must be greatly upset by the loss of your prototype, and the tragic disappearance of your secretary and two members of your crew.

Yes, of course.

All very sad, but what can you expect? That's life, you know. What really annoys me, though, is that I lost my hat: a pre-war Bross and Clackwell. And that's absolutely irreplaceable.

About the needle-marks found on your arm, Mr Carreidas. It seems that your companions didn't have these . . .

Naturally: I'm richer than they are.

I . . . er . . . precisely.

Captain Skut, you had to make a forced landing. Can you tell us something about it, and what happened afterwards? Your last radio message said you were flying over Sumbawa and had nothing to report.

Yes . . .

. . . yes, but is not possible to remember: is like gap in my mind . . . I not understand . . . Is like strange dream . . .

Me too. Just the same. Only I'd call it a horrible nightmare.

Blow me! Look who's here again. My old chum! The ancient mariner from Marlinspike! . . . The old humbug, he doesn't half come up with some comic turns!

I vaguely remember some grinning masks, and suffocating heat in an underground passage . . . Thundering typhoons, it makes me thirsty to think of it!

And how about you?

I . . . well, I had a similar dream. It's certainly odd, but . . .

And there's his pal, young Sherlock Holmes!

. . . the most inexplicable part of this whole business is . . . No, I think Professor Calculus will tell you . . .

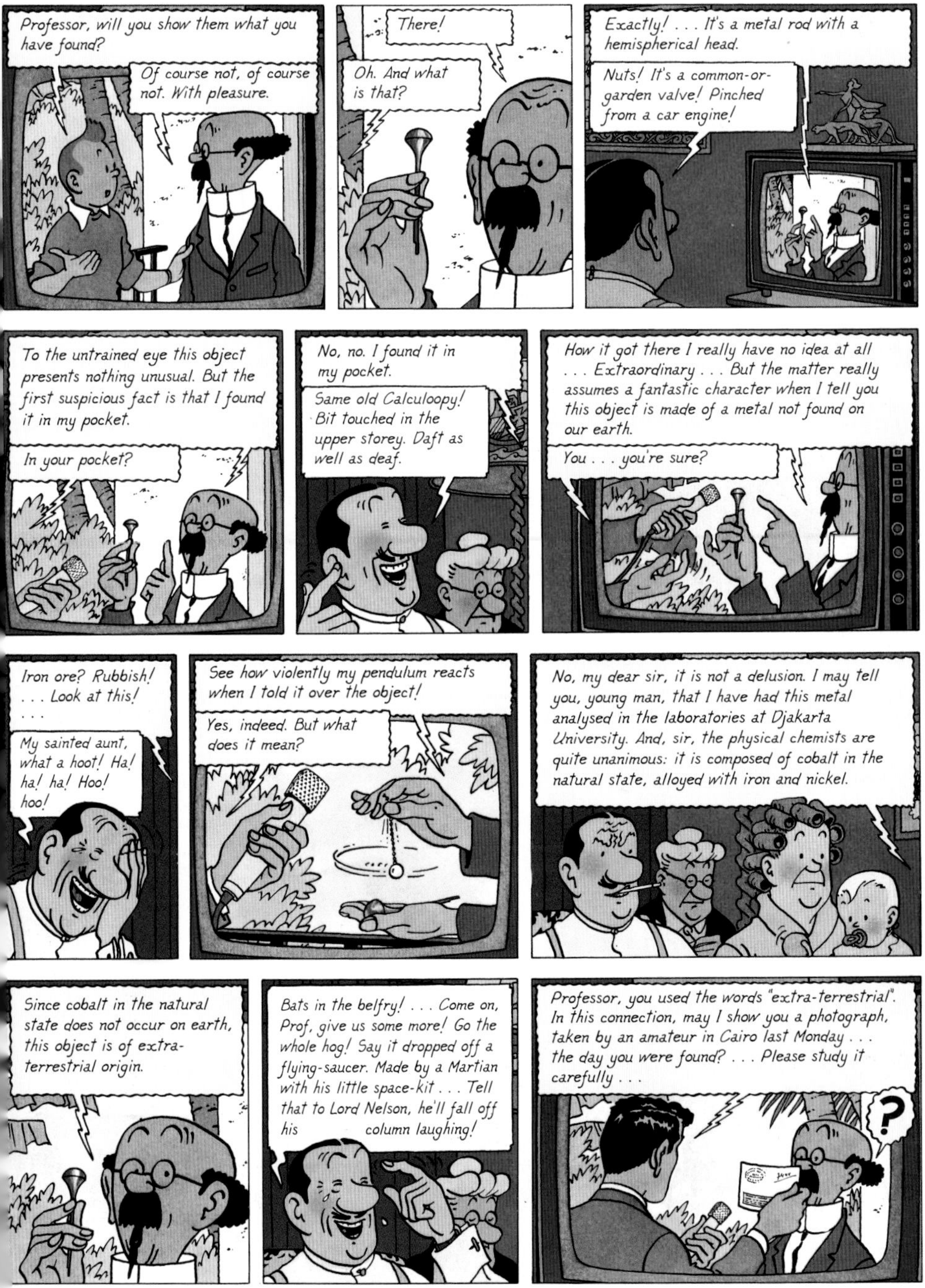
Professor, will you show them what you have found?
Of course not, of course not. With pleasure.
There!
Oh. And what is that?
Exactly! . . . It's a metal rod with a hemispherical head.
Nuts! It's a common-or-garden valve! Pinched from a car engine!
To the untrained eye this object presents nothing unusual. But the first suspicious fact is that I found it in my pocket.
In your pocket?
No, no. I found it in my pocket.
Same old Calculoopy! Bit touched in the upper storey. Daft as well as deaf.
How it got there I really have no idea at all . . . Extraordinary . . . But the matter really assumes a fantastic character when I tell you this object is made of a metal not found on our earth.
You . . . you're sure?
Iron ore? Rubbish! . . . Look at this! . . .
My sainted aunt, what a hoot! Ha! ha! ha! Hoo! hoo!
See how violently my pendulum reacts when I told it over the object!
Yes, indeed. But what does it mean?
No, my dear sir, it is not a delusion. I may tell you, young man, that I have had this metal analysed in the laboratories at Djakarta University. And, sir, the physical chemists are quite unanimous: it is composed of cobalt in the natural state, alloyed with iron and nickel.
Since cobalt in the natural state does not occur on earth, this object is of extra-terrestrial origin.
Bats in the belfry! . . . Come on, Prof, give us some more! Go the whole hog! Say it dropped off a flying-saucer. Made by a Martian with his little space-kit . . . Tell that to Lord Nelson, he'll fall off his column laughing!
Professor, you used the words "extra-terrestrial". In this connection, may I show you a photograph, taken by an amateur in Cairo last Monday . . . the day you were found? . . . Please study it carefully . . .
?

Would you agree with the photographer, who claims that it is indeed a flying-saucer? . . . And would you say that this machine is of extra-terrestrial origin?

A bottle of gin? . . . Frankly, I can see no connection . . . To me, the photograph would appear to show an unidentified flying object, popularly known as a flying-saucer.

Do you think this "machine" is connected with the object you found?

Round? That goes without saying. A saucer is always round, is it not?

Er . . . of course . . . One final question, Professor. I understand that you and your companions are suffering from amnesia . . .

If you wish, but I always take a glass of water with milk of magnesia.

I beg your pardon? . . . I . . . hmm . . . the point I want to make is that occasional cases of amnesia are not uncommon . . . There's one reported in the paper today. The head of a psychiatric clinic in Cairo, Dr Krollspell, has just been found wandering near the outskirts of the city. He'd been missing for more than a month, and he has completely lost his memory.

But in your case, how do the doctors account for the fact that you are ALL suffering from amnesia?

They don't seem able to give an explanation . . . any more than we can.

I could tell them a thing or two! . . . But no one would believe me!

And finally, what are your plans? Where do you go from here?

We're catching the next plane for Sydney. We shall just be in time for the opening of the Astronautical Congress.

Well, I hope there will be no further interruptions to your journey. Good luck from Scanorama, and thank you . . . Goodbye, Captain!

Goodbye!

DONG This is the final call for Qantas Flight 714 to Sydney. All passengers please proceed immediately to gate No. 3.

THE END

HERGÉ
★
THE ADVENTURES OF
TINTIN
★

TINTIN
AND THE
PICAROS

LITTLE, BROWN AND COMPANY
New York Boston

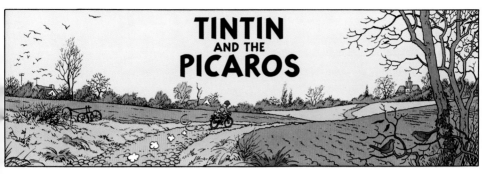

TINTIN
AND THE PICAROS

Ah! there you are . . . Come on in. I want you to read something. Look what I found in the latest "Paris-Flash" . . .

"Opera star Bianca Castafiore continues her brilliant progress through South America. After triumphs in Ecuador, Colombia and Venezuela, she visits San Theodoros, where she will be received by General Tapioca."

General Tapioca . . . Didn't he topple our old friend Alcazar?

Yes, with the help of the Kûrvi-Tasch regime in Borduria. They say Tapioca's a real tyrant . . . he's cruel and he's vain . . .

. . . In fact he's so vain he changed the name of the capital from Los Dopicos. He called it Tapiocapolis after himself. As for poor old Alcazar, he's gone underground with a band of partisans.

Oh, yes: the famous Picaros.

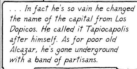

That's right, the Picaros. It's the name adopted by the guerrillas who've sworn to get rid of Tapioca and his mob. They're said to be backed by another great power . . . commercial and financial this time: the International Banana Company . . . A rare old mix-up, as you see!

Blistering barnacles, Tintin! What a lecture! . . . All that talking makes me thirsty . . . Here, have a whisky . . .

No, thanks. Not for me . . . You know that.

Oh well . . . Cheers!

PFOUAGH!

Billions of blue blistering barnacles! ... Some anamorphic aardvark switched my whisky for this ... this cleaning fluid!

Cleaning fluid?!?

Well, bottled bilge-water, then ... it all tastes much the same, I dare say ... Here! Try some!

I ...

?

?

I'm no expert like you, of course, but it does seem to me to taste just like whisky ...

Like whisky?!

My poor young friend, if that's a glass of whisky, I'm a jellied eel! And as you so rightly pointed out I'm an expert and I know a bit about it!

Of course, of course ... But still ...

I don't know what that hogwash is, but it certainly isn't whisky. However, just to please you, I'm prepared to give it another try ...

Pfouagh! ... Filthy! ... Foul! ... Disgusting! ... Disgraceful! ...

AH! ♫ ∭ MY BEAUTY PAST ∮ COMPARE ... ♩

NO!

FORTISSIMO

... THESE JEWELS BRIGHT I WEAR ... Everyone knows the golden voice of the famous Bianca Castafiore ...

Oh yes! We know it all right!

... who continues her triumphant tour through Latin America. Today she arrived in Tapiocapolis, capital of San Theodoros ...

SANTAERO

... where she met with a tumultuous welcome. As usual, she is attended by her faithful   maid, Irma ...

... and her accompanist, Igor Wagner. Also in her entourage, to watch over her jewels ... insured for millions   of dollars ...

BRAVO
ENCORE
BRAVO
BIS
BRA
BIS

... are two certified detectives, always on the alert, always following discreetly in her footsteps.

RRRRING

RRRRING

Hello? . . . Yes . . . WHO?

Jolyon Wagg, yes! . . . Hi! . . . Now look here, I just saw old Castanette on the telly . . . And what do I hear? Blow me if she hasn't got her knick-knacks insured now . . .

. . . and for a pretty penny too! . . . Strikes me you could have pushed the business my way . . . for old Rock Bottom insurance! What's the use of having friends, I say to myself, if they let you down at the first opportunity? . . . Come on, when you want to do someone a good turn, there's always a way! . . . Yes, I do! . . . And I don't mind saying so! . . . And while I'm on . . .

What? . . . But I . . . How . . . Well I'm . . . But . . . Excuse me . . . Look here . . .

Well I'll be . . . !! That's beyond a joke!

SLAM

In fact it's the thundering limit! . . . I'm taken to task by that weevil Wagg because he wasn't asked to insure Castafiore's jewellery!

PFOUAGH!

Billions of bilious blue blistering barnacles! . . . PFFF! . . . It's poi -son!

POISON ???

Nonsense, Captain! Who on earth would want to poison you? I know you've got a few enemies, but not as deadly as that.

Maybe . . . Anyway, I don't feel at all well.

Something wrong with this whisky? It tastes pretty good to me!

Have a lie down, Captain. It'll go . . .

Good night! You'll feel better in the morning.

All the same, I wonder . . .

SNOWY!

Snowy, you're hopeless! You've drunk all that spilt whisky!

Showhat? . . . Wassa matter? Wassamatter with a drop of whisky?

HIC

Still, it certainly proves the whisky isn't poisoned.

Come on, off to bed, you old dipso! Sleep off the booze!

HIC

Next morning . . .

I look horrible this morning . . . Must have been that wretched whisky I had yesterday.

Oh well, too bad, can't be helped! . . . It's time for the news . . .

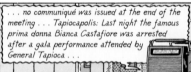

. . . no communiqué was issued at the end of the meeting . . . Tapiocapolis: Last night the famous prima donna Bianca Castafiore was arrested after a gala performance attended by General Tapioca . . .

. . . Statements by the authorities in San Theodoros have accused the star of plotting against the government . . .

Tintin! . . . Tintin! . . . Something marvellous just happened to General Tapioca!

He's arrested Castafiore, silly fellow! He doesn't know what he's let himself in for!

Arrested Castafiore? . . . No! . . .

He has you know: arrested her at the end of a concert . . . What a turn up, eh?

You could say so, yes . . .

Tintack! . . . Capock Hatpin! . . . Terrible news! . . . Dreadful!

Read this! In the "Daily Reporter"! Bianca Castafiore has been arrested!

Do they give any details?

That poor child! . . . In prison! . . . Just imagine! . . . I'm absolutely shattered!

GROOAHH!

Listen to this, Tintin: it's positively hilarious!

Go ahead, I'm all ears.

STAR IN TERRORIST PLOT

BIANCA CASTAFIORE ARRES

TAPIOCAPOLIS, T
International oper
Bianca (Milanese
Castafiore was a
tonight by the S
Theodoros poli
is accused of
against the s
Members of
entourage
taken into

". . . A search of her luggage revealed documents which prove conclusively the existence of a plot aimed at the removal of General Tapioca and the overthrow of his regime . . .

. . . The San Theodorian government have let it be known that the plot is centred in a West European country, where the singer was staying before her departure for South America."

It's just like a cheap thriller!

Castafiore in a conspiracy! A conspiracy of silence, let's hope!!

DONG

Excuse me, sir, but there are two reporters downstairs . . . asking if you will see them.

Already?!

All right. Just let me put on a dressing-gown and I'll come.

Why, it's Christopher Willoughby-Drupe and Marco Rizotto of "Paris-Flash". What can I do for you, gentlemen?

Good-morning, Captain. Forgive us for calling so early, but we wanted to be the first to ask what you think of this Castafiore business.

What do I think? . . . Perfectly simple! . . .

I think it's a load of old rubbish! Blistering barnacles! Accusing Castafiore of conspiracy! . . . Ridiculous!

Yes, but what about the accusations made against yourself?

Accusations against ME???

Ah, so you don't know about that yet? Here, look . . . in today's "Trumpeter" . . .

Impossible! . . . Those San Theodolites must be off their tripods!

Oh, it's you. Here, read this. It concerns you, too.

Me?

Yes, you! Read it! . . .

courageous action which will bring widespread benefits.

CASTAFIORE CONSPIRACY

TAPIOCA GOVERNMENT MAKES NEW CHARGES

Tapiocapolis: The Castafiore conspiracy was masterminded from Marlinspike in Western Europe, claimed a government spokesman today. He accused supporters of General Alcazar, and named as principal figures in the plot: Captain Haddock, Tintin the reporter, and Professor Cuthbert Calculus. All three are long-standing friends of General Alcazar. It is known that Signora Bianca Castafiore was recently a guest at Marlinspike Hall, country home of Captain

What is all this? They must be crazy!

You're telling me!

You deny it then?

I'll say we do! The whole story is bilge! Bilge from stem to stern!

DONG

'Morning squire!

"Daily Reporter"! Hi!

A few words for "Radio-Round", Captain . . .

. . . and for "Radio Rave-Up" . . .

Gentlemen, these accusations are as grotesque as they are false! Us? Conspirators? . . . Blue blistering bell-bottomed balderdash!

Seriously . . . Here comes Professor Calculus. Look at him, then tell me whether you think he's capable of taking part in a conspiracy!

Perfectly, my dear sirs! And proud of it!

 Perfectly! . . . And I weigh my words. It's a shame, I tell you! A scandal! . . . Imprisoning a poor, weak woman like that! We must take her case at once to the International Court of Justice!

 You deny the allegations, Captain. All the same, General Alcazar is one of your friends, isn't he?

One of my friends? . . . I've met him two or three times, that's all.

 If you say so. But I take it you won't deny that Signora Castafiore has been a guest here, at your invitation? . . .

Invitation? You mean invasion! But from that to conspiracy . . .

 Still, let's not discuss it any more. I tell you, the accusations are insane . . . Now, gentlemen, let me offer you some whisky . . .

 Let's drink to the release of the Milanese Nightingale, and . . .

 . . . your good health!

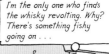 EURK!

 Stop! Don't touch it! . . . There must be some mistake. This whisky is quite undrinkable!

Undrinkable? On the contrary, it's excellent!

Velvet!

Mmm . . .

 You mustn't drink it, I tell you! It tastes like poison!

 Of course, of course: a poison that kills slowly! It's a known fact! Ha! ha! ha!

 And that's no problem: as it happens, we aren't in a hurry! Ha! ha! ha!

 I'm the only one who finds the whisky revolting. Why? There's something fishy going on . . .

 Unless . . . That's an idea . . . Maybe it's a new brand Nestor bought.

 I must ask him . . .

 I can't understand the master: I find this "Loch Lomond" superb, as always.

  I say, Nestor . . .

Well, Nestor?

I . . . er . . . to tell the truth, sir, I was making sure it really is "Loch Lomond".

And your conclusion, my friend?

It is "Loch Lomond", sir. Indubitably!

I don't understand, not one little bit!

That evening . . .

What about having one more try?

No! Enough is enough! Don't let me hear any more about whisky!

Are you depressed? Does the day seem long? We have the answer!

Ah, yes?

LOCH LOMOND

Impossible! They're doing it on purpose! It's a plot!

On the subject of plots . . . Listen!

. . . and to start our round-up, we bring you the latest on what is known as the Castafiore Conspiracy . . . with international reactions, and particularly those in San Theodoros. There, naturally, the response is particularly violent . . . as viewers worldwide were shown in this television interview with the San Theodorian president . . .

. . . General Tapioca, in Tapiocapolis. The general commented on what he called the "pantomime plotters".

. . . Let them tremble, I say! . . . Cowards, skulking in their dusty mansion . . .

. . . puppet-masters in this vile conspiracy! . . . Tremble, crooked Captain Haddock! . . . Tremble, treacherous Tintin and crafty Cuthbert Calculus!

Crafty yourself, you pachyrhizus! . . . And no one's more treacherous than you, you guano-gatherer!

I'll give him a piece of my mind all right, fancy-dress fascist! . . .

But . . .

Hello, International? . . . Give me South America . . . Tapiocapolis . . . General Tapioca! . . . What? . . . Tapioca, yes, as in tapioca . . . exactly!

I'm sorry, sir, but we don't stock tapioca. This is a butcher's shop, sir . . . Cutts the butcher! . . . Not at all, sir!

Thundering typhoons! Cutts again! Why do I always get him?

Why not send a telegram, anyway?

A telegram . . . You're right! . . . That's a very good idea: a telegram!

Wait, I'll give you the number . . .

And a few minutes later . . .

I'll repeat that: General Tapioca, Tapiocapolis, San Theodoros. Message reads: Profoundly shocked by false accusations made against us Stop We register formal and absolute denial Stop No regards Signed: Haddock, Tintin and Calculus.

Good! Thank you very much. A greetings telegram, sir?

ARE YOU MAD?

Next morning . . .

Daily Reporter

HADDOCK: I DENY!

CAPTAIN FURIOUSLY DENIES PARTICIPATION IN ANY PLOT WHATSOEVER

TAPIOCA: I ACCUSE!

GENERAL CLAIMS IRREFUTABLE PROOF OF COLLUSION BETWEEN MARLINSPIKE CONSPIRATORS AND INTERNATIONAL BANANA COMPANY

General Tapioca, Tapiocapolis. Oh! You know that . . . Good. Message reads . . . er . . . Downright lies Stop Will make you swallow false allegations . . . Yes, in the plural . . . one day Stop You will end up hanging from yardarm. Yes, y as in yashmak . . . Stop.

Two days later . . .

Daily Reporter

TAPIOCA
OFFERS
HADDOCK
ROUND TABLE TALKS IN TAPIOCAPOLIS

At a press conference today, General Tapioca announced that he is inviting Commodore Haddock and his companions to Tapiocapolis for a full, free, frank and fair exchange of views. Each visitor would receive a safe-conduct through the good offices of the embassy. "My only aim," asserted the General, "is to seek . . . out the truth."

You know, he isn't a bad old stick really . . . I've a good mind to accept his invitation. That way, we'd show everyone our good faith.

Or else we'll find ourselves in prison, like Bianca Castafiore. Thanks very much!

Oh, you! Always suspicious! . . . Anyway, we've a safe-conduct.

I'm not in the least impressed, Captain. The safe-conduct could be nothing more than a decoy!

OOOH!

Have you seen? We've been invited there. We must go, Captain.

?

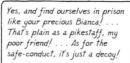

Yes, and find ourselves in prison like your precious Bianca! . . . That's plain as a pikestaff, my poor friend! . . . As for the safe-conduct, it's just a decoy!

Bravo! Well spoken! I'll pack my things and we'll go!

Next morning . . .

Daily Reporter

TALKS DRAMA
WILL HADDOCK & CO. RESPOND TO TAPIOCA INVITATION?

The following day . . .

Daily Reporter

HADDOCK SENSATION
NO!
I WON'T GO TO TAPIOCAPOLIS

And the day after . . .

Daily Reporter

HADDOCK BACKS DOWN
SAYS TAPIOCA: HE FEARS TRUTH

I'm backing down! . . . I'm afraid of the truth! All right, you dictatorial duckbilled diplodocus! I'll show you what sort of stuff I'm made of!

Calm down, Captain.

Calm down! Calm down! . . . I'm as cool as a cucumber!

He'd challenge me . . . that ostrogoth! All right, we shall see what we shall see!

Hello, Telegrams? . . . Yes . . . yes, naturally, for General Tapioca. Message reads . . .

Send safe-conducts (in the plural, safe-conducts) Stop Arriving by return of post . . . Signed: Haddock . . . Good. No! Ordinary rate!!!

The die is cast! . . . He'll find out what sort of fish he's hooked, that puffed-up Punchinello! . . . Tintin . . . we're going!

YOU may be going, Captain . . . I'm staying right here!!

?!

What? What did you say?

I said I'm not going, Captain. You're quite free to fall into the trap they're trying to set for us, but as far as I'm concerned it's NIET!

Oh! You and your suspicions! They're an obsession! According to you, the world's composed of nothing but scallywags and scoundrels! . . . Why shouldn't General Tapioca be an honest sort of chap, eh? . . . Why? . . . Go on, tell me!

It's always possible, but . .

. . . I still think they're trying to entice us over there . . . I don't know the reason . . . but it positively reeks of trickery.

Ah! So that's it!

All right, stay here, Mister Mule! Stay tucked up, all safe and warm in your bedroom-slippers! Cuthbert and I are going out there to defend our honour, and yours too, against that thundering herd of Zapotecs! Finish!

Hm!

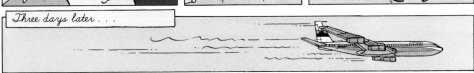

Three days later . . .

Ladies and gentlemen, in a few moments we shall be landing at Tapiocapolis. Please fasten your safety-belts and extinguish your cigarettes . . .

We're coming in to land, Professor.

Thailand? . . . Really? What a surprise . . .

141

D'you see? We're arriving in Tapiocapolis just in time for the famous carnival week . . .

In Greek??

"Taking part will be many performers from overseas including . . ." Why, look! There's a troupe from back home: The Jolly Follies!

Iced lollies? Now?

Aha! There's the reception committee . . .

Commodore Haddock?

Er . . . just captain . . . er . . .

Such modesty! Here, a man of your gallantry would be an admiral! . . . Allow me to present myself: Colonel Alvarez, aide-de-camp to His Excellency General Tapioca.

Delighted!

Professor Calculus, I presume? To you also, welcome to our country!

I'm sorry, officer, but I cannot shake a hand which grinds underfoot the imprescriptible rights of the human individual!

I . . . er . . . his little joke, of course! . . . Unfortunately, the Professor is still suffering from 'flu . . . as a result, the infection . . . er . . . you . . . you follow me?

So there!

Perfectly, Captain . . .

And this is our good friend Tintin, no doubt?

Welcome to San Theodoros, my young friend . . .

You're mistaken, Colonel! . . .

It's like, man, we're the Dripping Tap . . . Like we're here for the carnival.

But then . . . Where is Tintin?

Well . . . er . . . I . . . He couldn't come . . . 'Flu . . . him too . . . Asian, of course . . . So, for fear of infection, you understand . . .

Yes, yes, I understand very well . . .

Won't you get in, gentlemen?

WHOWOWOWOWOW

Unfortunately, the General is unable to grant you an audience for two or three days. He has had to go on a tour of inspection in the north and he begs you to excuse him . . .

That's exactly the question I was going to ask you, officer.

What question, señor Professor?

22-23-24 DE FEBRERO

That's no answer, soldier! I ask you, where is Signora Castafiore . . . Her spirit must be totally crushed, I'm sure, poor little thing . . .

On the contrary, dear Professor. I assure you, the morale of that charming lady is extremely high!

To Shanghai? . . . She's gone to Shanghai? . . . You dare to make fun of me?

No, no, Professor. I tell you she is delighted with her stay in San Theodoros . . .

. . . and next time, don't overcook my pasta!

Ah! Our hotel, I imagine?

No, señor Commodore. We thought you would prefer the peace of the countryside to the hubbub of the city. Besides, the carnival will be starting shortly . . . Then there'll be incessant noise round here, all day and all night. You wouldn't get a wink of sleep . . .

Did you know, a party of your compatriots are joining the festivities this year?

Yes, I saw . . . The Jolly Follies.

CAR NA VAL
WOWOWOW
22-23-24 DE FEBRERO

Half an hour later . . .

Here we are . . .

You've got us well guarded . . .

Just a simple precaution . . . Ah, yes, the swimming-pool is over the other side . . .

And Tintin was suspicious!

These are your apartments, señor Commodore: I hope they will please you . . .

I'm sure . . .

Of course, a servant will be at your disposal throughout your stay with us . . .

Too kind, Colonel.

Ah, here he is now!

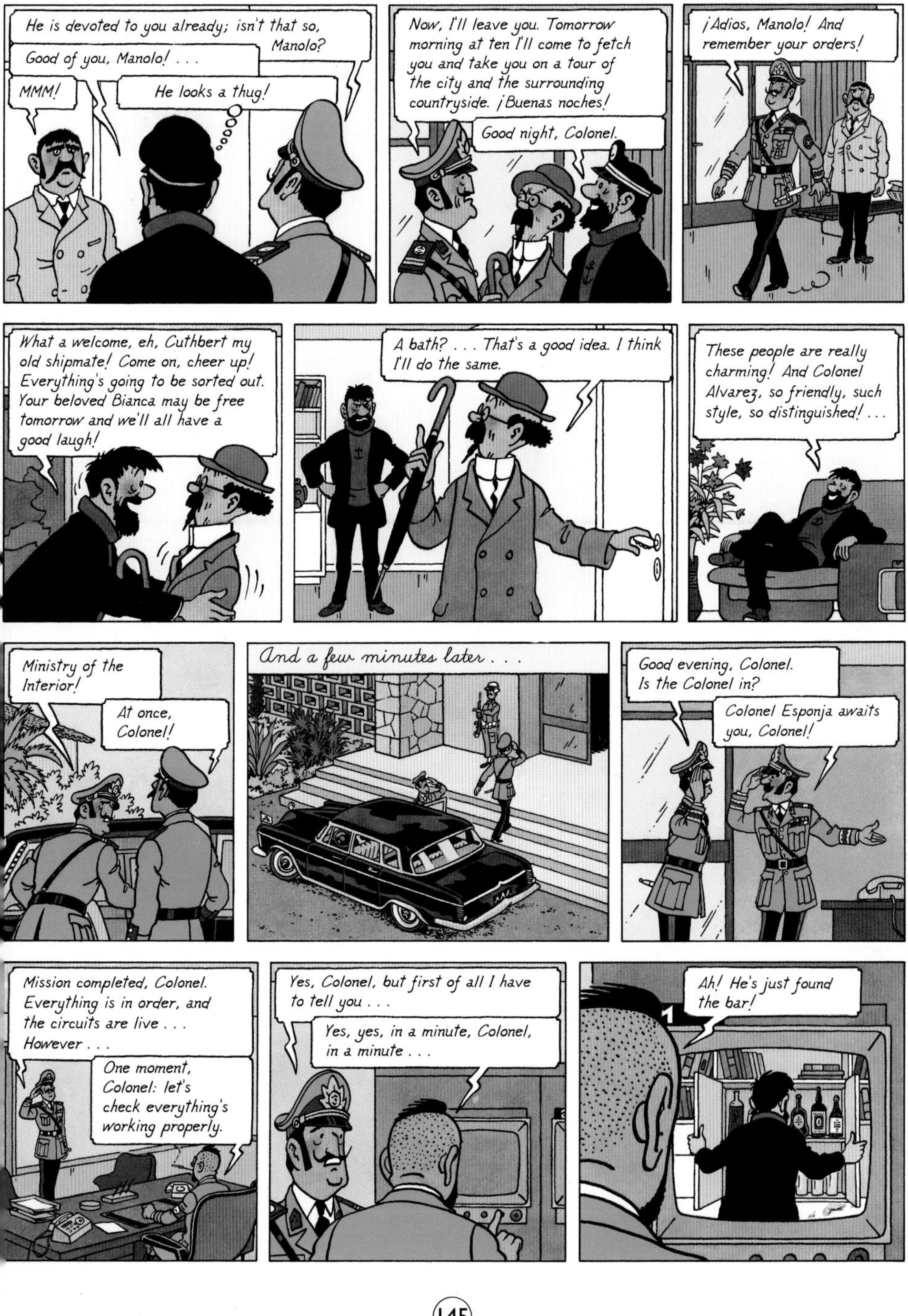
He is devoted to you already; isn't that so, Manolo?
Good of you, Manolo! . . .
MMM!
He looks a thug!
Now, I'll leave you. Tomorrow morning at ten I'll come to fetch you and take you on a tour of the city and the surrounding countryside. ¡Buenas noches!
Good night, Colonel.
¡Adios, Manolo! And remember your orders!
What a welcome, eh, Cuthbert my old shipmate! Come on, cheer up! Everything's going to be sorted out. Your beloved Bianca may be free tomorrow and we'll all have a good laugh!
A bath? . . . That's a good idea. I think I'll do the same.
These people are really charming! And Colonel Alvarez, so friendly, such style, so distinguished! . . .
Ministry of the Interior!
At once, Colonel!
And a few minutes later . . .
Good evening, Colonel. Is the Colonel in?
Colonel Esponja awaits you, Colonel!
Mission completed, Colonel. Everything is in order, and the circuits are live . . . However . . .
One moment, Colonel: let's check everything's working properly.
Yes, Colonel, but first of all I have to tell you . . .
Yes, yes, in a minute, Colonel, in a minute . . .
Ah! He's just found the bar!

Oho! "Loch Lomond". These Tapiocans certainly do things in style!

SNIFF

PFOUAGH!

Hello, that doesn't seem to please him . . . Yet they assured us that was his favourite whisky.

Unbelievable! . . . It's still happening! . . . What's gone wrong? Why can't I take whisky any more?

Let's try something else . . . gin, for instance.

PFOUAGH!

He doesn't like that either? Just his bad luck! . . . Now for Channel No. 2 . . .

Colonel, I must tell you . . .

Ah, there he is! A pity he didn't agree to work for us . . . But who knows, he may change his mind some day . . .

Good. Now, Channel No. 3 . . .

Colonel, I must . . .

You must what, Colonel?

I must tell you . . . Number Three has not arrived, Colonel.

Not arrived?! . . . Szplug! Why not? . . . Where is he then?

He never left Europe, Colonel. Number One told me he had influenza and that . . .

And you tell me that now! . . . By the whiskers of Kûrvi-Tasch!!

Influenza! . . . So, he was suspicious! . . . But it's absolutely necessary for him to come! . . . And if I know him, he'll be coming anyway!

Good, I'll think about it. Meanwhile, you'll have to stall the others. Tell them everybody's got influenza . . . that the Castafiore's lost her voice . . . tell them anything you like . . . to gain time.

Very good, Colonel.

Meanwhile . . .

What a beautiful evening. It must be lovely outside . . .

Hello, what's this? Rusted up?

Come open . . . you stupid . . . stubborn . . .

CRACK

Billions of bilious blue blistering barnacles! Why does everything happen to me?!

¿Que pasa?

¿Que pasa? . . . Que pasa is that I tried to open that confounded window! . . . And kindly put away the blunderbuss: those things have a habit of going off!

No good to open, señor . . . air conditioning . . .

That may well be so, but I don't happen to like canned air. Kindly open the window, por favor!

Windows, they do not open, señor . . . Buenas noches, señor.

ZZING

Thanks, friend . . . really, you try too hard!

Have you quite finished chucking your guns out of the window?

?

Is this yours, eh?

Yes, is mine! . . . Excuse me . . . er . . . small accident . . .

I . . . er . . . I go and sweep up . . .

You do that, old chap . . .

Ah, now for a nice pipe . . .

I'm sure I must have . . .

. . . some tobacco somewhere . . .

Not in my jacket either . . . Thundering typhoons!

Ah, come to think of it . . . I must have left it on the plane . . . Confound it!

Never mind, I'll buy some more . . .

Hé, señor, where you go?

Me?

I'm out of tobacco: I'm going to buy some.

Tomorrow, señor.

You buy some tomorrow. Today, is too late!

Too late? . . . But it's barely eight o'clock!

Stop, señor! Return to your room!

?

Ten thousand thundering typhoons! You dare forbid me to go out? . . . Me, the guest of General Tapioca! . . .

Not go out, señor.

Señor not go out tonight! . . . Tomorrow . . . Too late tonight . . .

And why not, if you please? . . . Aren't I old enough to be out at night?

No, señor, but . . . er . . . Sometimes Picaros make attack around here . . . Is muy dangerous, señor . . . So you see, is best for your own protection . . .

Tomorrow, Excellency . . . tomorrow we bring tobacco for Your Excellency . . .

Certainly not! I want to buy my own tobacco!

As you wish, Excellency . . . Buenas noches, Excellency . . .

. . . 'night!

SLAM

That young whippersnapper Tintin was right, by thunder . . . The cage may be a gilded one . . .

. . . but we're well and truly behind bars!

Ah, there you are, Cap . . .

FLOP

When are you going to stop these childish pranks?

Next morning...

RAT TAT TAT

...MMM...yes...
C'm in...

Buenos días, Excellency...
Your tobacco, Excellency...

My tobacco?...
Tobacco?...
What tobacco?

Tobacco you order last night, Excellency.

I told you I'd go and buy it myself, ten thousand thundering typhoons!...Myself, d'you hear?

Very good, Excellency.
I go and get escort ready, Excellency...

What escort? An escort to go and buy tobacco?

Yes, Excellency, must have escort... Is necessary, because of terrorists, you understand: los Picaros...

WHOWOWOWOWOW

An hour later . . .

Ah, you're back. Would you believe that Tintin . . .

Tintin? He was jolly sensible to stay in Marlinspike!

He was absolutely right: we're prisoners, lock, stock and barrel!

I can see our hosts have a true sense of hospitality. That's what I just said to him . . .

. . . and he entirely agrees with me.

WHO agrees with you??? . . . And about WHAT???

Exactly, and what's more, he'll tell you so himself!

Won't you, my friend?

¡Buenos días, Captain!

Tintin, where in heaven's name have you sprung from?

Well, I've come straight from Marlinspike . . . You don't look very pleased to see me!

Why didn't you stay there, you silly fellow?

Let's say I was missing you, Captain . . .

. . . and the Professor too, of course.

On a horse? We came by car.

You'd hardly left when I began to blame myself for not having gone with you. I thought of all our friends in prison and the need to try to save them . . . So I took a plane . . . It's quite simple . . .

And it's crazy!

Because you were right! Would you believe . . .

Ssh!

Ah! You've got a record here I simply adore! . . . May I put it on, Captain?

AH! MY BEAUTY

Have you gone raving mad?

(151)

Come, I want to show you something.

What?

There, look!

A microphone! The pirates!

And there's another! . . . The place is bugged, Captain!

And I'm pretty sure they'll have cameras hidden in every corner . . . I'd bet my life on it . . .

Behind a two-way mirror, for instance, like this one perhaps . . .

Aha! He's no fool, that boy!

No fool! He uses his head. But as I foresaw, that didn't stop him following the others into the trap I prepared for them . . .

A trap, Colonel?

A trap, yes . . . You see, before I was appointed by General Kûrvi-Tasch to be technical adviser to General Tapioca, I was Chief of Police in Szohôd, and those three . . .

. . . busybodies subjected me to a bitter humiliation!

You, Colonel, humiliated?

Yes, me . . .

. . . and I've never forgotten it . . . But fate sometimes plays into one's hands . . . When I heard that Bianca Castafiore was planning a tour in South America I immediately . . .

. . . realised how I could take advantage of the situation. I only had to arrest her, after forging compromising documents and having them slipped into her luggage . . . I concocted an entirely fictitious . . .

. . . conspiracy against General Tapioca . . . it only remained for me to give an international slant to the affair . . . And there it was . . . a brilliant conception, eh?

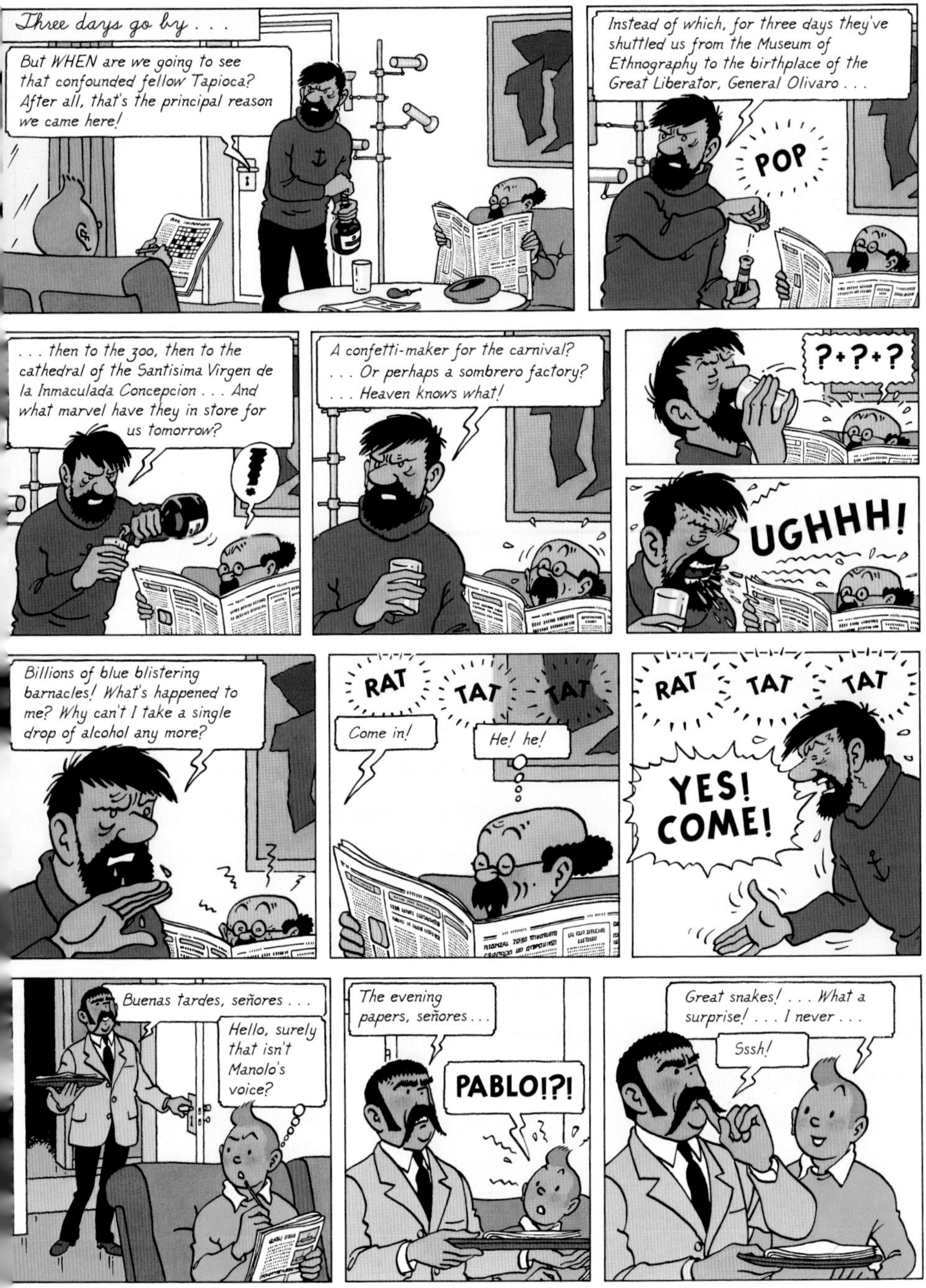
Three days go by . . .
But WHEN are we going to see that confounded fellow Tapioca? After all, that's the principal reason we came here!
Instead of which, for three days they've shuttled us from the Museum of Ethnography to the birthplace of the Great Liberator, General Olivaro . . .
POP
. . . then to the zoo, then to the cathedral of the Santisima Virgen de la Inmaculada Concepcion . . . And what marvel have they in store for us tomorrow?
A confetti-maker for the carnival? . . . Or perhaps a sombrero factory? . . . Heaven knows what!
?+?+?
UGHHH!
Billions of blue blistering barnacles! What's happened to me? Why can't I take a single drop of alcohol any more?
RAT
TAT
TAT
Come in!
He! he!
RAT
TAT
TAT
YES! COME!
Buenas tardes, señores . . .
Hello, surely that isn't Manolo's voice?
The evening papers, señores . . .
PABLO!?!
Great snakes! . . . What a surprise! . . . I never . . .
Sssh!

Good evening, señores. My name is Pablo. I've been sent to replace Manolo, who suffered a slight accident this morning . . .

THAT?

Nothing serious, luckily: just a sprain.

YES? . . .

. . . He'll be back in a day or two.

OK!

Waste no time, amigos! Your lives are in danger!

Our lives?   In danger?

Yes. The day after tomorrow a commando of Picaros, but not real Picaros, will pretend to attack this villa. In the course of the fighting, quite by accident, all three of you will be killed!

What?

The official version: the Picaros tried to kidnap you!

But anyway, why all the palaver? . . . And who wants to kill us?

Do you know who runs the Security Police in this country? No? . . . Well, it's Colonel Esponja, or, to give him his real name: Sponsz.

Sponsz! ! !   . . . Who was Chief of Police in Szohôd?

That's the one! He's been "lent" to General Tapioca to reorganise the Security Police in San Theodoros . . . and when he heard of Signora Castafiore's arrival, he dreamed up a plan to get rid of the three of you . . .

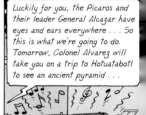

Luckily for you, the Picaros and their leader General Alcazar have eyes and ears everywhere . . . So this is what we're going to do. Tomorrow, Colonel Alvarez will take you on a trip to Hotuatabotl to see an ancient pyramid . . .

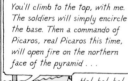

You'll climb to the top, with me. The soldiers will simply encircle the base. Then a commando of Picaros, real Picaros this time, will open fire on the northern face of the pyramid . . .

Ha! ha! ha! Success, success!

Under cover of the diversion you'll climb down the south face, having disarmed me and carefully tied me up. Two hundred metres away, right in front of you, one of Alcazar's trucks will be waiting . . .

Thanks, Pablo! Saving my life is becoming a habit with you. This is the second time!

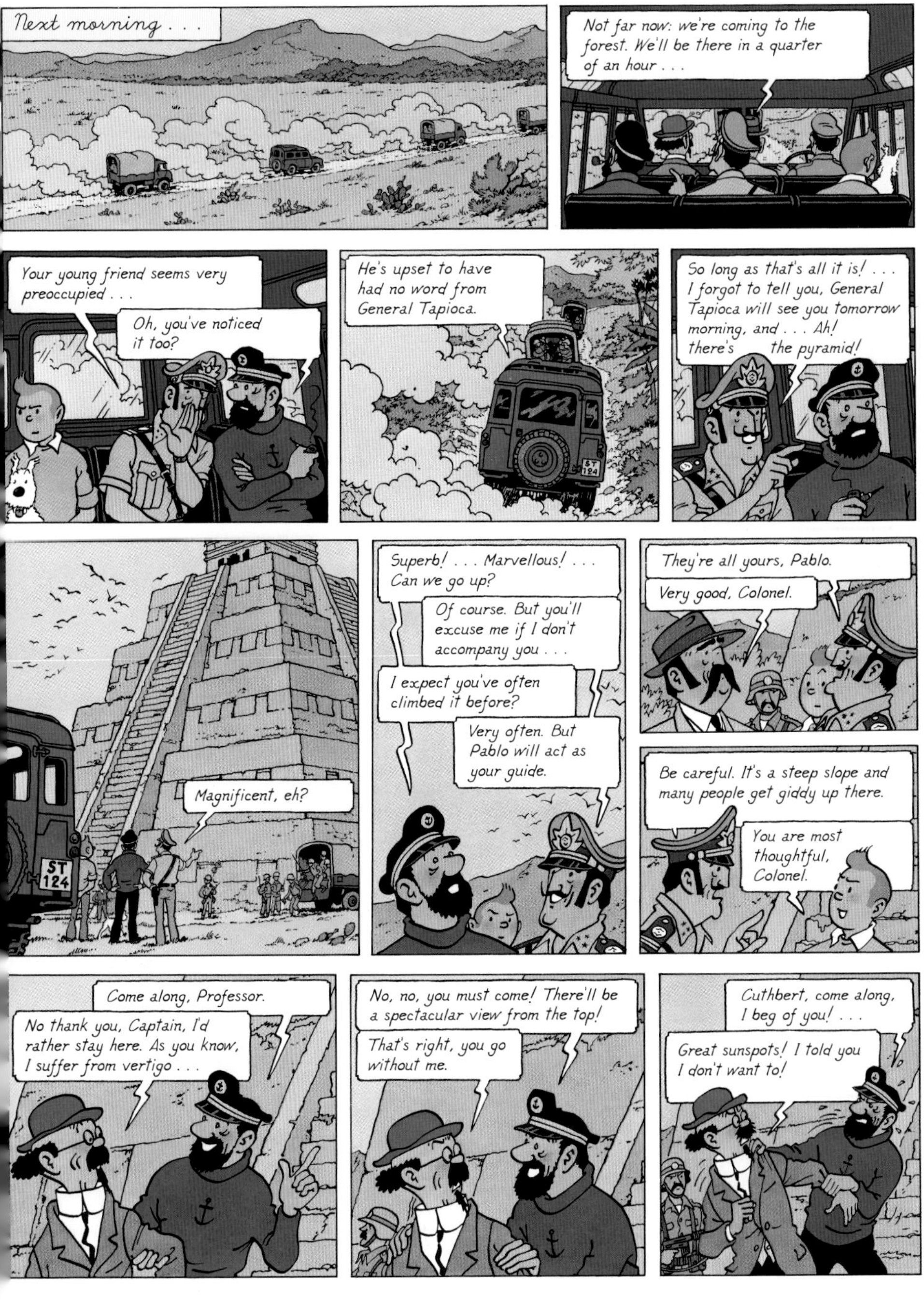
Next morning . . .
Not far now: we're coming to the forest. We'll be there in a quarter of an hour . . .
Your young friend seems very preoccupied . . .
Oh, you've noticed it too?
He's upset to have had no word from General Tapioca.
So long as that's all it is! . . . I forgot to tell you, General Tapioca will see you tomorrow morning, and . . . Ah! there's the pyramid!
Magnificent, eh?
Superb! . . . Marvellous! . . . Can we go up?
Of course. But you'll excuse me if I don't accompany you . . .
I expect you've often climbed it before?
Very often. But Pablo will act as your guide.
They're all yours, Pablo.
Very good, Colonel.
Be careful. It's a steep slope and many people get giddy up there.
You are most thoughtful, Colonel.
Come along, Professor.
No thank you, Captain, I'd rather stay here. As you know, I suffer from vertigo . . .
No, no, you must come! There'll be a spectacular view from the top!
That's right, you go without me.
Cuthbert, come along, I beg of you! . . .
Great sunspots! I told you I don't want to!

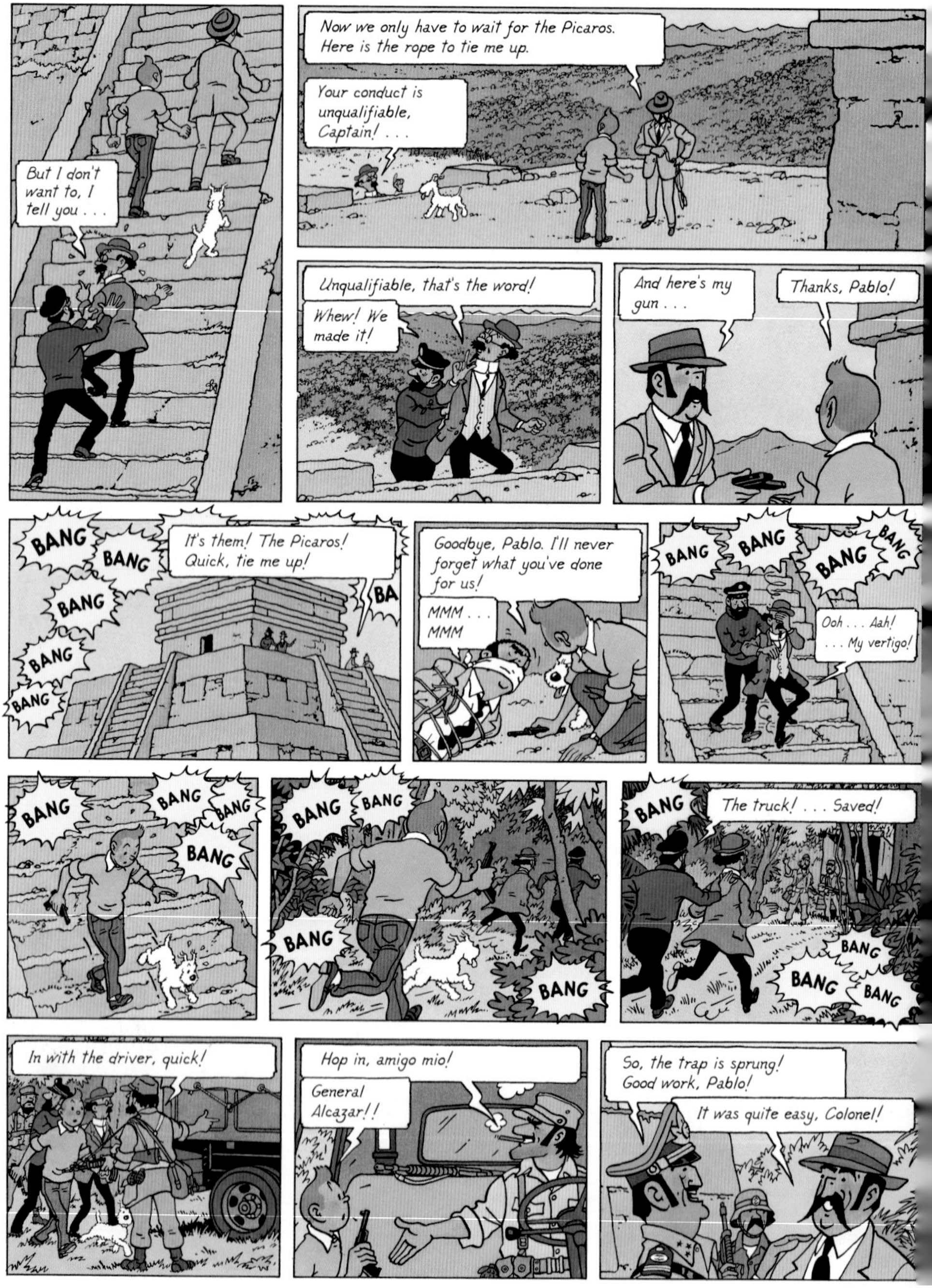
But I don't want to, I tell you . . .
Now we only have to wait for the Picaros. Here is the rope to tie me up.
Your conduct is unqualifiable, Captain! . . .
Unqualifiable, that's the word!
Whew! We made it!
And here's my gun . . .
Thanks, Pablo!
BANG
BANG
BANG
BANG
BANG
It's them! The Picaros! Quick, tie me up!
BA
Goodbye, Pablo. I'll never forget what you've done for us!
MMM . . . MMM
BANG
BANG
BANG
BANG
Ooh . . . Aah! . . . My vertigo!
BANG
BANG
BANG
BANG
BANG
BANG
BANG
BANG
BANG
The truck! . . . Saved!
BANG
BANG
BANG
In with the driver, quick!
Hop in, amigo mio!
General Alcazar!!
So, the trap is sprung! Good work, Pablo!
It was quite easy, Colonel!

Puma calling jaguar! . . . Puma calling jaguar! . . . Are you receiving me? . . . Come in now . . . Over . . .

Jaguar calling Puma! . . . Jaguar calling Puma! . . . Receiving you strength five . . . Over.

The truck's on its way . . . they'll be with you in seven or eight minutes . . . Mind you don't miss!

Be like missing an elephant at three metres in an alley, Colonel . . . And I've never done that yet!

You see, General Alcazar is true to his friends!

You can count on me! . . . So the minute I received your message I decided to move . . .

Our message? . . . You say you received a message from us?

Sure, the one Pablo brought me . . . What's the matter? You seem surprised about something.

I certainly am! . . . Because we never sent you any message . . . On the contrary, it was Pablo who told us, from you, that our lives were in danger but that you'd pull us out of trouble.

To me it stinks of treachery, General!

Treachery? . . . Impossible! . . . Pablo is dead loyal!

But Pablo lied to us, as he did to you . . . And with what object?

How should I know?

It bothers me, General . . . I've got a feeling someone's setting a trap for us . . .

Let's stop, General: we need time to think . . .

No way, amigo! We've a long trip ahead . . . and there's nothing to fear.

Jaguar calling Puma . . . We can see the truck now . . .

Careful, there's something in the road ahead . . .

You'll find binoculars there . . .

A monkey . . . He's stopped still, as if something frightened him . . .

. . . Now he's bolted back again!
. . . Stop, General!

Stop? . . . Are you crazy? . . . Why?

Stop! I tell you!

FIRE!

BANG

Quick! . . . Get out of here!
. . . The next one's for us!

Reload! . . . Get a move on! . . . Faster, you clumsy peasants! . . . And this time, don't miss!

FIRE!

BANG

BANG

Jaguar to Puma:
mission accomplished!

A direct hit? . . . Well done, Captain! . . . Are they all dead?

I've sent men to check, Colonel!

Colonel Esponja will be pleased with you, Pablo.

Jaguar calling Puma . . . Jaguar calling Puma . . .

Yes, I'm receiving you . . . What's that? . . . The truck's empty? . . . What?! . . . Because of the monkey . . . What monkey??? . . . Explain yourself, you imbecile!!!

No, they don't dare follow. They know we'll soon be in Arumbaya country . . . And that scares the living daylights out of them!

My other guerrillas who covered our escape while they pretended to attack will catch us up by another route . . . As for Pablo, that creep . . . Just wait till I get my hands on Pablo!

The dirty rat! I'll have him eaten alive by red ants!

I must admit I never suspected him for a moment . . .

A charming walk, isn't it, Captain?

Charming: you've said it! . . . To think we could be home at good old Marlinspike, downing a cool glass of beer!

But Captain, I ask you: why did you make me climb to the top of that pyramid and then rush me straight down the other side? . . . You must admit it's very odd . . .

Mmm . . .

I'm not really cross with you because the view certainly was spectacular.

There on the ground! . . . Columbus! Am I dreaming?

"Loch Lomond"?

Here, in a tropical forest? . . . Unbelievable!

Stop! Don't drink that!

!

I was only going to taste it . . .

They all say that . . . and swig the lot!

There!

Oh!

Wooah!

The next thing is a splitting headache!

A headache? . . . From "Loch Lomond"? . . . Never!

BONG

Over there . . .

?

I can't believe it! . . .

Wooah!

Look: a parachute!

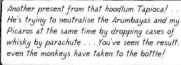

Another present from that hoodlum Tapioca! . . . He's trying to neutralise the Arumbayas and my Picaros at the same time by dropping cases of whisky by parachute . . . You've seen the result: even the monkeys have taken to the bottle!

ICEBERG DEAD AHEAD!

?

!

Hard a' starboard!

That crack on the head must have done it!

Look, Captain . . .

Who's captain here, you or me?

You, of course; you're Captain Haddock . . .

How ridiculous! . . . What's my first name, then?

Archibald, isn't it?

Even worse! . . . What's yours?

My name's Tintin.

Grotesque!

To crown it all, I've lost my ship . . . Perhaps it's flown away.

Look, Captain, ships don't fly!

Oh no? . . . That's what you think . . . Mine does! It's an airship, so there!

!Come on, vamos! We must reach the Arumbaya village before dark.

We'll stop and spend the night there . . . Have a cigar, amigo?

No, thanks.

. . . We'll move on again at dawn.

. . . As I said before, you will note that I am not reproaching you, for the view really was very fine from the summit of the pyramid, but . . .

As Napoleon said, "Think of it, soldiers, forty centuries look down upon you."

No, no, we're good pals with the Arumbayas. To begin with they gave us a load of trouble. But now there isn't any danger . . .

POF   POF

POF

THACK

Ridgewell! . . . You never get any better do you, you old joker! . . . Come on out of there!

Hello, General! . . . Hello, Tintin! . . . It's good to see you again!

Nice to be back, Doctor Ridgewell! . . . How are the Arumbayas? . . . Learnt to play golf yet?

Don't talk about it! . . . But on the other hand they've made great strides . . . in drunkenness, I'm afraid . . . By courtesy of General Tapioca!

LET ME GO! . . . TINTIN!!! . . . HELP!!! . . .

Tintin, help! . . . Save me! . . . Stop thief! . . . Fire! . . . Police! . . . Help, I am undone!

Ha! ha! ha!   Wotat it'fa!   Ha! ha! ha!

That's enough! . . . Gi'dahda vit!

You see? . . . Tapioca has a lot to answer for . . . Come, we must go. The village is still some distance away.

Dipsomaniacs! . . . That's what "civilisation" has done for those "savages".

That evening . . .

There's the Arumbaya village.

Excuse me, Captain . . . I see they are preparing some sort of meal over there . . .

He! he! . . .

OOH!!!

? ?

? ?

♪ ♪ ♪

Avakuki, chief of the Arumbayas, has invited us to share their meal . . . and to spend the night in his own hut.

Please thank him from us and tell him we accept with pleasure. Don't we, Captain?

Full astern!

Don't we, Professor ? . . . ? . . . ?

Oh! Now where's he got to? . . .

Ah, I see. There he is . . . just coming along behind . . .

That evening . . .

You may not fancy this very much, but pretend to like it: it's important not to offend them . . .

Don't worry . . .

Bon appetit, Professor!

Certainly not. On the contrary, I'm passionately fond of all exotic foods!

Owʒah g'rubai?

He's asking if you like it.

It's absolutely stunning!

Isn't it, Professor?

HHHH!

Oozfa sek 'unds?

He says you must have some more. And he's right: their "otnōsh" is particularly highly seasoned today.

I . . . I know!

Ava'n ip?

It's time for the toasts now. You must drink it straight down at one gulp . . .

Goes without saying!

Your very good health, mighty chief Avakuki!

Come on, make an effort . . .

PFOUAGH!

Young idiot! D'you want to get yourself murdered?

I'm . . . I'm terribly sorry . . . I couldn't swallow it . . . That whisky's simply disgusting!

Disgusting?!!! When you travel, you try to respect local customs! . . . Otherwise, you stay at home!

I'm terribly sorry, but I simply couldn't . . . It's too nasty . . .

PFOUAGH!

Goh'blimeh! Wa'samma ta, li li li va? . . . Lem eshohya!

Sum in'ksup wivit!

GLUG GLUG GLUG

Well I never! That's the first time it hasn't worked!

WAOAOAOW!

He! he!

WA LAAAAH!

". . . it seems that he too has temporarily given up whisky . . ."

The next morning . . .

Poor Captain, he doesn't seem any better . . .

Meanwhile . . .

. . . and our helicopters resumed their search this morning. But they have a difficult assignment as you will understand. Because of the forest terrain, the fugitives will be well hidden.   If, on the other hand . . .

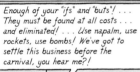

Enough of your "ifs" and "buts"! . . . They must be found at all costs . . . and eliminated! . . . Use napalm, use rockets, use bombs! We've got to settle this business before the carnival, you hear me?!

RRRRRRRR

A helicopter! . . . But there isn't any danger so long as we remain under cover.

RRRRRRRR

Hey, Captain! Stop!

RRRRRRRR

Stop! . . . Captain, take cover!

A man . . . at three o'clock!

RRRRRRRR

Captain! Stop!!!

SPLOSH

Hello . . . That's odd . . . I can't see anyone now . . . Yet I'm positive I saw . . .

OK, don't worry . . . We'll make another pass . . .

Well, where's your chap, eh?

FLOUFLOUFLOUFLOUFLOUF

GLUB

GLUB

There . . . You satisfied now?

Quick! . . . Get him out!

Still, I could have sworn I saw something move.

All right, we'll try again . . .

Oh no! They're coming back!

Sorry, Captain!

GLUG

?

FLOUFLOUFLOUFLOUF

GLUB

GLUB

That satisfy you . . . Convinced this time?

Mmmm . . .

Whew! . . . Saved!

You probably saw a cayman . . .

Look out! Behind you!...
A cayman!

What?... How?...
What did you say?

Caramba! You were lucky! That anaconda saved your life!

Look, he's coming round...

Well, amigo?...
Better now?

Look here, where's that bottle of whisky? Just you give it back, eh?... I found it, didn't I?

Hooray, he's cured!

Calm down, Captain...
We'll tell you what's been happening...

That's the limit!
I'll be...

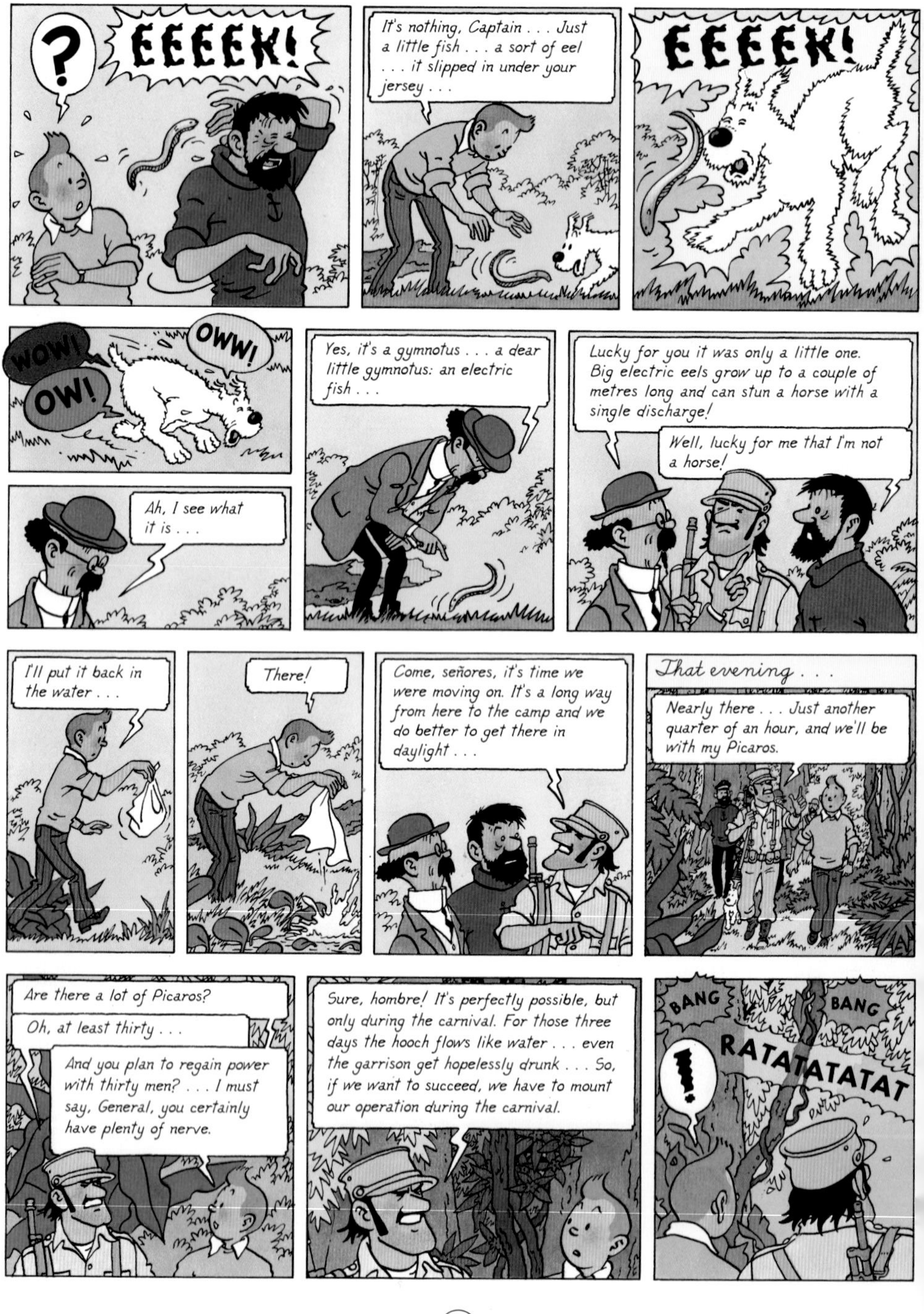
?
EEEEK!
It's nothing, Captain . . . Just a little fish . . . a sort of eel . . . it slipped in under your jersey . . .
EEEEK!
WOW!
OW!
OWW!
Ah, I see what it is . . .
Yes, it's a gymnotus . . . a dear little gymnotus: an electric fish . . .
Lucky for you it was only a little one. Big electric eels grow up to a couple of metres long and can stun a horse with a single discharge!
Well, lucky for me that I'm not a horse!
I'll put it back in the water . . .
There!
Come, señores, it's time we were moving on. It's a long way from here to the camp and we do better to get there in daylight . . .
That evening . . .
Nearly there . . . Just another quarter of an hour, and we'll be with my Picaros.
Are there a lot of Picaros?
Oh, at least thirty . . .
And you plan to regain power with thirty men? . . . I must say, General, you certainly have plenty of nerve.
Sure, hombre! It's perfectly possible, but only during the carnival. For those three days the hooch flows like water . . . even the garrison get hopelessly drunk . . . So, if we want to succeed, we have to mount our operation during the carnival.
BANG
BANG
RATATATATAT

BANG BANG BANG

BANG

BANG

The camp . . . it's under attack!

BANG BANG

BANG

BANG

Is something the matter?

Tintin, stop!

BANG

Stop! Stop! . . . Don't get yourself mixed up in it . . . you could be hit by . . .

BANG

BANG

BANG

Hold on, boys! I'm coming!

BANG

POP

PAF

PAF

POP

POF

POFF

PAF

?

RATATATATATATAT

LOCH LOMOND OLD SCOTCH WHISKY

¡BASTA!

¡Caramba, caballeros! ... ¡El general!

¿El general?

¡Ah, si, el general! ... ¡Viva el general!

¿Qué, el general?

¡Buenosh diash 'eneral! ... We wondered ... hic ... what'd happened ... hic ... t'ya! ... Shi! ... we were ... hic ... muy anshush ...

Thass why we ... hic ... hadda li'l drink! Shi! ... To forget ... hic that we were ... hic ... anshush!

But now that you've come, we aren't anshush any more ... Asholutely not!

Sho we'll have a li'l drink to shelebrate, won't we, amigosh? ...

HIPS

Enough! Touch another drop and I'll shoot!

So this is how we run a revolution? Don't make me laugh! ... You're nothing but a whisky-sodden rabble! You're canned! You're stinko! ... You pathetic tapioca puddings! ...

HIC   HIPS

Get to your quarters this instant! ... Parade in fifteen minutes in full combat kit! ... Dismiss!!

HIPS

HIC

You see?

Sadly, yes ...

Tapioca succeeded all too well with his parachute drops of whisky! ... ¡Caramba! How can one mount a revolution with that bunch of drunks?

Alcazar! ... So you decided to come back at last, did you?

¡AY!

Look who's here! . . . And just where d'you think you've been, Mr Big?
Good-evening, Peggy, my dove!
You promised me to be home the same night! . . . And you've been gone three whole days!
I can explain, palomita mia . . .
Yeah, yeah, I know: any excuse is better than none! And what about me, left to rot in a lousy mud hut? . . . That's real dandy!
The General promised me a palace in Tapiocapolis! And all the General provides is a beat-up palliasse crawling with bugs and roaches!
But . . .
These guys your friends? . . . OK, I warn them: they think they're gonna make the rules around here, they're mighty mistaken!
Thank you, gracious lady, for those kind words! . . . Please believe that we are extremely touched by your generous welcome, and allow me to offer you our most humble respects . . .
SMACK
That a weak woman should share the hardships and, let us admit it, the dangers of guerrilla life, commands not only our utmost respect but our profound admiration!
. . . And I speak in all sincerity, dear lady!
You coming, Alcazar?
Yes, my dove.
She seems a little . . . er . . . brisk . . . on first acquaintance, but she has a heart of gold . . .
Of course, General. One sees it immediately . . .
What a delightful lady! . . . So graceful . . . Such exquisite femininity! . . . As for that poor man . . .
. . . his revolution will never succeed with a collection of drunkards like that . . . Never, unless someone gives him a hand . . . And it is I who will do it . . . I, Cuthbert Calculus!
You?
You'll . . .?

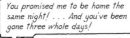

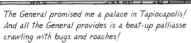

No, gentlemen, I am not a fool! I know exactly what I am saying!

You've missed a . . .

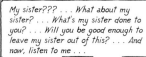

My sister??? . . . What about my sister? . . . What's my sister done to you? . . . Will you be good enough to leave my sister out of this? . . . And now, listen to me . . .

I . . .

Yes . . .

You see this tube of tablets? Well, it contains a product that I have recently perfected. It has a base of medicinal herbs . . .

The preparation has no taste, no smell, and is absolutely non-toxic. Having said that, a single one of these tablets administered in either food or drink imparts a disgusting taste to any alcohol taken thereafter . . .

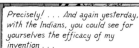

. . . And the very first person upon whom I tested it was you, Captain!

ME?

You dared to do that? . . . Borgia! . . . Cannibal! . . . Miserable blundering barbecued blister . . .

I tell you my sister has absolutely nothing to do with it!

And furthermore, you can thank me for being concerned for your health!

Please, Captain!

It's a disgrace! . . . A scandal! . . . A monstrous attack upon the personal freedom of the individual!

Precisely! . . . And again yesterday, with the Indians, you could see for yourselves the efficacy of my invention . . .

But I never knew you had . . .

No, young man, I am not mad! . . . And I would ask you to show a little more respect towards a man of mature years!

No, no, I insist . . . er . . .

And for heaven's sake stop talking about my sister!

My sister . . . just a moment . . . My sister???

. . . And another thing! . . . I don't have a sister . . . I never had a sister . . . And don't you forget it!

So there!

Stay with him, Captain . . . And for the time being stop him from doing anything hasty . . . I'm off to talk to the General.

RAT TAT TAT

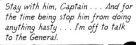
Come in!

Ah, it's you, amigo mio! Come on in.

I . . . I'm not disturbing you?

Alcazar, the dishes!

I'll carry on presently, palomita mia: I promise!

Sit down, hombre . . . What brings you here?

SCRATCH

Another cigar? . . . That makes three since you came back!

Does . . . does it, my dove?

I've been thinking over what you said to me earlier; a revolution is impossible while your Picaros have only one idea in their heads: whisky!

Alas, that's quite true.

But what would you say if someone succeeded in curing them of their bad habits?

Ah, that's impossible, amigo.

And yet, if you managed to do that . . . ¡Mil bombas! I'd give you half the gold reserves in the Banco de la Nacion! . . .

Ahem!

. . . er, let's say a third . . .

Ahem!

Well . . . er . . . ten per cent . . . What about that?

I don't want anything like that: not a centavo, General.

Then what do you want, amigo? Tell me . . .

A promise that you'll carry out your revolution without bloodshed . . . that there won't be any reprisals, or executions, or anything of that sort . . .

WHAT?

You're crazy! . . . Or else you're a traitor . . . and ought to be shot here and now!

A revo___ n without executions? . . . Without reprisals? . . . ¡Caramba! . . . It's unthinkable! . . . You must be joking! . . . And anyway, what about tradition? . . . Yes, what about tradition, eh? Answer me that!

No, what you ask is impossible, amigo . . . Tapioca and his ministers are bloody tyrants and villains . . .

They must be shot! . . . Every man jack of them! . . . Shot, d'you hear me?

Very well, General.

We won't discuss it further . . . And forgive me for bothering you . . .

Hey! but . . . Wait . . . Perhaps we . . .

Goodbye, General.

?

BOOM

What have you done? . . .

Ha! ha! ha! Funny joke! A teeny tear-gas grenade!

Who did that? . . . I'll have him shot!

One of your Picaros. Blind drunk, as usual . . .

Hmm! . . . Not easy to mount a successful revolution with that bunch of boozers, is it, General?

All right, you win! I accept your proposition!

You do?

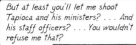

But at least you'll let me shoot Tapioca and his ministers? . . . And his staff officers? . . . You wouldn't refuse me that?

You won't shoot anyone, General!

No one but Tapioca and his ministers, then . . .

I said no one! You can take it or leave it!

But it's mean! You're taking advantage of the situation! . . . D'you realise I'll be nothing but a figure of fun if I do as you say?

GRRR

At least let me shoot Tapioca! . . . Just Tapioca, I implore you!

No.

I'll cure your Picaros of their drunkenness, and you'll promise me not to use any violence while I'm helping you to regain power . . . Agreed? . . . All right, say after me: I promise!

I promise . . .

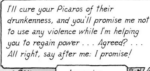

Good, I have your word . . . For my part, I promise that soon your Picaros won't touch a drop more alcohol.

Good! . . . But just you watch your step! If you've given me false hope . . . you'll be up against a wall, pronto! Understand?

Y . . . yes!

Ah, hello!

?

Has he lost something?

Yes, he must have lost something . . .

You seem to have lost something . . .

No, no, I've lost something . . .

The bottle of tablets I was telling you about just now . . . I can't find it anywhere . . . Isn't that curious?

Hey, you seem very upset that he's lost the tablets?

I'll say I am! I promised the General his Picaros would soon stop drinking!

You promised that?

Yes, it's obvious . . . if his men go on boozing, he won't ever get his revolution!

Well? We don't give a tinker's cuss for his revolution, anyway!

Yes, Captain, we certainly do . . .

. . . because our friends the Thompsons, Signora Castafiore, Irma and Mr Wagner are in danger . . . And the only way to save them is for Alcazar to defeat Tapioca and take over the government!

You're right, by thunder!

Oh, very well, here's his rotten old bottle! I pinched it from him, to stop him curing people of their pleasures!

Be a good fellow: give it back to him yourself. He'll be so grateful to you . . .

If you insist . . .

Is this what you're looking for, by any chance?

Captain, you're an angel!

SMACK

Thanks to you, those poor creatures will be delivered from their passion for alcohol at last! . . . Like you, Captain!

Tintin! . . . Tintin! . . .

That's the General!

Come quick, amigo! . . . The trial of your friends . . . it's on television!

Television? . . . Here? . . . They must have a portable generator.

. . . closing stage of the trial of the Marlinspike conspirators. This is being shown live on television on the orders of our beloved President, General Tapioca, so that the whole world may witness the impartiality with which justice is administered in our country . . .

That's a good one!

Sssh!

Recently, our beloved President generously invited Captain Haddock, Professor Calculus and the reporter Tintin to our country to put their case. He guaranteed their freedom. And how did they repay him? With cold cynicism! They took the first opportunity to flee into the jungle and join their accomplice Alcazar and his villainous Picaros!

This action alone is enough to prove that the grave accusations against the three defendants are entirely justified. But over now to the Palace of Justice where the Public Prosecutor is putting the case for the Republic . . .

. . . You have before you, gentlemen, two sinister characters who, more easily to accomplish their evil purpose . . . Do I need to remind you of it? . . .

. . . to assassinate our beloved President . . . did not hesitate to pass themselves off as honest policemen! . . . But their monstrous subterfuge deceived no one! Look at their low brows, their furtive glances!

. . . In short, look at their brutish faces! Policemen? Them? . . . Cheats! Imposters! Assassins!

. . . Men who, to appear as loyal supporters of General Tapioca and the noble ideology of Kûrvi-Tasch, carried their duplicity so far as to grow moustaches!

That's a lie! . . . We've been wearing moustaches since we were born!

To be precise: we're worn bearing them!

Silence! . . . You will speak when you are spoken to!

. . . Gentlemen, for these two wretches, who can have no claim to extenuating circumstances, I demand the DEATH PENALTY!

You see? None of your fancy scruples there, eh?

The death penalty!! . . . He certainly doesn't mince his words . . . He means to go the whole hog!

To be precise: his words certainly mean he's going to mince the hog whole!

But the real brains behind the plot . . . and we have here documents which prove it irrefutably . . . are those of a woman!!!

A woman . . . . or should we call her a monster? . . . who lent her talents, her undoubted talents to a criminal cause: her name is Bianca Castafiore, "the Milanese Nightingale"!

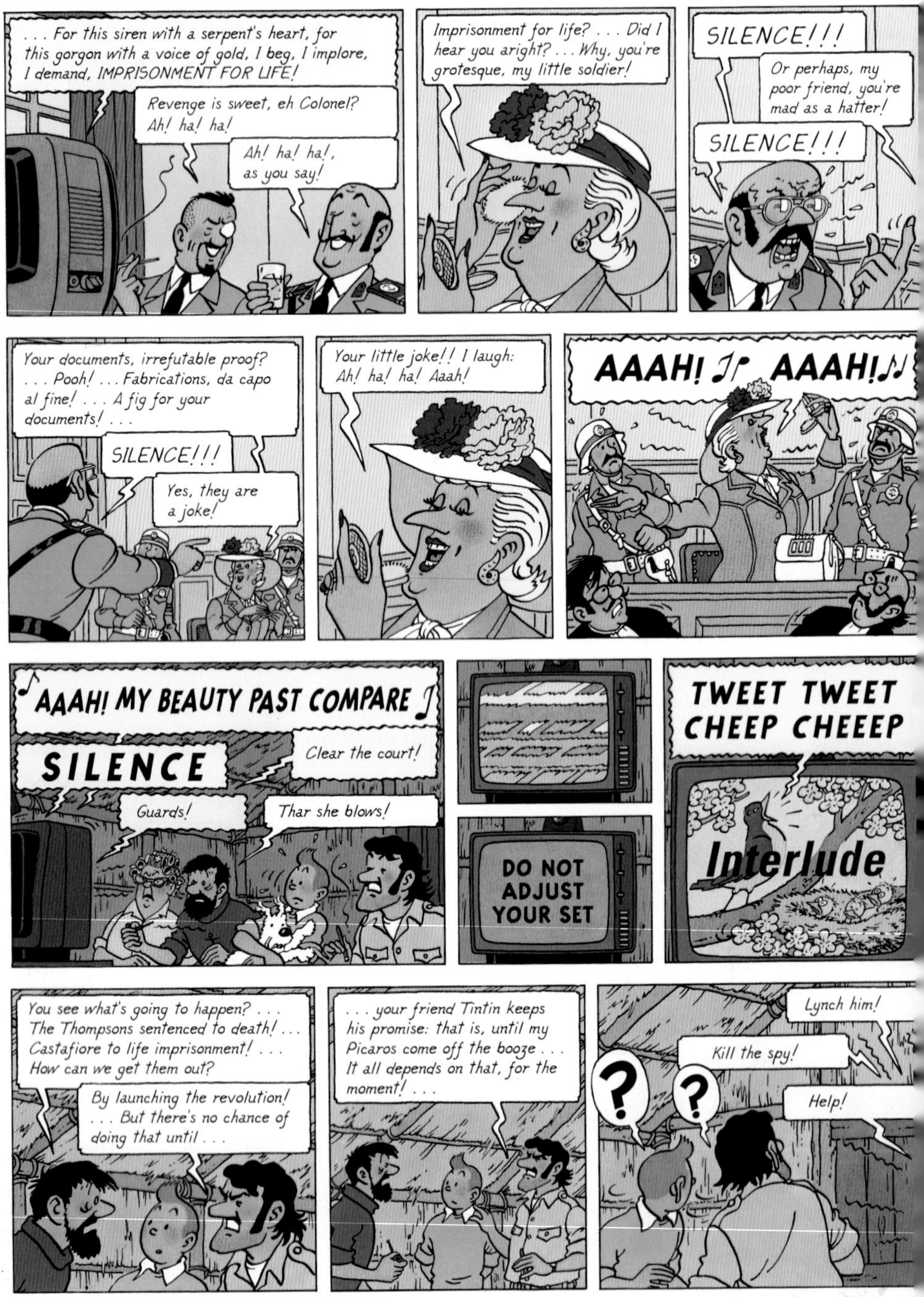

. . . For this siren with a serpent's heart, for this gorgon with a voice of gold, I beg, I implore, I demand, IMPRISONMENT FOR LIFE!
Revenge is sweet, eh Colonel? Ah! ha! ha!
Ah! ha! ha!, as you say!
Imprisonment for life? . . . Did I hear you aright? . . . Why, you're grotesque, my little soldier!
SILENCE!!!
Or perhaps, my poor friend, you're mad as a hatter!
SILENCE!!!
Your documents, irrefutable proof? . . . Pooh! . . . Fabrications, da capo al fine! . . . A fig for your documents! . . .
SILENCE!!!
Yes, they are a joke!
Your little joke!! I laugh: Ah! ha! ha! Aaah!
AAAH! AAAH!
AAAH! MY BEAUTY PAST COMPARE
SILENCE
Clear the court!
Guards!
Thar she blows!
DO NOT ADJUST YOUR SET
TWEET TWEET CHEEP CHEEEP
Interlude
You see what's going to happen? . . . The Thompsons sentenced to death! . . . Castafiore to life imprisonment! . . . How can we get them out?
By launching the revolution! . . . But there's no chance of doing that until . . .
. . . your friend Tintin keeps his promise: that is, until my Picaros come off the booze . . . It all depends on that, for the moment! . . .
?
?
Lynch him!
Kill the spy!
Help!

Help! ... Help! ... Save me!

The Professor!

Kill the traitor!

Hang him!

He's a traitor, General ... a saboteur! ... We caught him red handed, just as he was emptying a bottle of pills into the cooking pot!

There's no doubt about it ... he was trying to poison us! ... Let's shoot the nasty little reptile!

General?

Yes?

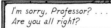

. . . . ? . . . .
. . . . . . ! . . . .
. . . . !!
!

No need to panic, boys! This man is a good friend of the Picaros: I can vouch for him. He isn't trying to poison you ... quite the opposite. He's giving you Vitamin C ... What for? ... Quite simply, to make you strong ... to beat the daylights out of that loathsome Tapioca!

Are you sure?

Ah! well ...

Sure as I stand here! ... Eat away! ... I give you my solemn word ... you won't come to any harm!

I'm sorry, Professor? ... Are you all right?

Take all night? ... Not nearly as long ... In a couple of hours at most my pills will take effect ...

From that moment, none of those men will be able to stomach a single drop of alcohol! ... Just like you, Captain! ... Isn't that marvellous?

GNNNN!

¡Gracias, hombre, gracias!

MBLL ...

And to show my appreciation, I create you companion of the order of San Fernando, first class!

A glass? ... How nice! ... A little iced water will be delicious ...

Whatever the General may say, I'm not eating that stuff ...

These new-fangled chemicals ... you never can tell ...

Look at them, Captain . . . They're obviously suspicious . . . And if they don't eat that food they'll go on drinking . . . So the revolution will fail . . . and our friends the Thompsons will be shot!

There's the dog . . . He belongs to the gringos. I'm going to give him some of that vitaminized stew . . . If he eats it, we will too . . . Otherwise . . .

He's right!

I agree!

Doggy woggy? . . . Come come come come . . .

Hello, what does he want me for?

Come come come! . . . Yummy yum! . . . Looky dere! . . . Looky dere, good for little dogsywogsies! . . .

He must be daft, talking like that . . .

Let's hope . . . let's hope he'll eat the food . . .

?

SNIFF SNIFF SNIFF

YEEEK!

You saw that, boys? . . . Are we going to eat what even a dog won't touch?

You're right!

We won't eat that muck!

Go back at once, Snowy, and eat it!

But . . .

That slop! It's full of pimentos!

SCHLOOP   SLURP

GLUP

SCHLOP

Hey, boys! Look! . . . He's changed his mind! . . . Now we can have some too!

¡Bueno! I'm hungry!

They're eating it! Now we can save our friends!

TOOT

! ?

Hello, a b-b-b-... hic... bus!

Ah! Not a pink elephant today, then?

Is it far to Tapiocapolis, chum?

Tapiocapolis?... Great snakes, you're hopelessly off the road.

Drat!... Could any of these soldiers escort us?... I've heard there's a risk of attack from guerrillas around here... they call them Picaros.

That's exactly where you are: among the Picaros!

No kidding?

Are these real guerrillas?

It's terrifically Tarzan, dear, don't you think?

I say, old man, where can we buy postcards?

Poshe... hic... cardsh?

They must have a souvenir shop somewhere about the place...

Blow me, look who's here!

Jolyon Wagg!

Doctor Livingstone, I presume! How are you, me old salt? On holiday?

No!

Don't tell me, you laid it on as a surprise! You're part of the welcome to the carnival! It's going to be a wow this year: thanks to us!

Thanks to you?

Bet your life!... Know the charity concert party, The Jolly Follies?... That's us!... And guess who's leader of the band: yours truly!

Ah! er...

Sunny Jim designed their costumes, too... Smashing, eh?

Very... original!

What's all this tomfoolery?

Who's that?

General Alcazar, leader of the Picaros.

Hi there, me old Field Marshal! . . . So you're the top brass for these boozy brigands!

What d'you think you're doing here, you and your busload of ballerinas? . . . And come to think of it, for all I know you're spies on Tapioca's payroll!!

A word with you, General, if I may . . .

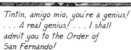

. . . . ? . . . .
. . . . ??? . . . .
. . . . . ? . . . . ??
. . . . ???. .

CLAC... TR2TRRRR...
RR... TING ½ CLANG
$\frac{m}{c}$ 2 ◖═ ◎ .. CLICK?
× 3.1416   !!!!

CLICK

Tintin, amigo mio, you're a genius! . . . A real genius! . . . I shall admit you to the Order of San Fernando!

Thanks, General.

Welcome to the Picaros,   señor.

Please forgive me, amigo mio: I didn't realise who you were! . . . But caramba! Friends of my friends are friends of mine! So make yourself at home, hombre!

And this evening, amigo, you and all your Follies will be my guests! Si, si! We'll have a grand fiesta, with whisky by the gallon! Just you wait!

What did you say to him?

You'll see in due course!

That night... What's the matter with this whisky? ... It's simply disgusting!

PFOUAGH!

You must be cuckoo, it's super!

♪ WE'RE THE ♪ JOLLY JOLLY FOLLIES ... ♪♫ ♪ HEY NONNY NO ... ♪ HEY NONNY NO ... ♪♫

The morning after . . .

Alcazar! ... Alcazar! ... Time for you to fix breakfast!

Alcazar? ... Where are you? ... Answer me this minute!

Alcazar! ... Answer me! ... I am not amused!

To Señora Alcazar

'Morning Cuthbert! ... Everyone still snoring in this palm court palais de danse?

Ants? Don't talk about them! Everywhere! A veritable plague!

Yiiijiiiiiiiii! THE MONSTER! HE'S GONE!

My dove,
I've gon to start the revulushun against the vial Tapioca. Wen its over you will have the pallis witch I've promist you.
Much luv from your
Zazar
I've borrowd the Jolyfoliz buss and have left sum Picaros to look after you.
Z.

⟨183⟩

¡Caramba! These Jolly Follies were sent from heaven! ... Thanks to them and to your friend Calculus I'll soon be back in power ...

It's a shabby way to treat those poor people, sneaking off with their bus and their costumes. But it's the only way to save our friends ...

Never mind, I'll be able to reward them with appropriate generosity as soon as I've chucked out that vile Tapioca: I'll admit them all to the Order of San Fernando!

Tomorrow afternoon we'll arrive in Tapiocapolis ... and that'll soon be renamed Alcazaropolis. It's the opening day of the carnival. Before we reach the city we'll rehearse our plans to the very last detail ...

We'll be dressed in the Jolly Follies costumes, with our guns at the ready ...

With orders not to use them!

The next afternoon ...

This is it, my brave Picaros! We're here! ... Now each of you guys: remember what you have to do ...

(184)

Meanwhile . . .

Are you sure it isn't dangerous, General, letting all these people assemble in front of the windows? You'll be a sitting target for the first Picaro . . .

No danger, Colonel . . .

. . . Even if by some extraordinary chance armed Picaros managed to infiltrate the crowd, they'd be far too drunk to shoot straight! . . . As you know, my parachute drops of whisky have been a total success.

My spies have been quite definite: Alcazar's men are never sober . . . And they'd be quite incapable of engaging in any serious action, poor fools . . .

This is it, boys!

Everybody out!

Watch it, Captain, remember you're a Folly!

Don't worry!

♪ WE'RE THE ♪ JOLLY JOLLY FOLLIES . . . ♩ HEY NONNY NO . . . ♪ HEY NONNY NO . . .

Where are those people from?

The programme says: "The Jolly Follies, a charity concert party from Europe".

Excellent! . . . Just listen to the beat! . . . They've even got our guards joining in the dance!

Ready! . . . On the next hey nonny no, out comes the chloroform!

HEY NONNY NO!

?

Put him with the rest in the porch. Your guns are there . . .

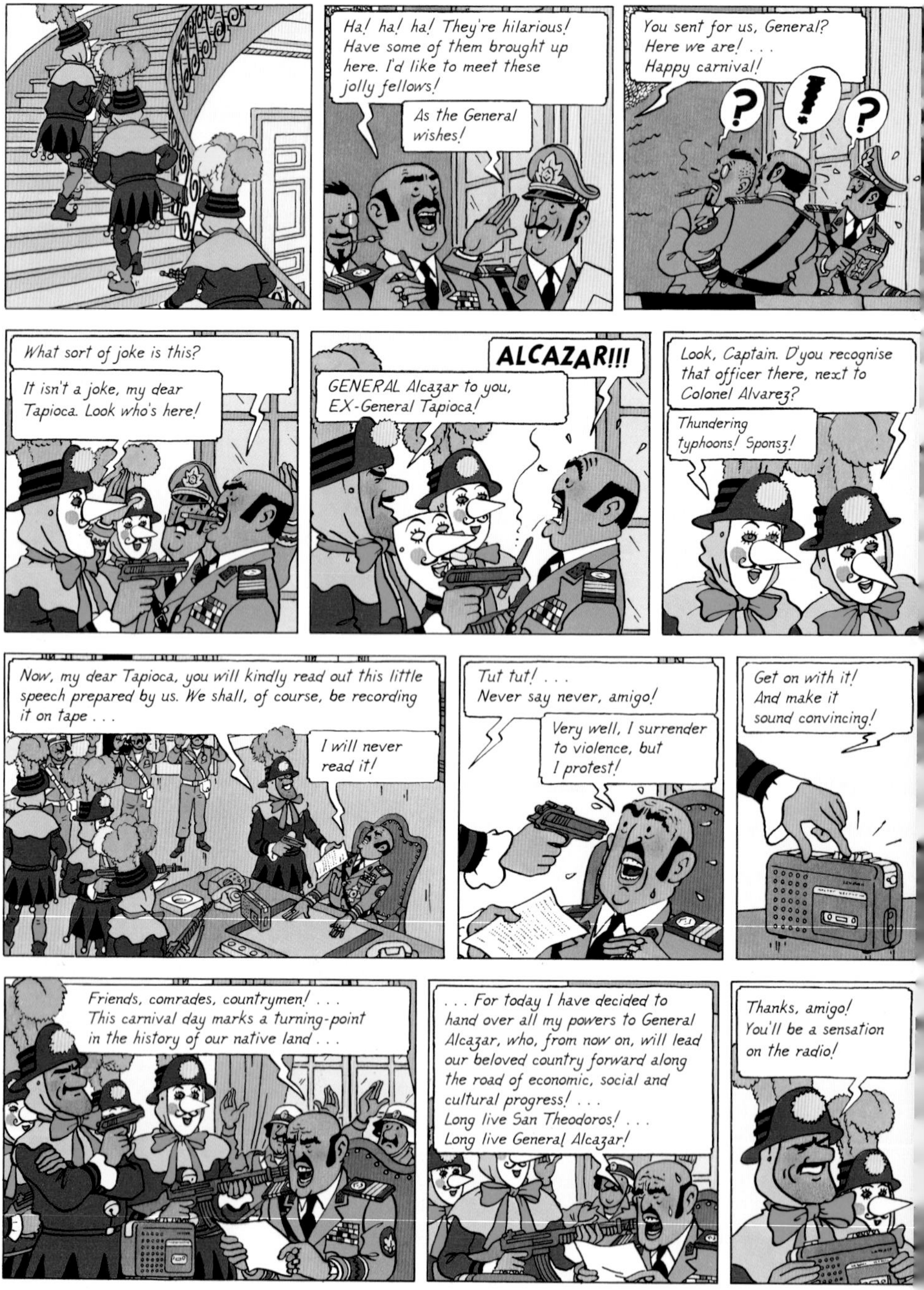

Ha! ha! ha! They're hilarious! Have some of them brought up here. I'd like to meet these jolly fellows!
As the General wishes!
You sent for us, General? Here we are! . . . Happy carnival!
What sort of joke is this?
It isn't a joke, my dear Tapioca. Look who's here!
ALCAZAR!!!
GENERAL Alcazar to you, EX-General Tapioca!
Look, Captain. D'you recognise that officer there, next to Colonel Alvarez?
Thundering typhoons! Sponsz!
Now, my dear Tapioca, you will kindly read out this little speech prepared by us. We shall, of course, be recording it on tape . . .
I will never read it!
Tut tut! . . . Never say never, amigo!
Very well, I surrender to violence, but I protest!
Get on with it! And make it sound convincing!
Friends, comrades, countrymen! . . . This carnival day marks a turning-point in the history of our native land . . .
. . . For today I have decided to hand over all my powers to General Alcazar, who, from now on, will lead our beloved country forward along the road of economic, social and cultural progress! . . . Long live San Theodoros! . . . Long live General Alcazar!
Thanks, amigo! You'll be a sensation on the radio!

There it is . . . in the bag! . . . Pedro, you and your section hop along to the Radio Building and see this statement is broadcast immediately . . . Understand?

Si!

My heartiest congratulations, General! . . . Death to Tapioca! . . . Would you like him shot at once?

Long live General Alcazar!

Shoot Tapioca!

Long live General Alcazar!

Executions are out! . . . His life will be spared.

But General, it's contrary to every custom . . . The people will be terribly disappointed . . .

The Colonel is right, General . . . For pity's sake don't pardon me! Do you want me completely dishonoured?

Permit me to insist, General!

My decision is irrevocable: your life will be spared! An aircraft will be placed at your disposal, to convey you wherever you may wish to go.

Are you mad?

No, I'm not . . . But he is! . . . This muchacho made me give my word that the coup would be bloodless! . . . I'm desperately sorry . . .

Come on, let's greet old Sponsz . . .

Ah, an idealist, is he? . . . Young chaps nowadays have absolutely no respect for anything . . . Not even the oldest traditions!

We live in sad times!

We meet again, Colonel Sponsz!

!

Don't worry, Sponsz, even you have nothing to fear. They're pining for you in Borduria, so your ticket to Szohôd is booked for the morning . . .

We caught this joker trying to escape . . .

It's Tintin! . . . I'm finished!

Pablo!

Mercy, Señor Tintin, mercy! Please don't shoot me!

That's less than you deserve, you subtropical sea-louse!

Don't be afraid, Pablo; no one is going to hurt you. You once saved my life, and I haven't forgotten that . . . You are free to go . . . Adios, Pablo!

You made a mistake there, Tintin, and you'll live to regret it. You're making a rod for your own back . . . To be precise . . .

Great snakes! The Thompsons!

The Thompsons, General! . . . The Thompsons! . . . They could be shot while we stand here talking!

Ah, yes . . . you think so?

Yes, General. The execution is due to take place in twenty-two minutes, precisely!

¡Mil bombas! Quick, call the prison and cancel the execution!

At once, General!

RRING
RRING

. . . fifty seconds . . . Pip Pip Pip . . . At the third stroke it will be five thirty-eight precisely . . . Pip Pip Pip . . . At the third . . .

You did it on purpose! Dial the right number this time, or I'll have you shot!

RRRRRING
RRRRRING

. . . precisely . . . Pip Pip Pip . . . At the third stroke it will be five forty and ten seconds.

If it doesn't work this time, I'll personally shoot the Minister of Telecommunications!!

The number you have dialled does not exist. Please consult your directory.

Only one thing to do: dash to the prison and save them ourselves!

Take B Section with you! The Colonel will guide you! I'll have his head if you're too late!

¡Rápido! . . . ¡Rápido . . . por Dios!

I'm terribly sorry, gentlemen, but we must go, please . . . It's time . . .

And one must be on time.

To be precise: time, gentlemen please!

Don't worry: it's a nasty moment, but you'll soon forget it . . .

This is San Theodoros National Radio. We are interrupting our programmes for a special announcement by His Excellency General Tapioca . . .

A car! . . . We must commandeer a car!

Useless! No vehicle could get through this crowd . . .

What can we do?

Look! That float . . .

What? You mean . . .

Yes! It's the only possible answer!

You! . . . Keep on playing!

Keep playing! . . . Don't stop!

Driver! . . . To the State Prison! And put your foot down!

Put my foot down? . . . With this crate? . . . You must be joking!

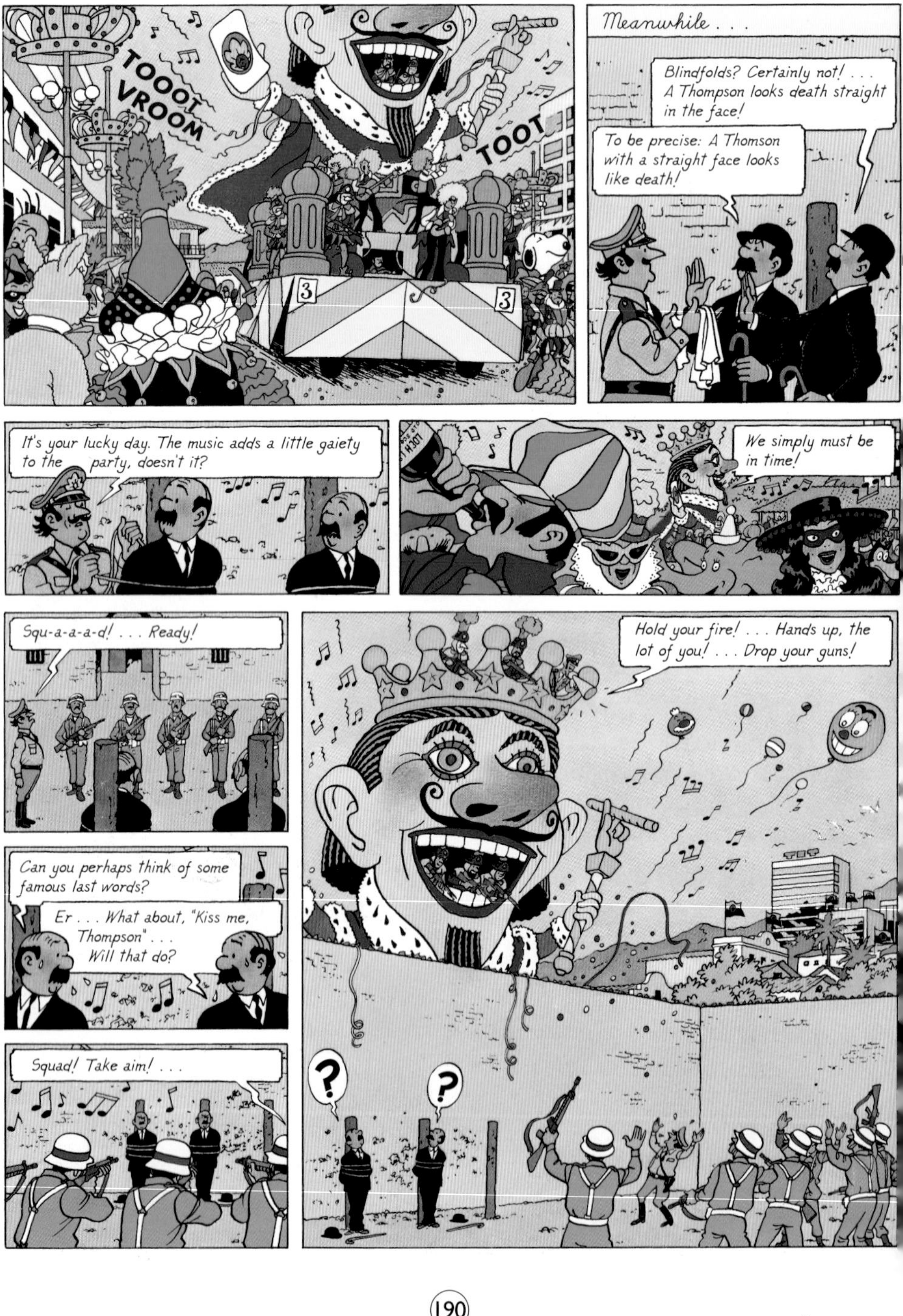
TOOOT
VROOM
TOOT
Meanwhile . . .
Blindfolds? Certainly not! . . . A Thompson looks death straight in the face!
To be precise: A Thomson with a straight face looks like death!
It's your lucky day. The music adds a little gaiety to the party, doesn't it?
We simply must be in time!
Squ-a-a-a-d! . . . Ready!
Hold your fire! . . . Hands up, the lot of you! . . . Drop your guns!
Can you perhaps think of some famous last words?
Er . . . What about, "Kiss me, Thompson" . . . Will that do?
Squad! Take aim! . . .
?
?

A few minutes later . . .

Saved by the bell, eh? . . .

Oh? I didn't hear it, with the music . . .

And the friends of these gentlemen . . . Where are they?

I'll take you there at once, Colonel!

They've been very well treated, Colonel. They'll tell you themselves . . .

I hope so, for your sake!

This is Signora Castafiore's cell. They've just taken in her lunch . . .

. . . and I'm telling you for the last time!

?

!

. . . I want my pasta cooked properly, d'you hear? . . . "al dente", as we say at home in Italy!

Ah, Madonna! . . . Captain Hemlock!

Come, caro mio! . . . Come to my arms!

No!!

I knew you'd come to rescue me from this dreadful place!

Ahem! . . . Here is Señor Igor Wagner, señora . . .

. . . and your maid . . .

Ah, my dear Irma, how I have missed you!

Ah, what joy to be all together again! I simply must sing!

No! No!

No!

Not that!

The army, the navy and the air force have come over to me! ¡Mil bombas! It's an overwhelming triumph!

And it's partly due, of course, to you . . . Si, si, si! . . . Alcazar is not ungenerous: you will be decorated with the order of San Fernando! . . . As for your five per cent . . .

Please forget that, General!

General, the bus you sent to the camp to fetch Señora Alcazar and the Jolly Follies has returned.

Good! Show them in here . . .

So there you are, Alcazar! What's the game, eh? You've been absent without leave again!

I can explain, palomita mia . . .

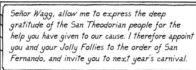

Señor Wagg, allow me to express the deep gratitude of the San Theodorian people for the help you have given to our cause. I therefore appoint you and your Jolly Follies to the order of San Fernando, and invite you to next year's carnival.

And Señor Professor . . . In recognition of the magnificent role you played, I appoint you Knight Grand Cross of the Order of San Fernando, with Oak Leaves.

No thank you, my friend. Never between meals.

Good old Alcazar! Give him a big hurrah!

As for you, my dove . . . I promised you a palace. Bueno, I keep my word. This is all yours, from now on.

Fine and dandy! . . . Anyone can see it isn't you who's expected to keep this dump clean . . . So for a start, stop dropping cigar ash all over the place! . . . You get me?

Blistering barnacles, I shan't be sorry to be back home in Marlinspike . . .

Me too, Captain . . .

Me too, but with a little mustard   if you please.

VIVA ALCAZAR

THE END